More Than a Man Can Stand
(A Novel of Fact and Speculation)

by

Richard DuRose

Published by Escarpment Press

Escarpment Press

www.escarpmentpress.weebly.com
INDIAN LAND, SC

More Than a Man Can Stand
(A Novel of Fact and Speculation)

By

Richard DuRose

Table of Contents

Introduction i

1 — August 25, 1927 1

2 — Columbia High (1917) 11

3 — Standard Aircraft (1917) 17

4 — Jersey Shore (1918) 29

5 — Toledo (1921) 41

6 — Chasing Moonshiners (1926) 51

7 — Flying to Rio (1927) 63

8 — Takeoff and Landing (1927) 73

9 — Rescue (1927) 85

10 — Settling In (1927-1928) 105

11 — Paul's Routine (1927-1928) 119

12 — Piarucu's Family (1929) 131

13 — Back to the *Port of Brunswick* (1929) .. 137

14 — The Waika (1930) 153

15 — We Must Find Paul (1930) 161

16 — A Platonic Wife? (1930) 175

17 — The Black Devil (1932) 187

18 — Attacked (1933) 193

19 — The Tall One (1933) 213

20 — The Haskins Expedition (1933-1934) .. 231

21 — Bitter Pickles (1934) 245

22 — Gold Prospectors (1935) 253

23 — Sururcu! (1936) 267

24 — The Final Chapter (1938) 287

Afterword I

The Expeditions III

Sources IV

The Port of Brunswick

Introduction

In late 1903, the year after Paul Reynaldo Redfern was born, the Wright Brothers, after intensive research, managed a fifty-nine second flight in their rudimentary airplane/kite on the beach at Kitty Hawk, North Carolina. However, no one really believed they had done it. Upon their return home, their hometown newspaper, the *Dayton Daily Journal*, refused to publish the brothers' claims. To the editors, the brothers' story of the flight seemed a hoax. But, a year later when the brothers invited the newspaper to a demonstration on the Hoffman Prairie, on the outskirts of Dayton, flying a full mile under control, the *Journal* ran a front-page story.

Once flying was shown to be possible, inventors and tinkerers all over the world began to experiment with various forms of flying machines. The Wright Brothers started a fire that could not be extinguished. Airplane development spread across the world. In short order, airplane design modernized, and engine design became more sophisticated.

In May 1927, Charles Lindbergh made a flight from New York's Long Island to Paris securing for himself the prize of $25,000 (approximately $300,000 in today's dollars) offered by hotelier Raymond Orteig for the first successful flight between New York and Paris. Lindbergh's unprecedented fame (and fortune) tempted many other pilots to replicate or exceed Lindbergh's intercontinental flight. There were at least a dozen such attempts in the remainder of 1927. Some succeeded. Many of them were unsuccessful and quickly forgotten.

Paul Redfern, an airman from Columbia, South Carolina, was one of the pilots who attempted to exceed Lindbergh's accomplishments. His solo flight from Georgia to Rio de Janiero was probably impossible. This is a largely fictional account of Redfern's adventure once his plane went down, placed in the context of known actual events.

1

August (1927)

With a quick glance through the window to his left, Paul Redfern's attention was drawn to the glowing turquoise waters of the Caribbean Ocean. There had been no change in the view for almost a full day. Paul was drawn to the beautiful sight. He had taken off at noon from the beach at St. Simons Island. Now, he was mesmerized by the brilliant azure hues compared to yesterday's dirty gray tones near the coast of Georgia. As he had done for the last two hours, he twisted his head sideways to see forward. The extra gas cans stowed in place of the passenger seat meant the two windows in the cockpit faced to the left or right, but there were no windows facing forward.

Paul had been looking for a recognizable landmark the past two hours when he spotted a steamship. He immediately began searching for writing materials in the zippered pocket of his leather flight jacket. As he fumbled with the pocket, he tilted the nose of his plane right at the ship. For fun, he came down within fifty feet of the smokestack. *That will get their attention*, he thought, as he saw a dozen crewmen scramble onto the deck. In all, he spent an hour and a half dive-bombing the steamship and dropping paper notes out the window. The first note inserted in an empty Crackerjack box, asked "Please point ship toward nearest land." He was hopeful the vessel with a German flag had someone aboard who could understand English. A second note inside a cookie tin missed the ship and dropped in the ocean. Luckily, it floated and was fetched by a half dozen of the ship's crew in a dory. Once back on deck the crew read the note, "Point ship in direction of land and wave once for every 100 miles." The captain ordered the ship into a southern heading and blew the ship's horn two times with each blast belching a cloud of white steam. Redfern immediately grasped he was 200 miles from shore. It was actually 168 miles, but the captain had no feasible way of indicating that exact distance.

Redfern dropped one more note, this one wrapped around a screwdriver, which landed on deck, "Redfern, thanks." Now that he knew land was about a couple hours away, he checked his watch and quickly calculated he had been in the air for twenty-three hours.

Paul took one last circle around the ship and jotted down the name from the lettering on its stern: *S. S. Christian Krohg.*

Redfern's goal was to fly non-stop, four thousand six hundred miles from Brunswick, Georgia, to Rio de Janeiro. He had calculated, based on his eighty-five miles per hour cruising speed, that it would take about fifty-two hours. His brand-new airplane, designed and built by Eddie Stinson, was outfitted with a Wright engine, the same engine used by Lindbergh to fly non-stop two thousand four hundred miles to Paris three months earlier. The plane, originally configured as a six-seater, was modified by Stinson to carry a total of five hundred gallons of fuel. There were tanks built in each wing, and in addition, six five-gallon gas cans stowed throughout the cockpit. There was barely room for its only passenger, Paul Renaldo Redfern the pilot.

After the excitement of the encounter with the *SS Krohg*, Redfern checked his compass heading and renewed the monotony of flying over the ocean. His mind wandered to the events that led to his flight toward Rio. It was during "prohibition" in the United States. For the last two years, he had flown for the U.S. Customs Service, taking off at sunset, hunting for moonshiners hiding in remote areas of the Southeast United States. At night, the bonfires used to boil the sugar water wash stood out against the darkness.

One afternoon, he met the head of the Brunswick, Georgia, Board of Trade, Paul Varner. The Board, made up of leading business leaders, was in an intense rivalry between Charleston, South Carolina, and Jacksonville, Florida to become the leading seaport in the Southeast. The Board was looking for a newsworthy promotion that would bring the port of Brunswick to the attention of businesses far and wide. The deep-water Port at Brunswick was accommodating, but not very well known.

Originally, the discussions were about an air show in which Redfern would fly under the Torras Causeway Bridge between Brunswick and St. Simons Island. Redfern described how he had flown under a railroad bridge over the Maumee River near Toledo with about nine hundred spectators watching. Flying under the causeway would be a piece of cake during low tide, except it would be difficult to get many spectators out there. That discussion was exploratory, and nothing had been agreed to when, on May 21, 1927, Lindbergh's sensational flight from New York to Paris became the center of attention for the world.

In a short week later, Redfern had a handshake deal that was put into writing and signed before the end of June. The Board of Trade would build a plane to Redfern's specifications and pay him $25,000 if he made it to Rio de Janeiro non-stop. Here he was now, in late August 1927, in the air toward Rio and about to become one of the most famous pilots in the world.

By late afternoon, Redfern noticed a string of islands dotting the bright green sea. He thought about going down and buzzing the buildings just to show everyone he was there. It was always enjoyable to bring people out of their homes and onto the street to gawk and wave. Redfern was, at heart, an entertainer. But, he realized, every minute he circled made his flight that much longer. The practical side of him concluded, "Let's keep our nose pointing at Rio." Soon the small islands were behind him.

He fought drowsiness all night. Fortunately, the plane would lurch or bounce occasionally which kept him alert. Almost suddenly, the sun rose over his left shoulder. He was back in the bright sunlight. There were no storms in sight in any direction. His spirits and energy made a comeback as the sun's warming rays covered him.

Then, in the distance, he spotted a large emerald-colored island. After staring at it for a couple of minutes, he realized it was the Island of Trinidad/Tobago just a few miles off the coast of Venezuela. He let out a whoop! The sight of land brought relief and satisfaction. Paul thought, *Now we're on the trolley.*

Unlike the chain of smaller islands, he had Trinidad on his hand-drawn map, and knew immediately where he was. There was no mistaking his location now. A slight turn to the right and there was the coast of Venezuela, only ten miles away.

As he crossed the beach near Capuano, the plane shuddered and bucked in the converging wind currents. With a smooth wave of the stick, he steadied the plane back to a level path. He thought to himself, *Well so far, so good. Everything is going according to plan. Everything's jake.* The first half of the flight gave him confidence that he could make it and collect the $25,000 prize offered by the Brunswick Board of Trade. It was the same amount won by Lindbergh three months earlier.

Once the ocean was behind him, Redfern checked his compass heading for Rio against his rough annotations on the handmade map in the clipboard resting on the shiny gas can next to his seat. When the compass reading was dialed in, he scribbled an "OK" on the map at the coast of Venezuela and glanced out the window once more. He then looked forward through the periscope placed directly in front of him. However, the view was blurry due to the vibration of the mirrors from the plane's engine. So, he concentrated on the view from the window next to his left shoulder.

After a few minutes, Redfern looked down again. He found he could not take his eyes away. He had never seen anything like it. For the last two years, flying for the U.S. Customs Service, he had flown over the Blue Ridge Mountains of Virginia and North Carolina searching for moonshiners. The terrain in the mountains was full of trees. Moonshiners tended to prefer uninhabited areas. But he had never seen ground cover like the thick blanket of green below. There was no view of the land, only green treetops. Occasionally, he caught a glimpse of a flash from the sun's reflection on narrow streams. The thick green covering of the jungle caught him by surprise. Paul unconsciously muttered, "Golly." It was evident there was no place to land in the jungle below.

It was Paul's habit, based on his barnstorming days crisscrossing the Eastern United States, to continually search for places suitable for a landing. Over the years, that habit saved him some anxious moments as the combination of a rather capricious engine and nighttime flying meant that landing quickly was imperative at times. He had to explain to several farmers in his career why his plane ended up in one of their fields. Usually a ten-dollar bill would settle any argument over crop or fence damage. Now, looking down at the jungle, he realized there was no place within sight to put the plane down; he had left the ocean behind, so that was not an alternative.

It was an uneasy feeling, but there was nothing to do but go on. He studied the blanket of green trees in every direction. The only clearings were on the sides of steep hills not suitable for a safe landing. Back in the States he could always find a spot to land within a few miles. Looking out over the horizon, thirty miles away, all he could see was the dense jungle. Off to his left, however, was a thin snake of an opening. It was a river sheltered by trees on both sides, also not safe for landing.

His mind wandered to Rio. The mayor had promised in last week's telegram that a fleet of military aircraft would escort Redfern to the airfield on the outskirts of the city as soon as he was spotted. In addition, extra searchlights would be set up around the field with their beams pointed skyward. Redfern knew he was still at least fifteen hours from his goal.

The weather for the flight was ideal. He had not seen squalls in any direction from the time of his takeoff from the beach. The stars had been thick and bright over the ocean, but now the sun was hidden behind a thick layer of clouds.

Over the years, Redfern had his share of mishaps while flying. He never actually crashed, but he had plenty of sudden, unplanned landings. He had built a plane in his backyard while in high school, based on an article in *Popular Mechanics*. Later, after high school, he added an engine and traveled the eastern states giving air shows. That plane, labeled the "World's Smallest Airplane" while funny to see, was dangerous to fly. The short wingspan meant it was dangerously unstable. He also toured in a World War I surplus Jennie, a simple plane used by the Army to train pilots. The hundreds of hours he spent in the sky made him attentive to the mechanical aspects of any plane he was flying. That is why he insisted on being an overseer during Eddie Stinson's construction of *The Port of Brunswick* in Detroit.

Based on thousands of flying hours experience, he did not need to look at the gauges to know how an engine was running. All he had to do was listen.

Lack of sleep was beginning to have its effect. A couple of times he quickly recovered from a nod of the head. He was aware that his second day of flying and staying awake would be the most difficult. The coffee in the thermos bottle was only a couple degrees above cold and not very tasty, but he forced another gulp down. He had already eaten eleven of the twenty sandwiches packed for him. He began to hum a popular song to himself. "Ain't she sweet. See her walking down the street . . ." But, far and away the most effective way to stay awake was to imagine himself waking up in mid-flight plunging into a death spiral. He had read about his friend, "Lonestar" Bill Erwin, in the Dole Race, who crashed in a spin three weeks ago while searching for three other crews that had been lost in the ocean. He tried not to dwell on negatives, but that story was chilling and brought him out of the doldrums.

It was tedious to keep going, but even if he wanted to stop for a while, he could not see anywhere below to land. He just *had* to keep going. He remembered that someone had told him the South American jungles would be difficult. Now he wondered why he had discounted those warnings. The wilderness of the Blue Ridge mountains in the states was a piece of cake compared to the jungle below. Glancing down at his watch, he saw he was now thirty-three hours into his flight. He tried, but was unsuccessful in estimating in his head how many additional hours it would take to reach Rio. He thought, *I could make that calculation easily an hour ago. What is wrong now? It must be lack of sleep. If I could, I'd land for a rest.*

As he was tackling the puzzle in his mind, he abruptly realized his engine was making a slightly different noise than normal. It was not anything drastic, only a slightly higher pitch added to the familiar low growl he had felt the last thirty some hours. Redfern sat forward in his seat. His attention was drawn to the needles in the dials in front of him. Fuel pressure, oil pressure, and engine temperature were normal, and remained steady. There was no change except for a barely perceptible whine from the engine. After about ten minutes of intense checking of the gauges, he sat back in his seat and loosened his nervous grip on the stick. Perhaps whatever was going on was not serious.

Ten minutes later, it happened. There was a loud "clunk" followed by a grinding sound from the engine. Instead of a steady, low rumble, the engine cut out every two or three seconds. Smoke poured out of the engine and flowed past his window. The propeller that had been rotating smoothly was now staggering intermittently. Paul abruptly exclaimed, "Oh no. Holy crap!" He knew instantly his engine had blown a piston—or two. A second later, Paul said aloud, "You lug head! You forgot to add oil today." It was the result of the lack of sleep. At each addition of fuel to the tank, he was supposed to add oil. Without it, the pistons would seize up. He recognized the signs and knew immediately he was not going to stay airborne much longer. His plane would not sink like an anchor, but it was certainly going to be on the ground in the next five or ten minutes. He turned his attention to seeing that he landed as safely as possible. From his previous observation, he knew it was going to be difficult. There was no safe landing area. However, as an experienced pilot, he would not panic, but would remain relatively calm.

2

Columbia High (1917)

During Redfern's elementary years, news coverage of flying and airmen began with a trickle and grew to a cascade. In junior high, Paul was enthralled by the idea of flight. By high school, he was obsessed with learning about aviation. His father, a college dean, had always encouraged him to read, but was bewildered by the fact that young Paul would only read about flying and airplanes.

For two years, Paul scoured every newspaper and magazine for articles about aircraft and flying. He visited the library at the University of South Carolina on a regular basis to search the periodical section for aviation news. His term paper in the seventh grade was a biography of the Wright brothers. He was mocked at his school for wearing an aviator's helmet with goggles during class change. As a sophomore, based on an article in *Popular Mechanics* magazine and pictures from the newspaper, Paul started a multi-year project to build a small airplane in his backyard. Most observers who saw it, thought it was a non-working replica of a plane that would never fly. And besides, it did not appear that the sprouting, teenaged Redfern could even fit in the open cockpit.

His classmates were aware of Paul's project, and it resulted in a good deal of kidding. "Hey Paul, can you take me to Chicago this weekend?" Or, "Have you tried out your parachute lately?" Paul would respond with a drawl, "As soon as it's ready, I'll take you."

For Paul, good grades came easy. The idea that he was one of the "brains" did not sit well. Naturally, his classmates resented "snobs" at the head of the class. Paul wanted to avoid being called a bluenose. Accordingly, Paul was always on the lookout for opportunities to be accepted. In grade school, he constructed a cigar box violin that he played with the box positioned on the floor like a cello. He entertained his classmates playing simple melodies.

He was known for the witty notes passed to his friends during class whenever a teacher turned to the blackboard. The trouble was the recipient could not keep from laughing out loud after reading the missive. More than once, he was caught and admonished for disturbing the class.

During class change in high school, Paul developed a technique for entertaining his friends. He would take three large steps down the stairs and pretend to slip and fall ending up on the landing on his back. During his performance, he would let out a loud groan as if he were injured. The trick was that while it appeared that he fell down the whole flight of stairs, he stayed on his feet most of the way down, and only leaned forward and tucked his shoulder in at the bottom of the stairs onto his back. His stunt never failed to bring a crowd of onlookers. Once he had a crowd, he would jump up, brush his pants, and take a bow. It never failed to bring some shrieks, followed by laughter, once the gathering crowd realized it was a stunt. That trick was good for a few performances. However, after a teacher happened to be on the stairs and sent him to the school nurse to check for hidden injuries, Paul was aware the performance would land him in trouble if he were caught doing it again. Anyway, it had served its purpose. He was not known to his classmates as one of the stuffed shirts, but rather as that funny guy who fell down the stairs on purpose.

After the summer between his sophomore and junior year, the plane in the backyard was practically completed. Except, there was no engine. That was going to be a problem. He did not have the skill to build one himself, and he did not have the money to buy one. The project was put on a hiatus.

To show off, Paul brought the full-sized homemade airplane to school. His shop teacher was overwhelmed, and arranged to have it attached to the wall at the gymnasium in the University of South Carolina for display. Paul had been spending his spare time at the university's library studying books and magazines about aviation. During those trips, he made a point to visit the cafeteria regularly and answered questions about his project.

During his fifteenth year, the "Great War" in Europe began, and in April 1917, the United States joined in. It was not long before all sides recognized the value of airpower to their war effort. In quick order, the role of airplanes in the war changed. First, aircraft were used for reconnaissance, reporting on troop and materiel movements. Then, aircraft were outfitted with simple one-shot rifles and flew to protect the reconnaissance flights from air attack. Finally, planes were armed and used to attack the enemy on the ground with rapid fire machine guns as well as bombs. All these innovations resulted in the need for more aircraft. By November 1917, the Army was intent on obtaining as many aircraft as possible for its own use and to lend to the allies.

Paul Redfern showing off his tiny airplane

Paul read about the fact that the Army was recruiting and training new pilots as fast as it could to join the war effort. Having no flying experience, Paul knew he could not immediately qualify for flight school. But, he reasoned, once he was in the Army, he could maneuver his way into pilot training. After all, he knew the flier lingo from all his reading. If he could meet the right person, he was sure he could talk his way into a pilot training program. The question was: how to approach his family? He knew if he let it slip that his goal was pilot training, his plan would be doomed. But a different approach might work.

Paul had been born in Rochester, New York in 1902, the same year as Lindbergh, but the family moved to Columbia, South Carolina, before Paul started school. Paul's mother, Blanche, and father, Dr. Frederick, were liberal minded, but not dismissive when it came to raising Paul. Both worked at Benedict College in Columbia. Frederick was an instructor and dean in the economics department. Blanche taught English. Benedict was a predominantly Black college. Frederick later was picked as an adviser to President Franklin Roosevelt on poverty issues in the South.

At the dinner table in late summer, Paul brought up his plan and asked his father for permission to join the Army. Paul pointed out that the country needed soldiers, and as a member of a patriotic family that loved the country, he was the logical one to volunteer. He pointed out that there were a lot of assignments in the military that did not involve combat. Paul purposely failed to mention his plans for flight school. He had another reason for volunteering. If his father were to serve, the family would lose its sole provider. If Paul were to join, the family would not lose any income.

Slightly different variations of the conversation were advanced three times. Each conversation had the same ending. Paul's father owned the last word: "The War is no place for a boy. You're only sixteen and you won't finish high school until next year. You are too young for combat. Joining the Army will delay your college. Who knows how long this blasted war will last? You will never get to college if you do not finish your high school studies.   I will not agree to allow you to join."

After the third request, and his father's increasingly forceful response, Paul's father and mother assumed the discussion of volunteering for the Army was concluded. Paul was not exactly resigned to that conclusion. But he realized Plan A, joining the Army, was dead.

3

Standard Aircraft (1917)

A few weeks later, Redfern read a story in *Collier's* magazine about the national war effort. In it, near the end of the article, a brief paragraph caught his eye:

> "Standard Aircraft Corporation has completed construction of a new factory in Elizabeth, New Jersey, where it will build a variety of aircraft exclusively for the U.S. Army. The project, consisting of five and a half acres under roof also has its own airfield for testing. It plans to hire 400-500 workers to work around the clock and will open its doors in three weeks."

"Alrighty!" Paul exclaimed in a half whisper, although no one else was in the room. That article was the genesis for Plan B. It was Saturday, and he had plenty of time to work out the details over the weekend.

It took him most of a Saturday to craft a letter to Standard Aviation asking for a job. Paul attempted to create a persuasive letter. He did not mention his age, but in 1918, it was not unusual for younger boys to become apprentices, sometimes even before they were teenagers. At the time, there was a shortage of factory workers because the draft had scooped up most of the young men. He did include a copy of his grade card from school that showed A's in mathematics and English. The fact that it showed Paul was in the eleventh grade would give the reader a clue as to his age. Paul's qualifications put him in high demand for the factory. The war had drained the number of available applicants. That left Standard Aircraft hungry to find eager workers.

In addition to the application, Paul submitted a letter of recommendation written by a lieutenant of the Army, who had seen Paul's plane in the university gymnasium. The lieutenant wrote, "Master Redfern is most industrious and has strived to educate himself about the construction of aircraft in exceptional detail."

If he could not join the Army to learn to fly, he could learn the ins and the outs of airplane construction. Paul sent the letter to Standard without telling his father. After a week, Paul let it slip at dinner that he had applied for a job in New Jersey. This precipitated several heated arguments among the family members. Paul and his sister thought he should go. Frederick and Blanche were against it. The argument only ended when Paul offered that he was not sure he would even be offered a position. It was premature to worry. He might not even be offered a job.

For the next several days, Paul was the first one to the mailbox in the afternoon. He was anxious for a reply. Finally, after a little more than two weeks, he saw the envelope he wanted. There it was: the letter from Standard Aircraft Corporation in Elizabeth, New Jersey. He ripped open the envelope to read the letter. It indicated if Paul could get to the plant in two weeks or less, a job would be waiting. This was good news. It was the answer to Paul's dream.

His next task was to convince his father to let him go. That was not going to be easy. The first time he brought it up, there was no discussion. His father merely said, "The answer is 'no'." However, Paul was insistent and argued that the country needed the support of every family, and he was willing to be the one from the Redfern clan to do his part. Paul added, "Benedict College can't run without you. It's only fair that I be the Redfern who can go."

His mother entered the conversation. She thought New Jersey was too far away. His big plan seemed to be going nowhere.

After the discussion, Paul was convinced his dream was dead. He went to bed, but hardly slept. In the morning while breakfasting on his Post Toasties and Ovaltine, he was joined by his father. Paul launched into his plea to take the job with Standard Aircraft. He promised that once the war was over, he would finish high school and apply to college. His grades were good enough that he would have his choice of schools.

This time his father did not reply unequivocally. Instead, he said he would "think about it."

A week later, his father asked Paul at the dinner table if he was still interested in going to New Jersey. Astonished by the question, Paul stood up and asked, "Really? Yes I am."

As a professor and dean of the economics department, his father had met plenty of other professors from around the country. One of them was Dr. Otis Smith of Rutgers College at New Brunswick, only eighteen miles from Elizabeth. His father had arranged for Paul to stay with Professor Smith and his wife in a small apartment in the basement of their home. The professor normally rented the place to a student, but this year, many would-be students had joined the war effort.

Paul was head over heels happy. He could not wait to leave on this new adventure.

Ten days later, his family saw Paul off at the train station. He had packed his suitcase with clothes and such, as well as about a dozen magazines with articles about aviation, along with his permission slip from the Board of Education. His mother had tears in her eyes as she handed him a tin of homemade cookies. His sister wished him "good luck," and his father shook his hand. "Don't forget to write your mother," he said. Then, it was off for a day and a half long train ride.

Whether it was the anticipation of the trip, or a deep fear of the unknown, Paul could not fall asleep on the train. Once he arrived at Professor Smith's home, he slept for twelve straight hours. Professor Smith had met Paul's father at an Economics conference several years earlier. Ever since that conference the two had traded letters and interesting academic articles.

Because of the draft, Smith had an empty room in his basement that he normally rented to a student. If it had not been for his friendship with Paul's father and the fortunate circumstance of an empty room in the basement, Paul would never have been permitted to leave Columbia for Elizabeth.

Unknown to Paul, his father had already made the financial arrangements with the Smiths. As Professor Smith explained, it was $9.00 per month which included two daily meals. His father had already advanced the first month's payment.

On the following Monday morning, Paul left his downstairs apartment at 5:00 a.m., walked to the train station and took the commuter train to Elizabeth Station. From there, it was a ten-minute walk to the plant. He arrived at 6:27 a.m. and reported to the office. He was called into the personnel office and was seated across the table from a large, overweight man with a two-inch long, unlit cigar drooping from the side of his mouth. The name plate on the desk said, *Raymond Carrabotta*. He had a stern look on his face.

As soon as Paul introduced himself, the man asked, "Where you from, boy?" And then, before Paul could respond, added "You sure are skinny." All the while, Carrabotta was looking down at Paul's letter.

Not knowing how to respond to the skinny comment, Paul hesitated, then blurted out, "Columbia, South Carolina, suh."

Carrabotta chuckled. "Columbia? I'll be doggone. Well, boy, I'm sending you to Receiving. Report to Petruzzi. I hope he can understand your accent. Go out that door over there and then turn left. He's at the far end. You'll check the lumber as it comes off the rail cars. Ya follow? Give him this paper. Atta boy. Now get out there." That was the extent of Paul's orientation. It was his first experience with brusque New Jersey conversations. Paul sat wide eyed. He replied, "Yes suh" as he got up to leave.

It was not the last time he would be reminded that he had an accent. Even though many of the factory men had accents of their own—German, Irish, or Italian— they laughed every time he spoke. By the end of the week, his name was changed to "Y'all." They would preface every request with "y'all." For example, "Y'all, come on over here." Most of the time the kidding was good natured. Paul realized that, either due to his age or his accent, the older men in the factory assumed he was quite dimwitted. He took that as a challenge. He would prove them wrong.

Petruzzi took Paul to the rail siding next to the open sided lumber warehouse. At the time there were a half dozen railcars at the siding, each open on both sides. Paul could see they were loaded with giant logs. Petruzzi handed Paul a clipboard and explained his job. Petruzzi had an Italian accent of his own that had nearly every word ending in a vowel. "Here's-a what I want-a ya to do. Write-a the number of the car. This-a one is nine, nine, eight, four. Then-a count the logs. When-a you done, write-a de number down here", pointing to a line on the form on the clipboard. "*Capisce?*" Paul had never heard that word, but he answered, "Yes, suh."

"Once-a you done, sweep-a de floor round de railcar. No loafing. I find-a you asleep—you done." Paul was enthused to get started and from that day on, he made sure his work was done thoroughly and accurately every day.

It was not two weeks before Paul figured out how to get along with the other working stiffs, almost all of whom were older, some by more than twenty years. Some of the working stiffs had come straight from Ellis Island. None of them were southerners. First, he began substituting the words used by the workers around him for the milder expressions he brought with him from South Carolina. For example, instead of "Blast!" or "Chicken Toes!", he substituted "Damn!" or "Shit", the normal epithets used by factory workers. Second, he began smoking Lucky Strikes. It took a week or two to quit coughing with every puff, but slowly, it became a second nature gesture to light up with the men before and after work. And, best of all he began to entertain his fellow workers with stories and practical jokes.

Paul recruited Dave, another sixteen-year-old sweeper, during lunch. It took him a week to convince the other boy to go along. He talked Dave into overcoming his shyness and participating in a prank. They spent their free time rehearsing for another three days. Then, at lunch on a Friday, Paul's plan was put into play. A tray was dropped to the floor. The two boys traded loud accusations. Then, Dave, the accomplice, threw a wild round house punch in Paul's direction. The punch did not land, but at that precise second, Paul put up his right hand as if to block the punch. That sleight of hand disguised the fact that Paul used his open left hand to thump his upper chest. The thump sounded like the punch had connected. Paul threw his head to one side and fell to the floor backwards, remaining motionless with his eyes closed.

Immediately, a crowd gathered in curious surprise. Dave knelt next to Paul and waved the growing crowd to stand back. It was nothing like anything they had seen. At the right moment, Paul jumped up and shook hands with the other boy and took a bow to the crowd, some of whom chuckled and lightly applauded before heading back to work.

Paul and Dave performed their stunt only once. Petruzzi heard about it and gave them a stern lecture about how the factory was not a place for a vaudeville act. "This-a is no place for play. Keep-a your mind on work." He mentioned the possibility of firing them. Paul did not know what a vaudeville act was, but understood immediately he did not want to be fired. Paul had his head down as he replied, "Yes, suh." Dave's whole body shook as they walked out of Petruzzi's office. He was the sole breadwinner of his family, since his father had joined the Army. The thought of being fired was terrifying to him.

It was also a message to Paul. He would have to act more like a responsible adult and less like a schoolboy. Paul's playful nature would have to be curtailed. From then on, no more silly stunts.

Paul was surprised at how many logs it took to construct an airplane. The logs came from Northern New York or Canada. They used only Sitka Spruce because of its strength and pliability. After the logs were unloaded from the rail car, they were cut into ten-foot boards. Any board with a flaw such as a knot hole was discarded. Then the boards were cured in steam for ten days. Next the steamed boards were cut into staves of various lengths, some for ribs and some for spars. More flaws were discovered at this stage and the defective wood was sent to trash. Some of the ribs and spars had to be curved by hand. Finally, they were distributed to the wing, fuselage, and tail departments to be formed into the skeleton of the plane. There were about one thousand staves used on every plane.

Counting logs and sweeping the floor were not what Paul had in mind. He wanted to learn how flying machines were made. At the end of his 30-day probation, his manager, Tony Petruzzi, brought Paul into his office. He had been impressed with Paul's ability to catch on to the job, together with his work ethic. Petruzzi called Paul over to his desk. "I'm-a gonna give-a you a new job. You are gonna be inspector. You think-a you can do it?"

Paul was ecstatic. Paul had no idea what an inspector was supposed to do. But that was just a detail. "Yes, boss. I'll do a good job for yah."

Paul soon discovered his job was to take three, seven-foot-long templates that were formed to demonstrate the correct camber and hold them against three spots on the upper and lower struts for each wing as it was completed by the workers. The wing should follow the curves of the template exactly. If there was more than an eighth of an inch deviation, Paul was instructed to put a big red X at that spot on the wing using a big red crayon. Petruzzi would follow up and inspect any wing with an X. Petruzzi would make the decision as to how to repair the flaw. Since Petruzzi did not look at a wing unless Paul caught the mistake, any wing without an X would go on an airplane without further inspection. Paul understood his job was vital to the safety of the airplanes sent to the War. He took his job seriously and placed an X whenever he had any doubts about the quality of a wing.

After a month working with the wing templates, he was assigned to propellers. Here again, he held templates at designated spots on the propeller and marked flaws with an X. In the process, he learned how the wood was glued together and then turned on a giant lathe to form the propeller. Paul was fascinated to work on the parts that went on the airplanes Standard was making.

Finally, after a month, he was given his dream job, replacing an incumbent who had been drafted. His assignment was to inspect the entire aircraft as it came to the end of the production line. He had a three-page checklist for each plane that he needed to fill out and make comments on. His were the last pair of eyes to observe each plane before it was wheeled to the airfield for field testing. There were four production lines in four separate areas, so Paul could wander almost at will and observe the men doing all the tasks required to build an airplane. Paul was aware of the importance of his duties, and he took them seriously.

Paul telephoned his parents and spoke to his mother to tell her of the "promotion." He did not mention the new job carried no increase in pay. All teenagers received the same pay. However, he was happy with the new assignment. The new job would teach him about the complete construction of airplanes. Engines had always been somewhat of a mystery to Paul. This job would provide insight into the secrets of engine manufacture. Before the end of the call, Frederick got on the line. He asked, "How's your arm?" Puzzled, Paul asked, "Pardon me?" Frederick responded, "Well I assume you broke your arm and that's why you have not written to your mother." Embarrassed, Paul agreed to be more diligent in writing letters to home.

The factory turned out several models of aircraft, including the Standard H-3, a reconnaissance plane, the Standard H-4 for the Navy with pontoons, and the Standard J-1, like the Curtiss J-4, the "Jennie", a trainer. Just before the War ended it produced a hundred E-1s, a trainer that could be fitted with a machine gun. The E-1 was distinctive due to the rounded cowling on its nose.

It was not long before Paul knew the name of just about every male worker with whom he had contact. He was too bashful to stop and talk to the women. None of his jobs involved women workers. His job took him to several areas of the factory, and he would ask questions everywhere he went. Some workers would wave him off so as not to be bothered. But there were others who would stop for a minute and go into detail as to what they were doing and why it was important to the process of building aircraft. Paul was determined to learn all he could about airplanes and how they were made. His encounters during work were naturally short. So, it was not unusual for Paul to search for the worker at lunch to continue their conversation in the dining hall. He took notes almost every day, and when he got back to his room at night, he organized them. His goal was to complete his own plane as soon as he got back home to South Carolina. He would use his knowledge learned at Standard to complete it. He realized that his crude little model of a plane at home would have to be re-started. He would have to reconstruct the model to a higher standard.

There was not much time for frivolity during his days in New Jersey. Right after getting to New Jersey, Paul was especially interested in observing the planes being manufactured. The Army was desperate to receive as many planes as Standard could deliver. The war effort was critical. Paul's workday went from 6:30 a.m. each morning until anywhere from 5:00 to 7:00 p.m. that evening. Usually, dinner was in the kitchen on his own since the Smiths had already eaten. Once he had walked to his room from the train station and had his dinner, Paul would take a few minutes to review his notes, but, by then, it was time to ready himself for bed. He was up the next morning at 4:30 a.m..

4

Jersey Shore (1918)

The airplanes being built at Standard Aircraft had a thick linen covering that was stretched over the entire exterior of the craft and then was treated with dope which strengthened the cloth. The cutting and sewing work on the fabric was done in a room next to the production floor known as the sewing room. There were two supervisors; one was male. The workers in that department were all women. While most of the females were older, some of them were close to Paul's age. Whenever he approached the wide door to the work area, there were remarks made to him that Paul could not decipher. When he looked up to see who was calling to him, he saw they were the younger females. The girls, sitting at their sewing machines all with big smiles, were speaking in a foreign language.

The sewing room workers were cutting and sewing the cotton covering that was glued to the exterior of the fuselage, wings, and tail of the planes. As it happened, the women working in the sewing room lived near the plant. That neighborhood was generally made up of families that had emigrated from Poland. It was unimaginatively called "Little Warsaw."

Unlike in other areas of the plant, the women in the sewing room always had something to say, especially to the young men working nearby. Paul's face would turn red whenever he heard them call out to him. "Hey Y'all.

Yakshemash synu," would ring out as he approached the area. He recognized the "Y'all," but he had no idea what the other words meant. But from their tone, he took it as a friendly greeting. Later, he learned it was a Polish greeting for "How are you?"

Women at work in the sewing room

One day, Paul paused just outside the sewing room door for a dipper full of cold water from a bucket. One of the girls pushed open the door wider and called out to him, "Hi! You want see how we sew?" Neither Paul nor the girls could speak the others' language very well. But since both Paul and the girl were interested in communicating, neither let that slight impediment stop them from using a few words and gestures to show their interest in each other. Paul decided he needed to speak quickly and incessantly to be understood. He had to decline the offer. He repeated three times that he was sorry to refuse her offer, but he had work to do. This was his first meeting with Liliana.

Women at work in the sewing room
at Standard Aircraft

In South Carolina, the girls in Paul's school had been shy and, while Paul liked to look at them, he never had the nerve to approach any of them for a conversation. The girls in the sewing room were anything but shy. They had things to say to him in Polish every time he came near, and from their cheerful expressions, he knew they wanted to become friends. After a couple of awkward weeks, Liliana approached him again at the water bucket, "You like go beach tomorrow? You like de vater? We all be there noon. Bring swimsuit."

Paul did not have to think it over. He was looking for something to do on Sunday, besides reading in his room, or walking around his neighborhood. Going to the beach sounded like fun. Back in Columbia, he had learned to swim in the Congaree River. He considered himself a good swimmer. Paul and a few friends from high school had a rope tied to an overhanging tree at the river and each would take turns swinging out over the water and letting go, landing in the water with a big splash. It was a way to cool off during the hot, humid South Carolina summers.

Paul spoke to Dave and convinced him to go with him to the beach. Dave lived with his parents, who had immigrated from Eastern Europe. His father was a butcher and expected Dave to assist him in the shop. However, after begging his father for a day off he was granted permission to go. Dave told Paul he would meet him at the beach.

Paul was not sure who all was going to be at the beach, but he was willing to take a chance. After getting directions, he boarded the bus and, with only one transfer, found his way to the famous Jersey Shore. As he stepped off the bus and looked out over the beach, he saw that there were hundreds of people crowded into the area between the street and the shore.

Once there, he changed to his two-piece bathing suit consisting of a black brief bottom with a white athletic style top. Putting his street clothes into a locker, he wandered down to the water. It took him ten minutes to spot anyone familiar, but there they were sitting and standing in an area of towels and portable chairs. Just as at work, the women were chatting away. Among the crowd were a lesser number of men standing together but not talking, some of whom Paul recognized as Standard Aviation employees.

Paul spotted Dave, and the two immediately began to chat. It was a beautiful sunny day with a steady breeze. They both traded remarks about the breezy weather and the swimming conditions. Dave pointed to the group of Standard Aircraft employees standing in the sand about twenty feet from the ocean. "There's the gang. Let's go join them."

As Paul approached, Liliana called to him with a big smile. "Good you come. Follow me." Paul had spoken to Liliana earlier that week when he was checking out the fit of canvas over the wing of a plane. He was concerned about some wrinkles near the area where the wing attached to the fuselage. Liliana had explained that the wrinkles would disappear once dope was spread over the fabric, causing the fabric to fit to the form of the struts beneath it. Paul checked out the dope and learned it was cellulose nitrate. He verified her explanation and was happy he had not put a big red X on the wrinkled end to the wing. It would have been a mistake. At the time of their encounter, Paul thought she was shy. But today, Liliana was bright and cheery as well as forward.

Paul was ready to join the conversation among his fellow workers. But he followed Liliana, who glanced back at him as she walked away. Dave watched as the two of them left him standing alone. After a short ten steps, Paul and Liliana were at the far end of the group near the seashore. Liliana poured some lemonade into paper cups as they sat down on the sand. The group made up of both boys and girls was busy talking and playing with a beach ball. Paul and Liliana sat and talked together for more than two hours. During that time Paul paid close attention. He guessed she was older, maybe even twenty. He was surprised at how forward she was. She spoke nonstop about a variety of topics: how her family came to the States; how they found New Jersey; and how she loved living here. She turned and pointed north, "Look it's Statue Liberty. I love statue." Paul looked out over the water and there it was. The Statue of Liberty looked almost mystical, like it was floating on the water. Paul whispered to himself, "Wow!"

When he got home that evening, Paul thought about Liliana and their conversation. He had never had more than a two-minute conversation with a girl before. He liked her. He wondered if she would agree to see him again.

Liliana told him she had come to New Jersey a year earlier, and that she started work at Standard about six months ago. Other members of her family had moved to New Jersey two or three years earlier. The Polish women had a reputation as good sewers. Liliana's mother was one of the first workers hired for the sewing room. Liliana said her mother had vouched for her when she was hired. Her father joined the Army almost as soon as they arrived in the United States and was stationed in Europe. Liliana said he was fighting in the trenches somewhere in France.

Paul was impressed at Liliana's accented English after being in The States only a year.

During the following week, Paul was reluctant to go near the sewing room. For reasons he could not explain, seeing Liliana made him nervous. He wanted to see her, but he was afraid. He did not know what to say. He was smitten. When he needed to go by the sewing room for work, he avoided speaking with Liliana.

The following Saturday, as he waited in line near the time clock to check out, he heard Liliana's voice behind him. "Halo Paul. Meet me by door." After a glance from the guard to make sure of his identification, Paul walked to the employee entrance after checking out and waited a minute until Liliana came out. She walked up to Paul. "Why you not talk to me?" she inquired. Paul was not sure how to answer. Liliana waited a second then asked, "Come to beach on Sunday?"

Dave was unable to go, since he had to help clean up his father's shop. But Paul was anxious to go, and decided he would not let Dave's absence keep him from going to the beach once again.

On Sunday, Paul caught the bus, made the transfer, and arrived at the beach bus stop at eleven thirty. He changed into his bathing suit and made his way across a swath of sand to the spot where the Standard employees had gathered the week before. But there were no employees. Paul's heart sank and his brain became fuzzy thinking he was not going to see Liliana.

Something had gone wrong. Walking back toward the changing room and showers he could not help but keep his focus on the sand under his feet. He could not look up. He was disheartened.

As he came within a few feet of the showers, he heard a voice. "Hey, Paul! Where you go?" Looking up, Paul saw Liliana coming toward him already in her bathing suit. "Where's everyone?" he asked. Liliana smiled and approached him. "Follow me."

Instead of walking toward the water like the week before, Liliana turned and walked up the beach to the right. She remained silent for ten minutes as they trudged through the sand. Finally, as they passed the last group of sunbathers, Liliana said, "Here." She rolled out a blanket and they plopped down. Paul wondered where the rest of the group was, but decided not to ask.

Liliana was the first to speak. "You like me?" Paul looked her in the eye and realized she was flirting. He also took her question to mean no one else from the factory was joining them. This was a new experience. "Ah sure do." They fell into a long awkward conversation about their respective plans. Paul explained he was going to become an airplane pilot and explore the world. Liliana talked about opening her own dress shop.

During a lull in the conversation, Liliana jumped up and started to run toward the water and shouted back at Paul, "Come!"

As they approached the surf, Paul looked at the waves as they crashed onto the beach. He had not seen this before. The week before the waves were barely a foot high. This week, the waves were almost over his head. He was not sure he wanted to go into the churning water. Waves that tall were something new to him.

Liliana was about five yards in front and as she raced toward the water, she turned and again shouted, "Come!" With that, she ran into the water and leaped headfirst into the crashing surf. Without hesitation, Paul followed her into the water. As soon as he hit the water, he found himself being tumbled head over heels in the wave. He started to panic, as the water was in control of his body, but before fear could take hold, he emerged on the shore as the wave retreated. He looked up to find Liliana. There she was standing over him. They both laughed as she sat down beside him.

Paul had never had so much fun with a girl. She was still laughing when he noticed something that startled him. Liliana's beautiful left breast had come out from under her bathing suit and was exposed. Not knowing what to do, Paul pointed. Liliana glanced down and saw her bare bosom. Paul half expected her to run off. She looked back at Paul and giggled. It crossed Paul's mind that Liliana did not mind that he saw her bare breast. Then she slowly turned one shoulder away and readjusted her suit to conceal her bosom in her bathing suit once again. There did not seem to be a hint of embarrassment in her reaction. Paul's heart was racing, his face was red, and his ears seemed to be burning.

It was the first day of Paul's first romance. He had a crush on Liliana. For the next few days, thoughts of Liliana crowded out all the others in Paul's brain. He thought of her upon rising every morning and just before sleep overtook his consciousness. They talked and laughed at every opportunity. He wandered into the sewing room to view the work being performed. In the few special moments outside of work when they were alone, there was necking and petting. All this was new to Paul as he awkwardly explored new frontiers. Liliana was mostly receptive.

Although the factory was making airplanes for the war effort, there was not much discussion among the employees about the progress of the war. Newspapers had descriptive headlines every day, but the war that had started in 1914 seemed to be dragging on without any end in sight. There had been advances by the troops toward the German border, but those advances were moving very slowly. As far as Paul could tell, the war was interminable. But then, in the fall of 1918, news of negotiations between the Allies and the Germans made it to the front page. On November 11, the Armistice was announced. The War and the fighting were suddenly over. The doughboys would be coming home.

The joy that the Standard Aircraft employees felt over the end of the war abated as the uncertainty of their future took hold. After all, their only product was military airplanes. With the end of the war, would the government still want the twenty airplanes per day that they were boxing up for Europe?

The answer was "no." The plant closed, and, in mid-February 1919, Paul found himself at the railroad station tearfully saying goodbye to Liliana who also was crying. They pledged to get together again at the first opportunity. They embraced for a long time on the platform. Liliana was Paul's first love. He had never experienced the feelings of devotion he was experiencing.

But then the train began to pull away. His stomach churned as he kissed Liliana one last time, let her go, and bolted a few steps to catch the train as it slowly pulled away. As he paused on the first step, Paul looked back and waved one last time. They had promised to see one another again, but it was never to be, as Liliana wrote to tell Paul of her engagement to another only about six months later. At the time, Paul was still desperately in love with her, but the fact that they had been separated from one another lessened the hurt.

5

Toledo (1921)

After returning to Columbia for his senior year of high school, Paul learned to fly. He had dropped out of high school at the beginning of his junior year to work in the airplane factory in New Jersey, talking his family into letting him go to work based on his desire to help in the war effort during World War I. However, the real reason was his desire to learn about airplanes. He had already built a small airplane based on plans he found in a *Popular Mechanics* magazine. He read every article he could find about flying. When he returned home after the war, he bought at auction an Army surplus Curtiss JN-4, nicknamed a "Jennie," with money he saved from his work at Standard Aircraft. Paul wondered if it was a plane he had inspected, but decided it was not worth his time to find out.

Paul quickly earned his high school diploma at Columbia High. Then, he took some college mathematics courses at Benedict College in anticipation of applying to the Massachusetts Institute of Technology. But the deadline for applying came and went. Paul deliberately let the deadline pass so he would not have to delay becoming a pilot. Finally, he and his father agreed on a one-year postponement of college. His father consented, but only after Paul agreed not to attempt any more dangerous tricks in the air. It was a promise he may not have kept depending on the definition of "dangerous."

Within that following year, Paul rented a pasture on the outskirts of Columbia and began a business, "Redfern Aviation Corporation" just off Adger Road. He offered a variety of services including aerial photography, aerial advertising, aerial training, and passenger travel. At the time, he was the only person in Columbia in the aviation business. The airfield was about five acres of cleared land with a barn that doubled as a hanger and workshop.

His year in New Jersey had given him maturity to go with his dream of starting an aviation enterprise. He was now a young businessman. To Paul, college was just an impediment standing in the way of his real career in aviation. He planned his business to cover all aspects of flying. His enthusiasm for his new vocation was unmistakable.

It is unclear whether he had any customers for his advertising and flying lessons. But he did have some businessmen as regular customers, flying them as far away as Massachusetts, or Nebraska, and the Canadian provinces to New Orleans. But a mainstay of his business was aerial photography, which was used especially to facilitate the sale of farms and other large parcels in the area.

Before long, he began taking fascinated folks up over Columbia at two dollars per hop to sample the thrill of flying. Paul would take his customers over downtown Columbia, or out to the countryside. To garner more interest, he added a few aerobatic maneuvers to his show, including diving and flying close to the ground. He was making more money than he could earn as a college graduate. To his father, the money was less important than getting a college degree. But Paul had his mind set on a career in flying. To him, a college degree was not germane.

Over the next year, in discussions with his father, choosing a college was brought up less and less. By the end of the year, the subject was no longer even mentioned in their conversations.

When Paul saw a growing number of "barnstormers" come to Columbia, he realized that if he traveled to other cities, he could increase his income. The Columbia market was drying up. In the next few years, Paul made out-of-state excursions. He would land in a farmyard on the outskirts of town, hitch a ride to town, and pass out fliers with the details of his performance. The public was fascinated by the concept of flying, and wanted to get a taste. At first, he concentrated on the South. But gradually, he expanded his territory to include Northern cities where he could draw bigger crowds with more pocket money. He flew north in the summer and south in the winter.

The working men, his best customers, were making better wages in Pennsylvania, Ohio, Michigan, and Indiana than the mill and mineworkers of the South. As time went by, to earn the most, he decided to concentrate on the North. Over the next few years, he traveled to most of the states to perform, concentrating on towns with factories.

As he travelled around the country, Paul developed several different "stunts" to wow the crowd below. After tightening the passenger seat belt, he would do loop the loops. His passengers loved a nosedive. He would point the nose toward the ground and only to pull up just as it appeared he would crash. Both maneuvers appeared more dangerous to the public than was the case. Paul had command over the plane during all his tricks. Over time, he developed into an excellent pilot. In addition, since he was on his own, he learned to do many of his own repairs.

Paul Redfern flying under a railroad bridge near Toledo
(note the crowd on the bridge)

Paul had a flare for the dramatic. In the Toledo area, he flew under a railroad bridge that spanned the Maumee River, while a crowd of close to a thousand watched from both banks of the river and from the bridge itself. He flew upstream and then downstream, as he skimmed over the water to cheers and applause. In Texas, he buzzed a train, causing chaos among the train's passengers. When he landed at a nearby town, Paul was arrested and spent the night in jail. As he was released from his cell, both Paul and the local sheriff had a good laugh. The amiable sheriff said, "I thought it was a neat trick, but one of the passengers watching fainted, so I couldn't overlook it." At another town, Paul threw a football dummy out of the airplane window causing several women to scream. He was reprimanded loudly by a handful husbands as he stepped out of the cockpit.

During his stay in Toledo, John Hilderbrand, a wealthy entrepreneur, hired Paul for some marketing activities. Paul dropped cigars attached to little parachutes over the downtown as a unique advertising ploy. Over the next few weeks, when the parachuting cigars became a hit and customers flocked to Hilderbrand's store, Paul and Hilderbrand became friends.

John invited Paul to Sunday dinner at his home. Their daughter, Gertrude, joined the Hilderbrands and Paul for dinner. Gertrude, a tall stately brunette impressed Paul from the start.

Once Paul met Gertrude, Toledo became Paul's northern headquarters. Her beauty, grace, and self-confidence were features Paul had not found in one person before. Gertrude's family was well to do. Her parents were friendly, but never hesitated to involve themselves in Gertrude's associations. They both liked Paul but were skeptical of his suitability as a husband. On more than one occasion, John cross-examined Paul as to his long-range plans. He was clear that he disapproved of barnstorming as a profession. Paul squirmed under the questioning. He had never thought about a life after performing. But since Paul was bitten by the love bug, he was willing to consider a change. He was stuck on Gertrude. When Paul approached John to ask for her hand, her father made him promise to find a safer way to make a living. Paul would have promised anything for the chance to marry Gertrude. He readily agreed to the condition.

After getting Hilderbrand's approval, Paul planned the marriage proposal to the last detail. He picked Gertrude up at the family home in the Old West End and they drove to a field in the Ottawa neighborhood. There, in the middle of a field, was Paul's Jennie. It was parked in a field of partially cut grass, not a regular airfield. Paul had paid five dollars to the owner to clear the field. Nevertheless, the takeoff was smooth, and they flew to Metamora, Michigan, a tiny village, a little north of Detroit. There, they landed in an empty pasture next to a small restaurant, the White Horse Inn. The Inn was a converted country home that was well appointed and comfortable, but not what would be called ritzy. After dessert, Paul, on bended knee, popped the question. Gertrude, surprised and red faced, readily accepted the ring to the polite applause of the other patrons. While flying back to town, Paul showed Gertrude a few maneuvers that demonstrated how happy he was. Gertrude, who was also in a good mood, giggled nervously as they buzzed some frightened cows.

When they arrived at the Hilderbrands', John was anxious to find out if his daughter had accepted. He said, "Come here honey, let me see the handcuffs. The photographer will be here next Saturday."

After a few months, plans were made for a Toledo wedding. Over one hundred attended the service at St. Joseph's church. Paul acceded to the requirement that

Gertrude showing off her engagement ring

he attend classes on Catholicism before the wedding. The honeymoon took the couple to a cabin on Lake Huron in the northern peninsula of Michigan. Paul, of course, flew the couple to the cabin.

Paul wanted to maintain his family headquarters somewhere in the Southern United States. By then, he was attempting to live up to his pledge to Gertrude's father that he would give up his aerobatic tours. A multitude of World War I veteran pilots were crowding the field. The traveling air circus business was winding down, since just about anyone who wanted a flight had already been up. As a result, what had been two-dollar flights now only brought in half a dollar. And, even at that price, customers were hard to find. Flying was no longer a novelty. The air gypsy business was on the decline.

Paul considered becoming an air mail pilot, but the mail routes were mostly between major cities, like Pittsburgh and Chicago. There were not any cities like that in the South in the twenties. And, Paul, a dyed-in-the-wool southerner, was not ready to live in the North.

Just as he was giving up hope of continuing his flying career, a job offer came his way that fit the commitment he had made to quit dangerous stunts. The U.S. Customs Service was charged with enforcing the Eighteenth Amendment, which proclaimed that alcoholic drinks were prohibited, and that brewing alcoholic beverages was a criminal offense.

Soon after the beginning of Prohibition, hidden stills popped up throughout the United States, and the South saw more than its share of them. At the beginning of Prohibition, in 1920, illegal stills were small and of little concern to the authorities. As time went by, however, the number of illegal stills grew. Their capacity now posed more of an affront to authorities. The number of illegal producers of liquor made the government look inept.

It was difficult for government agents on the ground to enforce the laws against distilling alcohol for several reasons. It was common for production activities to take place at night, hence the term "moonshiners." To further avoid detection, the distilling process usually took place in the mountains in locations not easy to locate from the roads. Usually, the stills could be found deep in wilderness areas. The U.S. was determined to put an end to bush whiskey. So, in 1926, Paul was hired.

Paul jumped at the chance to work for the U.S. Customs Service. The job was ideal. The pay was more than adequate, especially since he would receive extra compensation for the use of his plane. The hours left room for outside activities, such as flying. Gertrude was pleased that the job's fringe benefits included a paid vacation. Paul and Gertrude moved into their dream home in Savannah, a brick cottage on West 33rd Street.

6

Chasing Moonshiners (1926)

Paul's life now was quieter than at any time since he left Columbia. He was flying, but the distances were not great. He had a steady paycheck, and he was no longer taking the risks of a daredevil barnstormer. Gertrude had her doubts about living in the South. She was happy, however, to begin her married life with Paul.

Paul would fly from Savannah to his home base for the week on Monday morning. Home base was either Asheville, Kingsport, or Brunswick. On occasion, home base would be Savannah. From the weekly home base, he would fly to a location picked by the Customs Service. To keep the moonshiners on their toes, the Customs office would not decide where to send Paul until the last minute each week. A few of the moonshiners had developed illicit friendships with some of the agents. It was a challenge to keep Paul's flights a secret. Paul developed a reputation for flying in all kinds of weather and never suggested to delay due to storms or other bad weather.

Paul's new job entailed flying four nights a week over the mountains of western Virginia, North and South Carolina, Georgia, and eastern Tennessee, looking for the large fires the moonshiners used to cook the mash. Once found, Paul submitted a report to the Customs Service together with a map showing the exact location. He did not have to confront the moonshiners himself. His job satisfied the criteria set out by Gertrude's family. On the fifth day, he'd be busy with paperwork, writing lengthy reports for the government. The job did not involve dangerous stunts in the airplane and garnered a regular paycheck.

Paul's spy-in-the-sky work was a success. According to legend, he once pinpointed eighty-seven moonshiners in three days in southern Georgia. The Customs Service was pleased with his work. Moonshiners were violating the law and the Customs Service, with its revenue agents, was gradually putting them out of business.

Paul's nightly flying time started at six o'clock p.m. This was different than he had been accustomed to, but he was getting used to it. As a barnstormer, he usually flew at noon and was finished shortly before dark. Now he was flying in darkness regularly. This job was steady work—Monday through Thursday flying—and he could always get home to Savannah on weekends, as well as all week on occasion. For the time being, Paul thought this was an ideal situation.

Paul's success in hunting down moonshiners was partly because there were so many of them and partly because of the fires they used. The flames were so brilliant as to be seen for miles even though some of the distillers attempted to surround the bonfires with homemade fences and overgrown vegetation. This hid the whiskey stills from the ground. But flying overhead at night gave Paul a clear view of the bright blaze.

Typically, Paul would fly at about eight hundred feet over the mountains until he spotted a fire. Then, he would swoop down right over the operation to get a better look. Paul would then search for a nearby road. Sometimes that maneuver would draw angry gunshots from the elicit distillers. Paul had over twenty patched bullet holes in his plane's fabric during his first year. Upon his return to base, Paul would write a report on the location giving the Customs people the approximate number of stills, the location of nearby roads, and whether he had attracted any gunfire. The agents about to raid on the ground were more than a little interested if there had been any lead thrown at Paul since they could expect the same when they raided the distiller on the ground.

It was Prohibition, so there were no legal bars open. But, in the South, if you were interested, you could find a room at the local Elks or Eagles Club where an alcoholic drink, called "corn," was available. Paul thought it was amusing that he was tracking down moonshiners for the "revenuers," but sipping their product regularly at the social clubs. He was careful not to boast publicly about it though.

In November 1926, Paul was given an assignment to fly in the Brunswick, Georgia, area. There had been reports of moonshiners operating on some of the small, barely settled, barrier islands off the Georgia coast. While in Brunswick, Redfern met Paul Varner, the Chairman of the Brunswick Board of Trade, as well as a prominent Chamber of Commerce member. Paul found it convenient to dine at the Elks Club, where it was possible to order an illegal drink with your meal in a secluded area of the basement. It was also a spot where an out-of-towner could socialize with other club members. Eating in a public restaurant did not offer such advantages.

After running into each other a few times, the two men hit it off. Paul was the talkative one, and he never tired of telling stories about his flying accomplishments during his barnstorming days traveling around the country. Varner had never wandered extremely far from Brunswick. In fact, other than a few trips to New York City, his longest trip was his monthly visit to his banker in Atlanta. Varner ran an import business down at the docks and was interested in promoting Brunswick as an import destination. At the time, Brunswick was the up and comer, while Jacksonville, Florida, about seventy miles to the south and Charleston, one hundred and seventy-five miles to the north, were the more established locations for importing and exporting commodities in the Southeast.

Varner introduced Redfern to Howard E. Coffin, who was a founder of the town of Sea Island as well as a wealthy businessman. The three of them were regulars at the dinner table, as were the other businessmen who occasionally joined them.

Their discussions were generally about the status of business in the United States, which, at the time was booming. Everyone, it seemed was prospering. Unemployment hovered at or below three per cent. Stock prices, as well as real estate prices were doubling every few months. A wide range of people were borrowing money to buy up shares from Wall Street or local real estate, with the intention to sell at a profit in a matter of weeks. No one in 1927 foresaw the Great Depression that would decimate the country in 1929. They were living in the midst of the "Roaring Twenties."

Paul told Varner and Coffin about his life as a barnstormer, crisscrossing the Midwest and South putting on exhibitions. Paul had a way of telling stories that made him look good, but without bragging. He told of his conversations with Clarence Chamberlin, a pilot renowned for his flight across the Atlantic. Chamberlin had explained how to recover from a death spiral: "Point the nose of the plane down and then pull up." Paul joked about his first attempt at the maneuver and how his laundry bill had spiked immediately afterward. The men had a good laugh.

Over the next weeks, Varner introduced Paul to several other local businessmen. Varner was anxious to show off his new friend, the airplane pilot. The after-dinner discussions grew from small groups of one or two, to up to as many as ten men.

Varner usually led the evening's discussion. Once they were through with the main course, Varner would order a bottle of moonshine, which came in a mason jar. He would ceremoniously pick up the bottle, turn it upside down and shake it for about ten seconds. He would then hold up the bottle for all to see. It was a test to determine the alcohol content of the illegal brew. The bubbles were small and lingered only a few seconds before disappearing, showing an alcoholic content of about forty-five percent. If the bubbles had been large, it indicated a stronger alcoholic content, almost undrinkable. If there was anyone new at the table, Varner explained that the distiller supplying moonshine to the Elks used copper equipment that was not salvaged from an automobile. It was common for illicit brewers to use automobile radiators containing traces of methane and lead, both poisons. The jar was then passed around, followed by a pickle juice chaser to alleviate the burning sensation in the throat. As the evening progressed the mason jar and chaser would make several passes around the table.

During one of those discussions, Paul recounted the story of his flight earlier that evening. He had been flying over one of the offshore islands reachable only by boat between Brunswick and Savannah, when he spotted a large fire. As he came down for a closer look, his attention was on the fire, until he saw the muzzle flashes from the rifles. By then. the plane was cruising dangerously low. He was taking fire, and, before he could pull up, he noticed a wide hole in his left wing from a shot on target. He quickly banked to the side before sustaining further damage. Everyone laughed as Paul remarked how he was all of a sudden unintentionally imitating the Red Baron.

When Paul was in the middle of telling the story, the restaurant manager and a delivery man with three cases of illegal whiskey in mason jars on a dolly, walked by their table on the way to the kitchen in the back. As it happened, the delivery man was the owner of the moonshine still that had fired on Paul. He obviously heard Paul's story, so he stopped and announced, "So you are the son of a pup that flew over my operation earlier? If you try that again, you'll be mincemeat." His face was red with anger as he confronted Paul. The manager attempted to step in between the two men.

At first there was silence. Paul stood up, but hesitated to speak. The diners around the discussion table were worried a fracas might erupt. Then Paul responded. "Well, I did not know it was your operation," he drawled. "If I had, I would have looked on the other side of the bay. For Pete's sake, I wouldn't want to spoil my dinner here at the Elks. Lucky for you I haven't turned in my report for the night. I'll be careful next time." Everyone at the table laughed, including the manager. The moonshiner reluctantly chuckled.

Paul left the table and followed the moonshiner to the kitchen for a private discussion. Once Paul verified where the still was located—Pompei Island—he agreed not to disclose its location to the Feds. In addition, Paul agreed not to mention the earlier shooting incident in his report to the Customs people. In return, Paul extracted a promise from the moonshiner not to disclose Paul's subterfuge. The two men shook hands and parted. From that date, Paul never flew low over the moonshiner's island again. The Elks Club was their normal meeting spot, but the encounter with the moonshiner cemented the relationship.

Howard Coffin was probably the richest man with whom Paul had ever had a conversation. It was during one of their dinners that Paul realized that he could talk to anyone. He was a natural born talker. Growing up in Columbia with an academic father, working at a young age in New Jersey, living the life of an air gypsy, and stalking moonshiners were all experiences that made him unique. He liked to talk, and he was a good storyteller. The combination of his easy-going nature and his southern accent made him approachable, and enabled him to gain the confidence of listeners of any social class.

After about a year, Paul, Varner, and Coffin had developed a good relationship. Paul had been assigned to the Brunswick area several times, for a week or two at a time. Varner, a bachelor, ate dinner at the Elks Club most evenings. Coffin, a grandfather, was also invited. Each time Paul was in Brunswick, he ran into Varner. When Paul arrived at Brunswick just after Memorial Day in 1927, Varner told him that the Brunswick Board of Trade, as well as the Town of Sea Island, were interested in sponsoring an event that would bring renown to the Brunswick area. Varner asked, "Do you know anything about the cost to bring an air circus to town? We want to sponsor an event that will help to bring attention to Brunswick—and coincidentally to our great shipping port."

It was less than two weeks since Lindbergh's flight and Paul, ever on the outlook for business opportunities, ventured that a single aerobatic stunt would fit the bill. Paul explained that one solo aerobatic stunt could attract a crowd and generate some good will for Brunswick. He suggested a flight under a bridge like the stunt he had performed at the Maumee, Ohio, railroad bridge. Paul explained, "For that stunt, we publicized the event so everyone in town knew about it. Then we arranged for the trains to be held up for an afternoon to keep the bridge clear. There must have been at least five hundred people who showed up on that bridge to watch. Everyone in town and nearby Toledo was talking about the stunt." Varner and Coffin were intrigued. Coffin suggested a flight under the Torras Bridge. Before a plan could be arranged, Paul left town for Kingsport, Tennessee, on word of recent moonshine activity.

On the way to Kingsport, Redfern flew over the Torras bridge connecting Brunswick to St. Simon Island to check out the possibility of flying under it. It did not take long for Paul to discover this proposed stunt had drawbacks. First there was little room between the bridge and the water. Except during low tide, which varied every day, the opening was too tight. The stunt was still doable, but it would be at the mercy of the tides. Plus, there was limited room for spectators, and the bridge would have to be closed to traffic for the show. With the bridge closed, walking to the bridge meant about a mile trudge. In Paul's estimation, flying under the Torras bridge lacked the pizzazz the Board of Trade was looking for. When he arrived at Kingsport, Paul called Varner and gave him the bad news. They agreed the limitation on spectators was fatal.

By then, the news of Lindbergh's flight from New York to Paris had electrified the nation. Lindbergh collected $25,000 for his efforts, an amount equivalent to about $300,000 today. In city after city, thousands lined the street to get a glimpse of their hero, "Lucky Lindy."

On his next stop to Brunswick, Paul made a point of having dinner with Varner and Coffin. While eating, they discussed the news of the day. Lindbergh's flight came up, and they noted the wild adoration that he was receiving during his victory tour of the country. Paul told them of the similarities between Lindbergh's and his background. They were the same age, twenty-seven, and both had gotten their start in aviation as traveling air gypsies performing stunts around the country flying a World War I surplus Curtiss "Jenny." And both gravitated to more conventional employment after several years of performing. Lindbergh took a job with the U.S. Mail Service, and Redfern was employed by the Customs Service.

Varner was impressed by the report that Redfern had once met Lindbergh. As Redfern explained, they both appeared at the same Air Circus in Springfield, Illinois. It was six years earlier while Redfern was performing air acrobatics, and Lindbergh was putting on a parachute show. Lindbergh's most famous trick was to jump from a plane, open his chute, and as he approached the ground, disengage from the chute, and let it fall to the ground. The crowd below would gasp in unison. Some of the women would scream. Then, after what seemed like an eternity, Lindbergh opened a second parachute that he had hidden under his coat and continued to float all the way to earth. Redfern remarked that all the pilots admired Lindbergh's trick, but urged him to come up with a safer routine. Lindbergh took the advice and confined his tricks to the loops and spins inside his plane. Later, Lindbergh gave up performing and took a full-time job was flying mail between St. Louis and Chicago.

In the aftermath of the unbelievable outpouring of celebration over Lindbergh's triumph in Paris, a flurry of aviators attempted to cash in on the public's fascination with overseas flights. Millionaire Charles Levine, with pilot Clarence Chamberlin, made it to Germany in May, surpassing Lindbergh's mileage, only to crash outside Berlin. The plane was seriously damaged, but the aviators were unhurt. A month later, explorer Richard Byrd attempted to copy Lindbergh's flight with a crew. He made it to France in late June, but after getting lost, landed in the fog about one hundred feet offshore in the Atlantic Ocean.

Newspapers covered these flights, often sensationalizing the details. The public was enthralled by the daring aviators and was eager to hear any detail the reporters could offer. There were aviation reports in the news every day. However, many articles disregarded any accuracy. For example, when Charles Nungesser from France took off for New York, several newshawks reported on their progress claiming sightings from Newfoundland to Long Island. Finally, a report appeared in the paper of Nungesser's remarks upon landing on Long Island. It turned out he had never made it past Newfoundland. All the reports of sightings and conversations were bogus. His plane with the crew was never found, much to the consternation of the French public.

Naturally, when Varner, Coffin, and Redfern got back together to tip a few in Brunswick, they each offered their own views on all the aviation stories. Paul pointed out that he could undertake a long flight if he had a modern plane, with a reliable engine, rigged to carry sufficient fuel. Airplanes right out of the factory would fly about three hours and no more due to the capacity of their gas tanks. Unlike the Byrd and Levine flights, Paul said, "I can fly solo like Lindbergh. I have the experience. In fact, I probably have more than Lindbergh. Charles flew a mail route, so he flew over the same route day after day. My flying has been over unknown terrain and wilderness where I have to do my own navigating."

In the following days, Paul was in serious negotiation with Coffin and Varner planning a flight to show off his skills.

7

Flying to Rio (1927)

Over the next three weeks, Redfern, Coffin and Varner continued to discuss details of a rough plan. The goal of Varner and Coffin's was to bring positive, nation-wide publicity to the Port of Brunswick. Paul's suggestion seemed to fit the bill. A deal was struck. The Board of Trade, or some of its members would buy Redfern a new plane built specifically for a long-distance flight and award $25,000 to Redfern if he were successful. The plane would be named *Port of Brunswick* and fly to a distant location. Redfern offered the idea of flying to a South American city as it was something no one had done. Looking at a map, the three men agreed on Rio de Janeiro as the destination. After Coffin dealt with Redfern, he negotiated with several members of the Brunswick business community. They were quickly sold on the idea. The businessmen conjured up the picture of a ticker tape parade like Lindberg's to celebrate his triumphant flight. They were delighted with the prospect.

In setting Rio de Janiero as the destination, Paul was looking to smash Lindbergh's records. Lindbergh had flown thirty-four hours and two thousand four hundred miles. Paul would fly over the Caribbean Ocean to Rio de Janeiro in Brazil. Paul was attempting a flight of four thousand six hundred miles, which would take at least fifty hours. He predicted flying almost twice as far as

Lindbergh would bring twice the praise to him and the city of Brunswick, his sponsor.

The more they talked, the more the plan took shape. Paul contacted Eddie Stinson an airplane designer and manufacturer in Detroit. Stinson's "Detroiter" aircraft had a good reputation for stability and reliability. The "Detroiter" model had just been named champion of the Ford sponsored, National Air Tour in which fifty-four planes visited twenty-four cities in June. That race rated each of the planes not only on speed, but also on durability and navigation competence. Stinson was the only airplane maker Paul contacted.

At the end of June, Redfern went to Detroit to supervise the construction of his new plane. Paul, after all, had been an inspector at the now shuddered Standard Aircraft factory. He had made the final inspection on all the models of airplanes produced in New Jersey. He felt qualified to do the same in Detroit. He took a copy of the three-page final inspection checklist from Standard with him to Detroit.

After about three weeks in Michigan, Paul journeyed to Flint to visit Bill Malloska, the sponsor of *Miss Doran*, the Buhl Air Sedan, a biplane, he planned to enter in the Dole Race to fly to Honolulu. The Buhl company was also located near Detroit. Paul was anxious to see the plane to survey the changes that had been incorporated into the plane to facilitate a trans-oceanic flight. He was interested in the petcock valve that had been added to allow the wing gasoline tanks to be quickly emptied so that if the plane ended in the water, it would float. As a result, Paul added that feature to his Stinson when he returned to Detroit.

While in Flint, Paul spoke to Augie Pedlar, *Miss Doran's* pilot. A coin toss at the local newspaper had determined Pedlar as the winner over Slonnie Sloniger. Paul, who knew Sloniger, was a little surprised that Pedlar had won the job. Paul thought Sloniger had considerably more flying experience. Paul was also surprised by Pedlar's comment that the flight to Hawaii would be a "piece of cake."

His "All I have to do is head West and put it down when I get there," seemed rather flippant. On his way back to Stinson's plant, Paul thought, *Boy, Pedlar seems rather flip. I'll be better prepared than that.*

Paul was not put off by the fact that the "Detroiter" had only one engine. As he explained, Lindbergh's Ryan aircraft had only one engine and if he were to take a two-engine plane it would increase training time as he had never actually flown a two-engine aircraft. Besides, flying a two-engine plane was not any safer since the amount of extra fuel would make landing and taking off that much trickier. Paul thought his choices were conservative and not at all temerarious. Besides, at the time, if one engine failed on a two-engine plane, it would not necessarily stay in the air. The chances of an emergency landing would not diminish using two engines.

The Board of Trade sent out press releases, and, sure enough, it was not long before the story was picked up by a myriad of newspapers and the whole country heard about Paul Redfern's plans to fly from Brunswick, Georgia to Rio de Janiero.

When Paul reached Detroit, Stinson showed him a partially constructed plane he planned to outfit with extra fuel storage suitable for a long-distance flight. The "Detroiter" so named to highlight the Stinson factory's recent move from Dayton, was a six-seater. They quickly determined that one seat was plenty, especially since the flight would require over five hundred gallons of fuel, as well as extra oil. The seats were removed to make room for the gas cans. Stinson ordered a Wright Aeronautic engine, an updated engine like the Wright engine used by Lindbergh.

One drawback to the extra fuel stored in the cockpit was the lack of a window facing to the front. Instead, a periscope was placed in the cockpit, to give Paul a ready forward view. Otherwise, he had to use side windows to look at his surroundings. Another drawback was the extra weight of the fuel, which would make the plane unstable during takeoff.

During construction of the plane, Paul used his *souvenir* checklist he had pilfered from Standard Aircraft. Paul went over his plane and checked the boxes. While doing so, he found a couple of minor errors. One mistake was that the bracket holding one of the ailerons was misaligned, and the other was the linen cover next to the doorway had a small rip, which could easily expand. Both made it to his dummy checklist and were corrected.

The plane, named *Port of Brunswick* was delivered to Paul in early August. In the next few days, he took it for short flights around the Detroit area, before heading to Georgia. The flight to Georgia on August 5th gave Paul and Eddie a good opportunity to test the new plane. They purposely did not carry a full load of fuel, so takeoffs and landings would be stress-free. While Stinson was confident that his design would handle five hundred gallons, they did not need to take any chances now. The extra weight would make the plane sluggish on the ground. There was no sense in putting the brand-new craft in any danger of a risky takeoff.

Paul Varner and Paul Redfern discussing the upcoming flight next to the Port of Brunswick plane

The flight from Detroit to Brunswick lasted ten and a half hours, and they landed among a crowd of at least one thousand. The size of the crowd was notable since their exact time of arrival was unknown. As it turned out, their overall average speed was a respectable eighty-six miles per hour, about what Stinson had promised.

The handsome craft was painted a bright green and gold, emulating the colors of the Brazilian flag. On each side, in large, white letters, were the words, "Brunswick to Brazil." As required, the license number NX-773 was displayed on both sides of the tail. By the time they reached Brunswick, news of the flight to Rio had been carried by all the news services across the country. They spent the next ten days flying around Brunswick, checking all the controls, sealing the compass, and practicing landings and takeoffs.

At the end of May, less than a week after Lindbergh's flight, James Dole, the "Pineapple King" from Hawaii announced that he would put up $25,000 for the first pilot to fly from California to Honolulu. Thus, the Dole Derby was born. Redfern initially was one of the first to send in his name to enter. However, before the deadline for an entry fee, Redfern dropped out. He withdrew because he had made a deal to fly his own record-setting flight.

On August 16th, nine days before Redfern's flight, the Dole Racers lined up to takeoff from Oakland for Honolulu. While two planes made it, five either dropped out or were lost. Two more airplanes crashed on takeoff. In all, ten airmen and one woman perished. Tragically, Malloska's plane was one of the ones that was lost.

As a withdrawn entrant in the Dole Race and based upon the tragic results of the contest, Redfern must have been aware of the calamity. Despite this, the three men in Brunswick, Varner, Stinson, and Redfern, pressed on with developing a publicity stunt involving a protracted flight over the ocean. Redfern thought if Lindbergh could do it, he had the expertise to pull off his flight over the Caribbean. In his mind, he was just as good a pilot as Lindbergh, who had just flown over the Atlantic Ocean.

Several news organizations sent reporters to Georgia to cover Paul's takeoff. Just about every day between landing in Brunswick from Detroit and his takeoff from the beach at St. Simons Island, Paul spent part of his day showing off the *Port of Brunswick* and answering questions. There was mention of the proposed journey to Rio on the front page of almost every newspaper in America.

Varner was also inundated with questions from reporters. He was surprised by the interest in the flight. He never failed to mention the Board of Trade when discussing the flight. Even before the flight, he felt the good publicity the Board was receiving was worth the effort of sponsoring the venture.

Paul received letters of encouragement from folks all over the world, including celebrities such as Howard Hughes, Mary Pickford, and Tom Mix. His most prized letter was from Anne Morrow Lindbergh, wife of Charles. She wished Paul success and invited him to lunch once his flight was completed. Paul suspected the thoughts expressed in the missive were from Charles. But Charles agreed to Anne's letter because he did not want any notoriety from the letter. Paul was proud of the fact that the Lindberghs were interested in his flight. The letter accentuated in Paul's mind the significance of his flight.

On August 24th, within two days of takeoff, while grounded during a summer storm, Paul and Eddie Stinson ducked into the Sunrise Café, a clapboard hash house on St. Simons Island. They discussed once again the details of the plane's specifications and features. Stinson reassured Redfern, saying, "I've gone over the entire plane and am satisfied it's ready to go. I'm sure you have enough petrol for the trip. The Wright J-5 is the best available engine. Just be careful not to spill too much when you pour the gas cans into the tank."

To maintain adequate fuel levels, Paul would need to periodically empty some of the five-gallon cans of gasoline into a funnel leading to the fuel tanks in the wings. Paul reassured Stinson that he had practiced emptying the steel five-gallon cans using water to get familiar with the process. And on the trip down from Detroit he had additional practice during their trip to Brunswick. Stinson, aware of Paul's ever-present pack of Luckies, also gave Redfern, a stern lecture about pouring fuel with a cigarette dangling from his mouth.

Stinson then asked, "Are you still planning to fly non-stop to Rio?"

"It's all set," replied Paul.

"And how long will it take?"

"I think the four thousand, six-hundred-mile flight will last from fifty-two to sixty hours."

Eddie had been aware of the answer before he asked the question. He remained silent for a long twenty seconds. He wanted Paul to take his next warning seriously. "Paul, you need to reconsider. That kind of flight is more than a man can stand. A flight to Caracas just across the Caribbean would be a more reasonable destination—and it would be a record setter. Brazil is just too far."

Redfern did not respond, as he was about to put a piece of apple pie a la mode into his mouth. It was too late to change the itinerary anyway. If he shortened the route it would seem like he was afraid. Besides, the mayor of Rio was planning a lavish celebration with fireworks and movie stars. Paul finished his pie and changed the subject without commenting on Eddie's warning.

8

Takeoff and Landing (1927)

Paul's takeoff was planned for Glynn Isle Beach on St. Simons Island on Thursday, August 25, 1927. The sandy beach was nothing more than a mile-long sand bar attached to the island at one end. The "runway" was the hard sand at the edge of the water. Due to its isolation, pilots occasionally used it for takeoffs or landings. It was not, at the time, a regular runway for airplanes. For Redfern's purposes, however, it was perfect. The sand was firm and flat. There were no trees or buildings to interfere with the customary northerly breezes. The weather that day was sunny.

At about 6:00 a.m. a crowd began to assemble. It was warm and humid as most August days were with a light, but steady breeze. The mechanic from Wright Aeronautical, Charles A. Morss, had been there since 4:00 a.m. for a last-minute check of the engine. Since Lindbergh had used a Wright engine, it had become a favorite of pilots for long-distance flights. Starting with Lindbergh, and continuing throughout 1927, Wright sent a technician to check the engine before every over-the-sea project using their popular J-4 or J-5 engine.

On the day before the flight, Morss talked to the press, saying that tests showed that the plane would use approximately ten gallons per hour, travel at about ninety-five miles per hour, and could stay aloft for a total of fifty hours. He added that they had intended to set an induction compass that day but had run out of time. The single magnetic compass would have to do.

Paul Redfern taking off in Port of Brunswick on Glynn Isle Beach

Redfern had decided against taking a radio, because, at over a hundred pounds, it was heavy. In addition, radios at that time were known to be quite unreliable. In any event, there was no room for the nine square foot box in the cockpit. Besides, radio directional beacons had not yet been installed along his route. He also decided against a parachute. He was confident he would make it without the need for one. Besides, he only needed a couple of hundred yards to land. Likewise, Paul passed on taking an altimeter. He was willing to rely on his own observation to avoid colliding with a hillside.

That morning, based on the recommendation of Professor Simon Breckinridge from the University of South Carolina, Stinson loaded a sturdy wooden wine bottle case onto the plane behind the pilot's seat. It contained items for survival, including a first aid kit, a fold-up rifle, a revolver, boxes of ammunition, knives, fishhooks, fish line, flares, and baubles and beads suitable for trading with the "savage Indian tribes." Redfern was unaware of the box until the morning of the flight when Stinson showed it to him together with the letter from the professor. Stinson said, "You'll have plenty of time to read this on your flight. Follow the advice of the professor. You might run into some hostile Indians down there." At the time Paul did not have a clue how savage a South American "Indian" might be. He had focused his preparations on landing at Rio. He had no intention of landing anywhere short of his destination.

Stinson reached in and fastened the letter to the clipboard mounted on the right side of the dashboard. Paul took a quick look at it and decided he would look it over once the flight had settled into its humdrum phase.

As another safety measure, the main fuel tank was rigged with a petcock valve which, when opened, could dump its entire contents in forty-five seconds to avoid a fiery crash. Then, if closed, the empty tank would aid in keeping the plane afloat on the surface should he need to ditch the plane in water.

Stinson also included an inflatable rubber raft with the new plane. Gertrude tested it in the surf at St. Simons and declared, "'Why it's a delightful craft. I don't think anyone could sink in it."

By ten o'clock, the crowd had grown to over three thousand at Glynn Isle Beach, with only Paul's closest friends and family inside the ropes, together with a half dozen news reporters and photographers. Many in the audience had flags and banners. It was a festive atmosphere. The people gathered at the beach were there to see history being made. Some had left their cars alongside of the road and walked to the beach. Another hundred cars were stuck in a logjam on the packed sand road leading to the beach.

Paul spoke to the crowd and expressed confidence. "It's going to be a long two days, and I better get started. My plane is checked out and ready to go. Don't worry about me. If you do not hear from me right away, I'll be walking out of the jungle, even if it takes two or three months." Several laughed at the remark, including Paul.

He then walked over to Gertrude to give her a farewell kiss. As he put his arms around her, he could feel her body tremble from head to toe. She was nervous but not crying, which Paul took as a good thing. He held her in his arms for a good minute. However, he had never seen her so emotional and distraught. It was too near the time to leave to start another conversation about the flight. They had discussed the venture over and over, and the more Gertrude learned, she became less and less happy with the situation. But she knew she could not keep him from going from the moment he came up with the idea of flying to Rio. When it came to his flying, Paul was never hesitant.

At noon, Paul trotted over to the plane and jumped up to the cockpit in one bounce. The plane was already running, and he taxied slowly over to the beach. After pausing to look over the gauges, the *Port of Brunswick* started slowly down the beach. As it picked up speed the crowd on the rise overlooking the beach began to cheer. The cheer increased in volume as the plane picked up speed. Then, a spray of water flew up behind the plane. It had gotten too close to the slow remnant of a wave. As a result, the plane lost speed. Paul pushed the throttle, a lever on the dashboard controlling the flow of fuel to the engine. The crowd let out a collective disappointed "Ohhhh." The plane immediately slowed to a crawl as he slowly made a U-turn. Someone got a truck to pull the plane back the half mile to the starting point.

As he got back, Paul Varner ran up to the side of the plane. He was concerned as he did not want his friend Redfern involved in an accident, and perhaps just as important he did not want the Board of Trade to get any bad publicity. "You OK?" he yelled. Paul shouted over the engine, "Yeah. I just need to keep my speed up with all this gas on board. I'll keep her out of the Atlantic this time."

Sure enough, the second attempt to take off at 12: 46 went smoothly and without incident. The crowd shouted and waved banners goodbye. Once airborne, Paul could not resist the temptation to turn back and take one last pass along the beach to the delight of the crowd. A spontaneous cheer erupted. The onlookers waved goodbye as the words "Brunswick to Rio" came into view. Paul dipped a wing in a gesture of farewell to the multitude of well-wishers. The bright green plane then turned to the South. Once out of sight of the beach, the plane cruised out to sea, directly over a fleet of three shrimp boats.

Gertrude walked slowly to the limousine Coffin had lent to her. She sat down on the back seat, leaving the door open. As she reached for the door handle, her strength drained out of her, and she slumped across the back seat. She quietly cried for the next ten minutes. She then ordered the driver to take her back to the Sea Island Club. As they drove to the Club a strong forlorn feeling enveloped her.

A lesson learned by any experienced pilot in the twenties was that sooner or later, an emergency landing would occur. Emergency landings were typically routine because they were so common. The landing itself could be accomplished in a farmer's field or on a straight stretch of road. The distance needed was short, since the plane's speed was reduced to about forty-five miles per hour.

The reliability of engines was far less than today due to a variety of factors, including the lack of precision metal-working machines as well as the fact that engine design for aircraft was relatively unsophisticated. In addition, for long range flights, a pilot needed to be aware of not only the fuel supply, but also the replacement of oil leaking into the combustion chamber.

Paul had forty gallons of oil aboard in five-gallon cans along with the fuel cans. Or, as Paul would pronounce it, forty gallons of "ohl."

Once he heard the thud, and saw the smoke, Redfern knew immediately he was going down. He turned off the engine. It was then that he remembered that he had not added oil for a good seven or eight hours. He felt like a fool, for that could have been the cause of his trouble.

His mind jumped to the present. What could he do? He could look for air currents to prolong the flight, but that would save a few minutes at the most. If he happened to get into an updraft, fine, but he would not spend time searching for one. He had other things to worry about. He maneuvered into a long shallow glide. The lack of noise from the engine was jarring after hearing the earsplitting rumble for more than a day. The only sound was the whoosh of the wind. He thought for a few seconds about dumping the fuel cans in the cockpit. He then realized the petrol might be needed for a takeoff later. Fire was a common danger in a crash landing. He decided the metal cans would be safe in his reinforced cockpit if he could continue to slow his speed. He worked the ailerons to maintain control. At the same time, he reached over and turned the valve to flush all the fuel from his main gas tanks from both wings. He continued to scan the landscape below looking for an opening in the canopy of green treetops. There were none for as far as he could see.

As looked back behind the seat at his petrol situation, Paul noticed the forty gallons of oil. Paul spoke aloud to himself, "Jesus, I forgot to check the oil." After flying for almost two days, he had not replaced the oil in the aircraft engine. The typical combustion engine in 1927 needed oil as well as gasoline infusions. That could have been a big mistake.

Paul tried to look forward through his periscope. But it was too jumpy to see clearly. The fact that there was no window to the front, and he could only view straight ahead through a periscope, hindered his ability to pick out a landing spot. But due to the vibration, he gave up using the mirrors. He pressed a cheek against the window to his left to see forward. Still after five minutes, he could only see the green trees in between the clouds and the smoke spewing out of the engine. As the seconds ticked off, he lost altitude but there was still no clearing in sight.

Just then, he remembered a conversation with "Daredevil" Dick Grace, a Hollywood stunt pilot famous for crashing airplanes on film. Dick had told him, "When I'm doing one of my stunts, I always maneuver so the right side of the plane hits first. I don't want those ash wood ribs to break off and puncture my heart. If that happened, I'd be a dead pigeon." Then, another Grace recollection came to Redfern: "I need to keep the plane at about half speed to maintain control. Anything less may result in a spin. If that happens you could end upside down. Any faster and you hit too hard." For a split second, Paul wondered how those words of advice came to the forefront of his memory. He then concentrated on his landing.

Thinking he was as prepared as possible, Redfern tightened his seat belt, stowed his clipboard and thermos. He was now about ten feet above the tree line. He waited two seconds as he continued to lose altitude, lifted the nose to the left, and stalled the plane causing it to sink into the trees on its right side. He had slowed his foreword movement, but even so he was traveling at about forty miles per hour.

As he crashed into the trees, there was a loud thump, and then what seemed like an endless series of very loud cracks and crunches as tree limbs and the plane both broke apart. He saw his right wing disintegrate, as chunks and splinters from the wooden spars and ribs flew in all directions. Paul was thrown against the control panel in front of him. He briefly felt an aching forehead, but then lost consciousness.

When he awoke several minutes later, he was disoriented. *Where am I?* he thought. He realized his brain was working in slow motion, and he wondered if the condition was permanent or temporary. *How long have I been here? What conked me?* Gradually, the mist behind his eyes began to lift. He started to recognize his surroundings: he was still in the cockpit. His left wing was pointing skyward, and he was scrunched in his seat to the right. He remembered the crash. Then, when he tried to slide over to look out of the window, he spontaneously let out a loud cry. "Owww!" Every slight change of position raised the pain level several degrees. He could not move. His right leg was on fire.

His forehead was aching. Looking down, he realized for the first time his leg was bleeding from two gashes: one on his thigh and the other just below the knee. He felt his forehead and found a large bump, covered with sticky, drying blood.

Just then, the plane rearranged itself with a thump in the treetop and dropped a few inches to a slightly more level orientation. His view was obscured to the right by a five gallon can resting on the window. Gingerly reaching over to his left, he opened the door latch and using his left heel, gave it a kick hard enough to throw it all the way over so it ended up resting against the fuselage. In doing so, he let out a semi-scream, "A-y-y-e-h-h!" The pain in his leg was intense. He looked out and realized he was in the top of a tree, too high to jump down. In addition, it was raining, his footing would be slippery.

Paul unwrapped the silk scarf from around his neck and wiped the blood off his leg. The bleeding from his thigh had stopped, but blood was still oozing from his knee. He tied the scarf around his lower leg to stop the bleeding.

He guessed he was about twenty feet from the grass below. As he assessed his predicament, he began to look around for something to stop the bleeding. He remembered the first aid kit packed in the wine case. It took three shaky swipes of his hand to dislodge it. He pulled up his corduroy pants leg. Finally, he retrieved the gauze and tape from the kit and arduously wrapped the two leg wounds. As he did, he realized the cuts had not severed an artery, because the bleeding was merely dripping and not pulsing in unison with his heart's beating. But, protruding from the skin below his knee, he could see glimpses of white bone. From his stint in the Boy Scouts, he knew he had suffered a compound fracture. *I survived the crash, but boy am I in a jam.*

Paul decided to remain still for a few minutes to plan his next move. He was relieved to observe there was no fire from his crash. He began to unbuckle his seat belt, but stopped. He was afraid he might fall out. His instinct was to exit the plane. He could not get help otherwise. However, it occurred to him that he was relatively comfortable sitting in the cockpit with a roof over his head despite the soft drizzle. He had some snacks and a thermos with now-cold coffee. He had no idea where he would go if he got to the ground. He could see no road, nor was there even a trail. All he could see were twenty- to thirty-foot tall trees surrounding him and thick underbrush of ferns and palms in between. He was astounded to see a few brightly colored flowers sprouting from the tree branches, not understanding that they were orchids.

As he sat there, he became aware of the loud call of the birds in the vicinity. Paul had never been a bird watcher, but he could not help being fascinated by the scene from up high. At the top of a tree, he was in their territory. Their calls were louder and more frequent than any of the birds in South Carolina. There were countless noisy parrots swooping hither and yon. Tiny hummingbirds flashed from flower to flower. Toucans with overgrown, gaudy bills flitted about. He felt the perspiration running down his back. He struggled to take off his wool-lined, leather flight jacket. As he was pulling his arm out, he was startled by the huge shadow of a twenty-pound Harpy Eagle with an owl-like face gliding directly over his head.

9

Rescue (1927)

After about twenty minutes, and no obvious solution to his predicament, Paul heard voices. He could not make out what was being said, but he was sure the voices were human. He instinctively called out, "H-e-l-p-p-p!" He could tell the voices were getting louder. He yelled for help again. Excited voices were getting closer. He called out once more just in case the approaching group had not seen he was high in the trees. His heart was racing.

Paul strained to see in the direction of the voices. Then suddenly appearing from the brush, three small brown personages came into view. Paul blurted to himself, "Holy smoke!" He blinked as he stared out of the open door. The three men were completely naked and barefoot. Their bronze-colored skin was glistening from the soft rain. Each one had a small necklace made of shells. Two of them had painted reddish and purple streaks over their bodies. Paul was by no means tall, but these men were quite a bit shorter, maybe a little less than five feet. By their stature, he assumed they were boys, especially since they had taken no steps to cover their genitals. None wore any clothes whatsoever. Each one carried a five-foot-long stick, which he would learn later was a blow tube. Paul was not sure what to make of these people. Anyone running around naked must be lacking in brainpower. On the other hand, they were the only hope Paul had of assistance. Paul shouted down, "Hello, can you help me?" The three men continued to talk in excited tones to one another. They looked up at him and pointed. Their conversation was indecipherable.

Suddenly, one of the men leaped from the ground, placed his feet on the tree trunk and hand over hand, scrambled up to Paul who was looking out of the open doorway of his plane. In about two seconds he was sitting on a branch just above Paul, looking down at him. Paul looked back at this person with coal black eyes and bright yellow feather arm bands just a few feet away. The man raised an eight-foot-long tube to his mouth and suddenly a short dart struck the fuselage near the doorframe, a small feather visible on the end. Paul had not realized the blow tubes carried by the natives were weapons. He was startled. Paul was afraid the next dart would be fired at him.

Professor Breckenridge in his note had warned him of poison darts. Instinctively, Paul raised his hands palms out to fend off an attack, saying "Whoa!" His raised hands had another meaning as well. Paul realized he was being treated as a potential enemy, or at least as a suspicious stranger. He kept his hands out and open to demonstrate his lack of aggression. The native slowly lowered the blow tube so it was pointing downward. Paul could not help but look down at the man's genitals. Why was he not covered? He saw that the penis was pointing up to where his prepuce was fastened to a string around the waist. Immediately Paul looked back at the man's face. All through this encounter, the two men on the ground continued a stream of loud and animated chatter. From this close-up view, Paul concluded that this strange small person was an adult and not a child.

Instinctively, Paul pushed his open hands forward and asked again, "Can you help me?" Paul always thought a direct approach was the one that was most effective. The man answered in what seemed like babble and then shouted something to his comrades below.

As he sat there, Paul recalled the letter he had received from Professor Breckinridge in greater detail. In it the professor had described the natives of the Amazon region. He had barely glanced at the nine-page letter during his flight. However, he did recall one sentence in which the professor had said, "The savages in the region are hostile to white men and can be vicious. Some tribes have been known to be cannibalistic."

The man with yellow feathers standing outside the door then made a gesture holding one hand palm up, and open while bringing the other down from above to the palm. Paul realized the man was mimicking how his plane had gotten to where he was. Paul replied, "Yes. Yes. Yes," nodding his head up and down while managing a smile. He mimicked the motion of one hand swooping down to the other. Paul did not know it, but the fact that he had fallen out of the sky was a factor in his favor. The man with the Yellow Feathers acted friendly as a result.

It was not the first time Paul had tried to communicate with someone who did not speak English. At the aircraft factory in New Jersey, there were several immigrants from Europe, including Liliana, who predominantly spoke their national tongue. As he had managed at the factory, he tried to smile and act as friendly as possible. He repeated everything he said hoping it would be understood. However, Paul was having a difficult time acting friendly because the pain in his leg was excruciating.

Paul started to move toward the door to better communicate, but as he started, the man vaulted down to a lower branch and in one more bounce was on the ground. Then, all three of the natives disappeared back into the jungle. Their voices faded. Paul did not know what to think. Perhaps by moving toward the door, he had scared the men off. Maybe they had gone for help at a nearby settlement. Or they would come back in a few days and find him dead. His heart was still racing. He did not want to be abandoned. He had never been in a situation like this, and he grasped how unprepared he was. He was sucking in air in big gulps.

Finally, after several minutes, he realized his emotions were taking over, and to survive, he would need to calm down. It was a lesson learned through flying and coming out of tight spots in the past. He thought, *OK, take it easy. Panic will not help. You have food and water and a roof over your head. You need to think clearly.* Gradually, he felt the hammering in his chest subside. He made a mental note of the spot where the men had melded into the forest. Turning awkwardly in his seat, he reached behind for the box of supplies. It was too heavy to lift so he concentrated on opening the lid far enough to reach in with one hand and grab two things, a flare gun, and a revolver. It took several minutes just to manage that task and he was breathing hard as he slumped back into his chair.

After a few minutes, he reached back behind his seat again and found some dried apricots to munch. He stuffed the excess fruit into his jacket pocket along with his Luckies.

As Paul attempted to relax, he thought more about his situation. He began to wonder what kind of men he had encountered. They certainly were primitive. Why did they not understand the importance of clothes? He wished he had studied the letter from the professor more closely. As he wondered, he nodded off in just a few seconds without realizing that sleep was overtaking him. He had passed out again.

About an hour later, he awoke to the sound of voices. The intermittent rain had stopped. He looked but could see nothing. As he listened intently, he recognized the voices were speaking the same strange language as the men before. Then, one man emerged from the forest. He was naked like the men before, except he had many more colorful bird feathers attached to his arms and ears. Then, one by one, about two dozen more men followed him out of the underbrush. Paul called out through the open door, "Help!" He held up his hands palms out. Startled, the men looked up and backed up a step or two. Paul saw a few of the men load the bows they were carrying with five-foot-long arrows.

This time, four men jumped up the tree trunk to a branch near the open door, including the man with the yellow feathers attached to his upper arms. One man carried a length of woven vine in his hand and started to unwind it onto the floor of the cockpit. When done, he threw one end over a nearby tree limb and tied it off. Then, without a word, he pulled the door all the way open and reached into the cockpit, looping the other end around Paul under his arms. He made a gesture to Paul to come out of the doorway. Paul looked down and thought he could easily fall twenty feet if he were to take a step.

Several men crowded around on the ground and grabbed hold of the green rope. The man next to him gestured again. Paul realized they wanted to lower him down with the rope. Paul wondered if these diminutive men were strong enough to keep him from falling. Paul hesitated for a moment and concluded the men were trying to help him. They would not drop him, at least not on purpose. *I don't have a choice if I want to get out of here,* he thought. He was willingly putting his life in their hands. (A few weeks later, when Paul saw the men build a sophisticated bridge with ropes and heavy tree branches, he realized he had nothing to fear. But now, he was wary of what was happening.)

First, he gathered up the remaining snacks from the floor of the cockpit. There were chicken sandwiches, peanuts, dried fruit, and a half bottle of juice. He finished the juice with one gulp and put the other items in a paper bag that he let drop to the ground below.

Then, he gingerly slid over to the door and stood with his left foot on the edge of the door frame. To test the situation, he held the inside of door frame and bent his knees, so his full weight rested on the rope. The men below held steady. Paul thought, *Good thing I only weigh about one hundred twenty-five pounds*. He then stepped out of the plane and let himself fall forward into the air. The men held tight and slowly lowered him to the ground. As he set down, he first put weight on his left foot then his right. As soon as it touched the turf, his right leg collapsed. He let out a sudden yelp and was on his back looking up at a dozen sets of black eyes staring down at him. Out of nowhere, an illustration from the book, "Gulliver's Travels" made its way to his brain as the pain receded.

Looking up at the group, he observed the men closely. All had bronze-colored skin, black hair and eyes, and stood under five feet tall. Their hair was cut as if a bowl had first been placed on their head. A small bald spot was evident at the crown of the head. Their bodies were clean, and they had no body odor. Each one carried a stick with a string attached to the top and bottom, or a hollow tube. He could see that each one also had a small container tied to a cord around his waist with what appeared to be twigs with feathers attached. Some of the men wore some sort of decoration attached to their earlobes in the form of a tattoo and small feather. Some were adorned with arm bands made of feathers. Paul observed the brown men each had thin legs and muscular shoulders, as well a small pot belly.

One man had more elaborate decorations consisting of bright red feathers worn in his hair and others attached to his arm bands. Paul was surprised to see a live toucan with a black body and bright orange bill sitting on his shoulder. He noticed that this man was the one giving orders, which the others obeyed. He was the head man in charge.

Paul listened intently for a few seconds to attempt to decipher a word or two, but he was at a loss to comprehend the conversation. He could not grasp anything. He waited another moment, with the expectation that time would bring some understanding, but still nothing said was decipherable. He sat up and asked, "Speak English?" There was no comprehensible response. He thought, *How am I going to find out what's going on?* He concluded he'd have to use sign language—talking with his hands. He needed to speak to be understood. He rattled on about his leg, explaining that it was broken.

Paul reached down and tugged at the small rip in his pant leg. It separated with a *z-z-i-p-p-p!* Simultaneously, he said, "Broken," and pointed to the out-of-place bulge of a bone that was now obvious. This brought a round of talking from the men, but again Paul had no idea what they were saying. About half the men then left and trotted into the woods. Paul sat up in the grass. His mind wandered to the appearance of the men. Why were they not wearing any clothes? What had he gotten himself into? Were these savages dangerous?

About five minutes later, Paul heard a rustling in the underbrush, and two men appeared, carrying four sticks, each about three feet long. Without hesitation, they wrapped palm fronds around the open wound and then tightly lashed the sticks to his leg, using a strand of vine. *It's a splint*, Paul thought, *exactly what I would have done for my leg if I were able.* It assured him that the intentions of these natives were not hostile.

Paul observed that these short men had stern and unsympathetic facial expressions. However, they had been treating him well. This mixed message, based on physical characteristics, was confusing. Did their facial expressions convey a hostile opinion? He would need more time to figure out what their attitude toward him was. But the good news was he had been treated well so far. He had no choice but to trust them.

Two men maneuvered Paul between them and picked him up. One put his shoulder under Paul's armpit and the other looped an arm around his waist. Paul started to warily step forward. He felt the strength of the smallish men at his side. They had no problem lifting him up. Walking was painful, but he had no choice but to follow the silent orders to hike as best he could with their assistance. He did not want to be left alone, which seemed like the only alternative. While the two helping him walked at a slow pace, the other men bounded ahead into the jungle.

Paul took one small hop with his good left leg and tried to keep the broken leg elevated. He let out a howl of pain when he inadvertently stepped on his right foot. He decided the only way to make headway was to hop on his left foot, keep his right foot off the ground, and endure the pain. He continued taking more hopping steps. Paul noticed they were following a narrow trail through the wilderness. He was surprised that the small man on his right was able to hold him up with each small move forward. Paul decided he would take it "one step at a time" and not think about his aching shin.

After about fifteen minutes, Paul spoke up and announced that he needed to rest. He made a gesture with his face demonstrating that he was tired. Apparently understanding, the two men assisting him lowered him to the ground.

After a short respite, the three men continued their walking and resting routine for the next two hours. It was midafternoon, but the profuse tree branches created an umbrella of sorts that protected him from the sun. During the journey, Paul continued to listen intently to the chattering of the men around him but could still not understand what they were saying. He *did* feel that their treatment of him was relatively gentle, and did not sense any hostility. He noticed that while his shirt became wet with perspiration, none of the men around him seemed to be sweating, even though it was hot and markedly humid.

As they continued forward, Paul felt his body begin to weaken. The adrenalin rush from the plane crash had long since disappeared. He could feel the ache in his broken leg, and wondered how much longer he could go on. But he decided he must press on. He worried that if he stopped, the men would just go on without him and drop him in the jungle to fend for himself. As he pondered whether he could last long enough to get to shelter, the group came to a clearing in the wilderness. The open area had obviously been stripped of trees, but some tree stumps remained. Paul judged the clearing to be about an acre in area, and in the middle was a low hut with a thatched roof. His spirits rose when he realized that his walk was apparently over. There were only about fifty yards to go. Paul could hardly hold his head up, but as they continued moving forward, three dozen unclothed children ran up to him, yelling, laughing, and pointing, and Paul could not help smiling at the cluster of curious youngsters, who showed unrestrained joy at his arrival. He was the center of attention.

Then, one of the boys came closer and reached out with his palm, patted Paul's hand, and quickly ran away. One by one, the rest followed suit using their hand or fingers to gently touch him. Paul noticed a few of the girls were cradling small monkeys as if they were dolls. All the while the children continued to jump and dance all around him, laughing, pointing, and shouting unintelligible words.

A few seconds later, there was another commotion as a group of women approached and ordered the children away. Again, all of them were naked and barefoot. The women were shorter than the men by five or six inches and had the same bowl-cut-with-bald-spot hair style as the men. Some had painted squiggles on their bodies and faces. All the body parts one would expect to be covered were there to see. In addition, the women each had two to four white tubes protruding from their cheeks or chins. Paul looked down and away. This was embarrassing. How was he to handle this situation? The admonition of the professor came back to him: "The natives in South America can be vicious and some are known to be cannibalistic." As he stood propped against two men, the women circled him and chatted among themselves. A few of the women approached him, and, like the children, reached out with their hands to touch him. Again, he felt no danger, but he was wary.

Finally, the group made its way to the village. Paul surveyed the opening in the jungle. He would later learn the name for the clearing was *shabono*. In the clearing was a hut where the tribe slept. It was about one hundred feet long, and contained a compartment for each family. It had a thatched roof and was open on the side facing the clearing. The other sides were open about five feet to the thatched roof line. Smoke could be seen curling up from inside some of the compartments.

The main feature of the room was a hammock hanging about a foot off the dirt floor. There were several clay pots and woven baskets strewn around the room on the ground.

Several fires, some burning brightly, and others merely smoldering, could be seen in the courtyard. A layer of mist hung over the clearing. Some of the families wandered into their own cubicle, while others remained in the clearing squatting around a fire. There was a low level of murmuring from the families' conversations, interspersed by an occasional laugh. Other than the men who had rescued him, the tribal members were no longer paying much attention to him. He thought that was a good sign.

Paul heard someone bark orders in a loud authoritative voice as he and about fifty natives marched up to an open doorway. The procession stopped. In the hut opposite them was a twenty-five-square-foot room. The two men holding up Paul guided him to the edge of a hammock and lowered him into it. It was comforting to relax after the arduous walk from the plane. He noticed the sky was darkening into evening. The crowd of rescuers stood just outside the doorway.

The headman with a toucan on his shoulder appeared. He was still giving orders and Paul noticed they were obeyed. It was the man with bright red feathers in his hair and on his upper arms. This man gave the appearance of being perpetually in a hurry. He wore a necklace around his neck that was made of shells. Paul made a note to himself to find this man he named Red Feathers and make friends with him. He was an important person.

The headman called out to another man in the crowd, who immediately stepped forward. This man had small dots on his body resembling spots on a leopard. He immediately inspected Paul's leg. After a few seconds, he went to the foot of the hammock and lifted Paul's right foot about six inches. He began to chant in a low voice, all the while shuffling his feet from side to side. As his song progressed, he raised his voice and looked up at the sky. Paul thought to himself, *What's going on?*

The man's voice was high pitched and, while he was not singing, whatever he was saying had a slightly melodic sound to it. He came directly over to Paul, waving both hands and taking ever faster steps from side to side. Paul stared back at the man in amazement. After a few seconds, the man reached down and opened the torn pant leg, making a waving motion with a bouquet of indigo feathers. This went on for about a minute, at which point he shouted toward the crowd, and two men stepped forward.

One man approached Paul from behind and placed his hands under Paul's armpits. The other man grabbed Paul's right ankle. Paul quickly realized they were going to set the broken leg bone, but before he could protest or say anything, the leg was being pulled and the bone was restored to its intended location. The pain was insufferable, and as Paul moaned, he lost consciousness for the third time that day. He was oblivious as the two tree branches were tightened with a thin vine rope around his leg. Paul was also unaware as the agitated man turned and left.

It turned out that the setting of the broken leg was only partially successful. Eventually he would be able to put his weight on the right leg. However, he would continue to have some pain and would limp for the rest of his life.

Paul noticed it had started to rain again, and it fell unimpeded through the porous roof. There was water dripping down everywhere. It was obvious that this compartment had not been in use for some time and needed repair. The man with yellow feathers, who had been standing nearby, noticed too. He scampered up to the roof and spread a couple of layers of palm fronds on the roof to stop the rain. Paul sat on the hammock, and was thankful for the new roof. He did not think he could sleep with rain falling on him. Now, he put his head back on the damp hammock.

The crowd quickly dispersed and went about its evening activities.

As Paul closed his eyes to sleep, he was startled by the man with the yellow feathers, who called out, "*me-a-re.*" With a broad smile, he handed Paul two sticks approximately four feet long. Paul was puzzled. The man retrieved the sticks and put his shoulders over a short perpendicular branch at one end of each of the sticks. Paul then realized the man was offering him a pair of primitive crutches. Paul got up and put each one under an arm and began to hobble a few steps, keeping his right leg off the ground. The props were shorter than he would have liked, but, with some effort, he was able to achieve some mobility. He wouldn't have to spend his days sitting in a hammock as he had so far. Paul said "Thank you" three times, and the man smiled again before walking away.

* * * * *

GERTRUDE AWOKE WHEN she heard the knock on her door at the Sea Island Club. She called out, "Who's there?" She really had not had much sleep since Friday and, at 6:00 a.m. on that Sunday she was wide awake. It was Paul Varner and Eddie Stinson. She called for them to wait by the door for a minute.

After she freshened her face and put on a robe, she let the men in and offered them a chair in her suite.

"Have you heard from Paul?" Their expression was grim. Gertrude was a stately woman with upper class upbringing. She smiled warmly at the two men in front of her in contrast to the look on the two faces in front of her. Her attention was heightened.

Gertrude Redfern waiting by the radio
for news of Paul

Varner and Stinson both responded, sometimes individually and sometimes concurrently. Their message was not good. Paul had not shown up in Rio the previous day and it was almost impossible that he could show up there now. His fuel had to be gone, so one way or the other, his plane was on the ground or in the ocean. If he had landed in a city on his way to Rio, some sort of radio message would have reached Georgia by now. If he were in the water, his plane could be floating. Or not. But no one had reported seeing him. Therefore, he was either in the ocean or in the wilderness north of Rio. They informed Gertrude that since Paul had no radio, he would have to find someone with broadcasting equipment before they would hear from him. When they had finished, there was silence.

When it was clear Gertrude had no questions, the men explained: The Mayor of Rio de Janeiro promised to send his military planes from the Army base at Macapa to the north to do a thorough search. However, no one had a good idea of where to look. A general inquiry was being broadcast throughout Central and South America in the hope that someone on Paul's route would report a sighting so they would know his direction at least. The mayor said he would contact the Venezuelan and Guiana governments to join the search, but he did not think there were any spare government aircraft in either country. Private pilots would be recruited to search. Both Varner and Stinson reported they did not anticipate much help from any South American nations other than Brazil.

The men expected Gertrude might break down with the news, but she remained stoic. She had shed all her tears on Friday and Saturday. Her final words to Varner and Stinson were, "I'll wait here for a few days, and then head home. Call me if you hear anything."

Before they left, Stinson passed on one ray of hope. "Radio stations, ships, and lighthouses sprinkled on or near his route across the equator are alert to his voyage and plan to flash to the world the first news they have of Paul or his plane. Amateur wireless operators throughout the southeast, as well as powerful government and commercial stations are keyed up and listening in for the slightest bit of information about his whereabouts."

Two weeks later, on September 3rd, the steamship, *Christian Krohg*, pulled into the docks at Kingston, Jamaica. Unaware of Redfern's disappearance, the captain had not publicized his August encounter with the *Port of Brunswick*. Once he heard about Redfern's disappearance, he visited the newspaper office and told the story of his encounter with Redfern one hundred and sixty-eight miles from the shores of Venezuela.

When the news reached Gertrude, it gave her hope, since Redfern was less than two hours from the coast when he crossed paths with the ship. It was unlikely he had gone down in the ocean. Gertrude's hopes were higher now after hearing this report. She recalled Paul's words: "Don't lose hope, because it might take several months to walk out of the jungle."

Within the next month she decided to take an extended visit back to Toledo to be with her parents for comfort. She was happy to return to familiar surroundings.

Unbeknownst to anyone in Georgia, George Henry Hamilton Tate of the American Museum of Natural

History went to look for Paul in late September. Tate, who was born in England and worked in New York for the museum, was an expert in the study of rare warm-blooded mammals. Tate was already in Brazil on an expedition for the museum cataloging South American wildlife when he received orders by cable from the museum's board to change his itinerary and go to the Mount Roraima region to search for Redfern. The leaders at the museum had read about Redfern's flight and thought they should help since Tate was already in the vicinity. The huge tabletop mountain, Mount Roraima, is in Guiana near its border with Venezuela and Brazil. It was originally discovered by Sir Walter Raleigh.

Tate reluctantly pulled his party away from northern Brazil and circled Mount Roraima. After a week, he canceled the search for Redfern and resumed his pursuit for rare animals in Brazil.

He did not report his lack of success in finding Redfern until he finished his expedition a month later. Once back in Georgetown, Tate wired the museum in New York and tersely described the results, "Sorry to report, no sightings of Redfern." Only then, did word of the failed search make it to the newspapers.

While Gertrude was troubled that there was no good news, she kept her hopes up. Paul had always been a good aerobatic pilot and that meant he was an expert at getting out of tough spots. She told everyone that she was still optimistic. Tate's story, which she read in the newspaper, was discouraging, but not so much as to make her anxious. She told reporters, "Paul is going to pop up sooner or later."

10

Settling In (1927-1928)

Paul awoke just after dawn. The voices and laughter from the open area just outside his hammock were enough to draw him out of his sleep. He rolled over in his hammock to get a view of the courtyard. He grimaced from the pain of his broken leg, which remained tender. As they were the day before, the men, women, and children of the village were all engaged in a variety of activities. From his hammock, Paul could see about one hundred inhabitants.

Paul thought the scene was peculiar. He had never witnessed anything close to this. He was fascinated. Here he was, living with natives that he hadn't even known existed before yesterday. He thought, *Until now, I've never known anything about these people. Now I'm* living *with them.*

As he stared out at the natives, Paul realized he was in the care of the tribe. They had saved him from certain death by taking him out of the plane and bringing him to their village. They had even set his broken leg. But right now, he was being ignored. No one was talking to him. Everyone seemed to be concerned with their own mundane chores. Paul thought, *The tribe does not appear hostile. I think I'm safe.*

As Paul studied the scene in front of him, the man with yellow feathers, who had engineered his rescue yesterday appeared. He handed Paul a makeshift bottle, fashioned from a gourd, filled with water, together with three bananas. Paul nodded his head and thanked him. As he peeled one of the bananas, he realized he was hungry. After gobbling down the first one, he quickly tore into the second and then the third banana. The man with yellow feathers darted off just as Paul was thanking him again.

Redfern was still fascinated by the natives' lack of clothes. Men and women of all ages, as well as children, wore absolutely nothing. They made no attempt to cover any part of their body. They did decorate themselves, however. There were flowers, bird feathers, and tattoos, none of which were covering any private parts. Women had white sticks protruding from their lower lip. Others had sticks piercing their nostrils. Paul had never imagined such a sight. He was raised in a conservative household and was stunned by the scene. He thought the folks back home would be scandalized.

Paul spent the morning in his hammock. In addition to peering out, he adjusted his clothes and studied his crutches. *What do I have to do to survive?* he thought. After thinking for a few minutes, he decided the people were friendly. *I don't want to annoy them*, he thought. *I should be as agreeable as possible. If they like me, they are less likely to be hostile. Whatever they tell me to do I will do.* Paul thought back to his days at Standard Aircraft. He dealt with many strange people there. He hoped his plan to remain friendly would work on the tribe.

That afternoon, Paul struggled out of his hammock and got onto his makeshift crutches. He had difficulty because the crutches were made to fit a smaller person, so he was bent over as he hobbled around.

Paul limped toward a group of women sitting nearby on the turf weaving baskets into shape. As he approached to within ten feet, two men intervened between Paul and the women, bounding in with a purposeful gate. Each of the two men carried a bow, and a blow tube. Paul realized they did not want him to have any contact with the women. It occurred to him "fraternizing" probably was not what they were attempting to prevent.

He spun to the left on his good leg and slowly made his way toward a group of men sitting on their heels in a circle at the other end of the yard. As he approached, he called out, "Howdy Fellas." The men looked up, and several said something to him, but Paul had no idea what their words meant. He stood for a few minutes and watched what they were doing. Then, he lowered himself to sit on a nearby log, from where he observed that all the men had something in each hand. Paul looked closer to see what they were holding. Each man held a stone in one hand, with which he pounded away at another stone held in the other hand. After a few minutes, Paul realized the men were making arrow or spear heads. He thought that it was remarkable that they had the patience and ability to chip away at a rock until it became a sharp weapon.

Once he understood what they were doing, he remembered the professor had told Paul the natives in South America were living in the "Stone Age." The professor was right about that. Paul thought, *These natives are literally chipping out stone implements. They don't have any wheeled vehicles, nor do they have any metal tools. Yet they have learned how to make weapons. What ingenuity!*

Paul stood and watched the men craft arrow and spear heads for an hour. By then, he had caught the attention of a group of children aged roughly three to thirteen. They hurried over to him and began to follow him, all the while twittering and jumping around. Paul had to laugh at the happy contingent. He led them around the compound, much like the Pied Piper. Then, he suddenly ducked behind a large tree, and the children stopped following him. He was suffering from the beginning of a weeklong bout of diarrhea.

In the days that followed, Paul observed that the men and women of the tribe each had separate—but equally as important—tasks from the men, who were the hunters and warriors. Men also oversaw the construction and maintenance of the *shabono*. They made and cared for the bows and arrows, blowguns, and spears. Heavy work such as making dugout canoes and clearing the land also fell to the men. Women, symbolically associated with fertility, primarily tended to the children. In addition, they gardened and made the baskets and pottery. Most of their time was spent gathering and cooking the food.

As Paul wandered throughout the village, he received the most enthusiastic response from the children. All he had to do to get a laugh was make a face or pretend to chase them, hobbling along on his crutches. To them, he was a bizarre personage with his clothes and white skin.

At the far end of the open yard, there were a series of cultivated gardens. Each family maintained a portion of the garden assigned to them for upkeep. Among the allotment were plantains, bananas, and another fruit that Paul later learned was peach palm. This fruit, called a *piliquao,* became Paul's favorite. He learned it was considered bad form for anyone to take fruit from another family's garden without permission. Occasionally, during Paul's stay with the tribe, a heated argument would erupt over accusations of someone poaching a garden. Paul was always careful to ask permission before picking a peach palm.

Every morning, a group of women gathered around a fire in the courtyard. Paul would hobble over to observe. The women would squat in a circle. In front of them were piles of roots, which Paul later learned were the tubers from cassava plants. Each woman had a small board with embedded stones and would rub the roots on the board. The result was a stringy pulp. The pulp next went into a press, and the juice was squeezed out. The resulting pulp was formed into a small cake and placed on a plaited basketry tray. The last step was to place the cakes on a tray and into a hot fire. The cakes were served at every meal. The chewy cassava cakes were a favorite part of the meal to both the natives and, after a few days, to Paul.

One afternoon, there was a commotion as a tribesman ran into the compound shouting excitedly.

The whole village quickly gathered around him and listened to the man's animated dialogue for a minute. Then a group of six or seven men ran toward an opening between two fire pits and slipped into the jungle. Paul was curious, but there was no way he could follow them. His injured leg dictated that he remain within a few steps of his hammock every day.

About two hours later, he heard voices coming from behind the thick underbrush. In a few minutes, a group of men entered the compound. The villagers rushed toward the returning men, shouting and laughing. Two of the men were carrying a pole like pall bearers. Dangling upside down from the pole by its feet was a large animal. Paul marveled at the strength of the men, because the animal looked to weigh over three hundred pounds. He did not recognize the animal immediately, but from the joyous shouting he understood its capture was a good thing. As he hobbled out toward the men, he soon recognized the beast was a wild hog. Paul knew some hunters in South Carolina who shot hogs for sport, but as far as he knew they never returned home with them. They served as props for pictures, but nothing more. This hog was more than a trophy; it was food. And unlike the meat of some of the other animals of the jungle, the hog's meat was fatty and full of calories.

The villagers were incredibly grateful to receive the hog. The returning hunters were met with appreciative looks, comments, and gestures. Paul took note of the respect shown to the hunters.

For the rest of the day, the whole community scurried about preparing to cook the giant hog. Smoking embers were transferred by the man with leopard like spots from a small campfire to the largest fire pit of the compound. Children of all ages were dispatched to the forest and returned with wood to fuel the fire. Paul watched as a few men began butchering the pig, eviscerating its stomach, and discarding its entrails. The excised pieces of un-skinned meat were placed on the flat stones surrounding the fire. A few men left and returned with fish. Women went to the edge of the clearing to the small plantain orchard and picked fruit. Small animals that had been captured earlier were place on the stones surrounding the fire.

The man with leopard spots painted on his body called out to the spirits in appreciation for the beneficial hunt. He appeared to be the man who led chants and songs. He would call out a line and the tribe would respond singing a similar response. He always was the first voice whenever the tribe launched into a singsong chant. The singing was spontaneous, and not everyone sang together, but everyone was serenading enthusiastically.

When Paul went to sleep that night, the village was busy preparing to cook the meal. When he awoke the next morning the women in the village were still cooking and preparing the meal. There was chanting and singing throughout the morning, and the men continued to tend the fires.

About noon, the meal was ready. Food was placed on woven mats placed on the ground. Several types of cooked plantain, sweet bananas, sweet potatoes, and yams were laid out. Next, smaller cooked animals were placed on the mats, including fish of several species and sizes, monkeys, anteaters, and deer. The cooked remains of the hog proudly dominated a heaped pile at the center of the mat .

Following what appeared to Paul as a preordained order, families orbited the feast, taking what they wanted. Then, they sat on their heels in small circles and ate independent from other families. Paul observed that each family seemed to have one husband and from one to three wives, together with children and grandparents. Paul marveled at the amount of food each family took. He would later learn that the natives would gorge on food whenever there was a successful hunt, but would eat mainly fruit, ants, grubs, and small animals in between bountiful hunts. The size of a meal depended on the amount of food available.

Once everyone had gathered their food, the man Paul called Yellow Feathers invited Paul to the feast. As the two men walked around the rows of food strewn across the yard on palm fronds, Paul, who was unable to bend over, pointed to his choices. Yellow Feather picked up whatever Paul pointed to and placed it on a woven platter. Paul ate heartily until his stomach was full.

Paul accepted his new diet. The food was different, but he decided he would learn to like the offerings without complaint. He told Piarucu, "The food here is different and for the most part it's good. But I sometimes get a hankerin' for a milk shake." Piarucu smiled politely, and Paul smiled too when he thought about explaining what a milk shake was. He decided not to make the attempt.

Paul had always been a thin person (he weighed only about one hundred twenty-five pounds on the day of his flight), and he was aware that he was losing weight while living with the natives. His new diet did not contain the sugar and fat of his former life. However, his energy level was good, and he saw no reason to be overly troubled about it.

After eating, Paul hobbled around on his crutches and talked to everyone he encountered. As he did, he smiled and laughed. In return, the children smiled back at him. From the adults Paul received mostly empty stares in return. This did not discourage him. He wanted to be known as a friend of the village, and the best way to do that was to be amiable. He understood it would take time for the villagers to become accustomed to his good nature. But he also knew he would be accepted faster if he was cheerful.

Soon after, the families filed into their respective shelters and were soon fast asleep even though it was mid-afternoon. Before Paul could fall to sleep, the man with leopard spots came and started a small fire in the hearth next to Paul's hammock. Temperatures were warm, and the fire was small. However, Paul had experienced the precipitous drop in temperature at night, so the fire was welcome. He would feed the fire in the evening. Later, Yellow Feathers explained via hand gestures that a fire would also keep dangerous animals away at night.

A few nights later, after dinner, a crowd gathered in the courtyard. Paul was curious. He made his way to the group, wondering what was happening. He noticed the audience was mainly comprised of men and some boys. They formed a circle. Next, two of the men entered the ten-foot ring. One of the two men was Yellow Feathers. The leader then made an announcement, and the men began to face off against one another.

First the men pounded their chests and bellowed loudly at one another. The yelling continued throughout the match. Next, they rushed each other and tried to throw their opponents down. Paul recognized the match as wrestling, but it was not like the wrestling he had seen in high school. At first, their movements seemed awkward and random. Both men were strong and quick. Either combatant could easily pick up and throw his opponent. Paul wondered how long the match would last as it seemed interminable. Finally, Yellow Feathers threw his opponent down and pounced on top of him. The headman said something, and Yellow Feathers jumped up. The crowd cheered. Paul was happy that his friend had won, and let out a two-fingered whistle that startled everyone. There was silence as the crowd stared at Paul. Paul was embarrassed, but thought he should not let it show. He smiled and pointed at Yellow Feathers. The crowd resumed its cheering.

There were about ten more matches that evening, with some lasting a short minute, while others lasted for more than an hour.

After the last match, an argument broke out. Two men were facing one another shouting. It appeared they were heading for a fight. A crowd gathered. One man was accusing the other of making untoward advances to his wife. It went on for several minutes, until the headman arrived. He ordered the men to stop their arguing. Paul noticed the headman was carrying a club fashioned from a tree limb with a knot on one end.

There was a brief discussion among the three. The spectators formed a circle around the two antagonists. The men then alternately hit each other in the chest with a clenched fist with as much force as possible. The recipient of the blow did not to flinch or step back. The winner of the contest was the one that took the most blows. Paul learned that chest pounding contests were the common way to settle disputes. The winner came away from the contest with more prestige than the loser. It did not matter what the dispute was about.

As he walked away from the contest, Paul thought chest pounding was an odd way to settle a dispute, since it only demonstrated physical strength together with mental fortitude. There was no attempt to determine the merits of either man's position on the adultery issue. Brute strength won the match.

Paul observed that both competitors in a wrestling or chest pounding match achieved status merely by participating in the contest. By standing there and taking the blows they acquired *waiteri*, a reputation for ferocity, an important virtue among the tribe. Men with *waiteri* were held in high esteem, and their counsel on issues of importance was well regarded

Paul soon realized this fit in with the belief that men with strength coupled with fierceness were to be admired and those men held leadership roles in the village. It was those men who won arguments in chest pounding contests—regardless of merit.

In every contest, after about ten blows, the men would begin to stagger after receiving a blow. Finally, one of the men would fail to get back on his feet. The headman would pronounce the standing competitor the winner. The man on the ground would crawl away. Paul never did learn which of the men was married to the woman involved in the adultery. But the chest pounding contest apparently settled the matter.

Paul was intrigued by the wrestling and chest pounding. But at the end of the evening, he was ready for sleep. The excitement of the fighting left him drained of energy. He was happy since his friend Yellow Feathers had been one of the winners.

As Paul drifted off to sleep, he thought of the scene he had witnessed. The entire population of the *shabono* had gathered for the feast, the wrestling matches, and the chest pounding. During it all, Paul was treated as a friend of the tribe. It assured him that he was being accepted by the village as a friend.

* * * * *

The Brunswick Board of Trade held monthly luncheons at the Rotary Club in Brunswick. To celebrate the one-year anniversary of Paul Redfern's flight, the Board organized and chaired a commemorative on the beach. The members had also discussed other ways to handle Paul's disappearance, but had not been able to decide on anything other than the beach affair.

On June 8, 1928, the waves of the Atlantic Ocean were crashing onto Glynn Beach and, despite the sunny skies, the warm winds were whistling. It had been almost one-year since Paul's takeoff to Rio. A group of friends and family invited by the Brunswick Board of Trade gathered to honor Paul. Among the guests were Frederick and Blanche Redfern, Paul's parents. Paul Varner acted as the master of ceremonies. A respectful crowd stood in the sand for the ceremony, dressed in their Sunday attire of suits and ties for the men and dresses and hats for the ladies.

Four Army planes flew overhead and dropped gladioli on the ocean opposite the beach. Redfern Airfield on St. Simons Island was dedicated in Paul's honor. A group of young girls placed bouquets of flowers around the flagpole.

The Honorable Clark Howell, editor of the newspaper, *Atlanta Constitution,* read an uncertain eulogy to Paul, since his fate was in question. Among the comments made, Howell said, "We pay honor today to the brave Paul Redfern . . . The airfield here at Glynn Beach is hereby named in his honor. From this day forward it will be known as Paul Redfern Airfield."

Paul's parents, who had traveled from Columbia, South Carolina, were introduced to the gathering on the beach. Paul's father remarked that the affair was ". . . solemn and unique, for a shadow hung over the desire to celebrate the triumph of their hero — the continuing mystery as to that hero's fate."

Blanche, his mother, read a poem she had written for her son. It was common in those days for folks to share poems written for deceased relatives or acquaintances. Her poem concluded with the following lines:

> *"We only pray that God reveal,*
> > *And to us here at home unseal*
> *The mystery, which seems so deep,*
> > *That bids jungle and stream their silence keep.*
> *A revelation is all we ask,*
> > *So that we better can fill each task*
> *Which comes to use from day to day.*
> > *Reveal, Oh Lord! Reveal we pray."*

Gertrude, Paul's wife, had declined her written invitation to the event from the Board of Trade. She told Frederick and Blanche that the format was "too dark." She felt if she attended, ". . . it would be like giving up on my husband ever coming home."

Paul Varner telephoned her on the morning of the gathering, offering to pick her up, but she again declined. She told Varner she preferred to repine in private.

11

Paul's Routine (1927-1928)

In the days following the feast, Paul spent his time in his hammock, or wandering around the compound. A group of children came to find him daily. He made faces and playful hand motions whenever they were there. He could get a giggle out of them without much effort. All that was required was a silly face, or occasionally a crazy one-legged dance with one crutch held high.

There was a group of older men that gathered each day in the yard. Paul sat with them as they chatted, or sometimes worked at making tools and weapons. He kept up a steady stream of chatter, all the while smiling. He recounted his exploits as a hunter of moonshiners, but no one indicated any understanding. He sat with the old timers and imitated them by tearing off chunks of meat with his hands before chewing it. There were no utensils. Paul always had something to say, and smiled while conveying his unstated message, which was "I am happy to be here."

The man identified by Paul as Yellow Feathers brought food one or two times a day. After a day or two, Paul concluded that the food he was given was good tasting and was satisfying. Whenever Yellow Feathers appeared, Paul would have something to say. At first it was banal chatter about the weather or the taste of the food. Over time, Paul would tell Yellow

Feathers stories about his life back in the States. As time passed, the stories became more thorough. And Paul tried to make sure Yellow Feathers understood.

After ten days or so, Paul's diarrhea had dissipated, and he found that he was becoming acclimated to his new diet. He was served a wide variety of cooked meats including tapir, deer, monkey, wild hog, ocelot, and armadillo. While meat was not always available, fish was plentiful. Fish caught in the fish traps was always available. When nothing else was obtainable, Paul would accept baked spiders and ants, although he was slow to partake of them unless there was nothing else. He flatly turned down an offer of roasted white grubs, although the natives seemed to relish them. They also served a limited variety of large birds. Birds that were cooked were always plucked, unlike the meat, which was cooked with the skin intact. He was never served his favorite breakfast of fried eggs, sunny side up, since the natives considered birds' eggs to be off limits.

Paul began to realize Yellow Feathers was seeking a relationship. He sought out Paul each day, bringing him food. As Paul ate, Yellow Feathers sat beside him and listened to Paul's chatter even though it was doubtful that he understood hardly anything. Paul talked about his flight to Rio and the fact that he had a lot of money coming, had he made it that far. It was clear that Yellow Feathers was interested in Paul and his well-being. Yellow Feathers was young and strong, and, as far as Paul could observe, he was well regarded in the tribe. He thought Yellow Feathers would be a helpful friend.

One morning, Paul stood up in front of the old timers and pointed to his chest, saying, "Me Paul." After repeating and pointing several times, a few voices repeated, "me Paul," mispronouncing "Me" as "Mih." Paul then pointed to each man and asked, "Who are you?" He received only blank stares in response. However, from then on, many of the natives in the compound used the term "Mih-Paul" when addressing him. Paul began referring to the men by some physical characteristic, such as "curly cue," for body decorations, "shorty," based on height, or "flowers," based on arm decorations. Paul was a little disappointed not to learn of the men's proper names, but decided he would keep trying.

Finally, one of the men responded to Paul's inquiry. He said, "Yanomami." Paul assumed it was the man's name. But, it turned out to be the name of the tribe.

Paul was a natural at making friends. He talked to everyone, smiled constantly, and asked a lot of questions. In response, the natives responded in three different ways. Some would laugh at every question. Others would stare at him with blank facial expressions. And those who responded would speak too fast for Paul to translate. However, the tribe slowly warmed to him, even though they did not communicate in detail. Body language and facial expressions demonstrated a hospitable mindset. Paul learned the greeting used to say hello or goodbye, "*me-a-re*" which he used profusely.

Paul was determined to learn Yellow Feather's proper name. He was confused by the reluctance on the part of all the natives to reveal their names. It was unclear to him why that was so. But after asking a few times, Paul learned Yellow Feathers' name was Piarucu.

Paul had another conversation with Piarucu the following week, and learned the tribe leader's name was Shapora, while the *shaman*'s name was Yanokiritana. Paul asked several people to reveal their names, but found everyone was reluctant to share. The usual response when asked for their names was "Yanomami."

A week later, Piarucu came to Paul and confessed the names he had shared for Leader and *shaman* were fraudulent. They were names used in place of their real names. Piarucu told Paul that it was a matter of status. All tribal members kept their names to themselves, except for their immediate family. The names, Shapora and Yanokiritana, were used to disguise their actual names, which they did not want revealed. Piarucu assured Paul that he had not lied about his own name. Paul thought this revelation was odd. But he decided to go ahead and use the fake names. Besides, they were the only ones he knew.

As Paul walked away, a joke came to mind. It went like this:

> *A man walked into the county clerk's office and announced that he was there to legally change his name. "What is the name you wish to change?" asked the clerk. The man replied, "Oliver Stinkfoot." The clerk wrote down the name, suppressing a smile.*
>
> *"What do you suggest as your new name?" asked the clerk. "Maurice Stinkfoot," said the man.*

Paul considered trying the joke out on Piarucu but thought there was no way he could tell it so that Piarucu would understand. He decided to let it go.

Paul noticed the men all had a slight bulge to their cheeks. Upon closer observation, he realized they were putting a wad of leaves in their mouth and holding it between their teeth and cheek. Paul wondered why. He asked Piarucu and was told the leaves from a coca tree, mixed with lime juice, gave the men superpowers. He was also told the coca leaves gave the men extra strength and stamina. Paul had never heard of coca leaves and was left wondering about them.

Yanomami native - Note mouthful of coca leaves

The man "named" Yanokiritana, who was covered with purple leopard spots, and who carried a bouquet of feathers in his hand, also visited Paul every day and looked him over from head to foot, stopping to prod his broken leg, until Paul let out a yelp.

Over the next few weeks, Paul's leg was getting better, but he still could not put his full weight on it. He knew from the experience of a boyhood friend that broken bones took about six weeks to heal.

Every week, Paul took slightly longer walks around the compound, hobbling along on his crutches. Since the crutches were too short, it made walking awkward. However, he increased the length of his walks in a few weeks from about two minutes to about ten, making two full revolutions around the camp.

After watching Paul struggle to walk, Piarucu brought him a lengthier set of crutches also fashioned from tree branches. Now, standing tall, they made Paul's daily journeys much easier. Six weeks came and went, but although he was walking more, and putting weight on both legs, his right leg was still sore at the end of the day.

During his strolls around the compound, Paul stopped to talk and gesture to any man who would listen. Paul's personality was to be a talker. Mostly, he talked about his plane and how it had let him down by blowing a piston. He explained how he had cleverly landed in the treetops, and joked about how the men had lowered him down from the plane on a rope, citing his trepidation before stepping out the door. All these stories generated interest but no comments. Each man to whom he told the stories listened intently. It occurred to Paul they were enthralled to hear a different language from their own. Undeterred, he spoke to everyone, never failing to smile while doing so.

By now, he was known throughout the village as "Mih-Paul." As he approached individuals in the community, they would say, "*Me-a-re*, Mih Paul." Paul would respond with "Howdy" or "Hi There."

In most conversations, Paul described his home in the States as well as his wife, Gertrude. He made clear he had a home elsewhere. There was never a response. In fact, it was not clear whether any of Paul's comments were understood. The natives also spoke to him. Much of their speech was undecipherable, except for one message that was quite clear. Paul was not to venture into the jungle alone. While he spoke to men freely, he did not attempt to communicate with women. Nor did any of them speak to Paul.

Paul noticed that whenever he approached the edge of the forest, one or two of the men would silently block his path so that he could not enter the wilderness. These men, as did all the others, had weapons in their hands. Paul was consistently being sent a body language message that said: "You cannot leave." Since these men were the same men who had blocked his path to a women previously, he concluded they had been assigned to keep him out of the jungle and away from females. He wondered if the men were acting to protect him from dangers hidden in the forest, or were merely keeping him confined. He could not tell, and he was in no shape to test their resolve. The fact was, the men had been ordered to protect Paul from the evil spirits that roamed the forest. He was, after all, an emissary of the sky spirits, who were most beneficial. Accordingly, the tribe felt he needed to be protected from the evil spirits.

Paul was in no position to argue. He did not know what dangers would confront him in the jungle. So, he obeyed and did not complain about being prevented from exploring the surrounding jungle.

Paul had asked Piarucu about the spirits. Piarucu offered that there were sky spirits and forest spirits. There were spirits in the animals and plants. Some spirits were inherently good and some evil. In addition, there were spirits that were good or bad depending upon what the tribe asked of them. Paul was confused but decided to accept the belief system of the tribe. If they wanted to believe in spirits, Paul would go along with it.

Yanokiritana was the one in the tribe who seemed to be most concerned about the spirits. Whenever someone was sick or injured, he would be at the person's side, chanting and singing. He would also give his patients chopped up herbs to aid in their recovery.

Once, when Yanokiritana saw Paul limping, he brought a mix of herbs to Paul, indicating they should be added to his drinking water. Paul was hesitant to drink the concoction, but his leg was aching. He added the herbs to the water in a gourd dipper and drank it in three gulps. It tasted sweet and went down easily. Within an hour, the pain in his leg disappeared. When asked, the *shaman* said the pain-killing formula had been known to the tribe for many years. From that day forward, Paul sought out the *shaman* for a taste of the mixture before every long walk. Yanokiritana never failed to find a way to take away the pain.

When Paul asked Yanokiritana about the spirits, Yanokiritana explained that spirits have the power to control the weather, the animals, and the plants. His explanation was slightly different than Piarucu's. He explained that his training to become a *shaman* gave him the ability to speak to and command the spirits. Yanokiritana explained the system of beliefs about spirits is called *hekura*.

Paul had been impressed with Yanokiritana's diligence whenever someone in the tribe was suffering. Once at their side, he would not leave until the person recovered or died. Yanokiritana impressed Paul with his dogged efforts, but Paul was not yet ready to personally believe in spirits. He felt the native's beliefs were naïve. But he certainly did not challenge his host's beliefs for fear of turning the tribe against him.

Over time, Piarucu talked to Paul about *hekura*, a word that Paul did not understand at the time. He soon realized it signified the spirits that permeated the area. Piarucu warned that Paul should not venture into the jungle alone because of the bad spirits. The bad spirits, he explained, could cause injury or death. Paul was skeptical. However, he realized that the native's belief in spirits was genuine. They mentioned the good spirits when describing a successful hunt. And if someone was sick or injured, bad spirits were blamed. Spirits were considered responsible for many events in their lives.

Paul observed that the adult men and women of the tribe were normally in a good mood. They went about their daily activities in a cheerful manner. Jokes were customary, and belly-laughter was commonplace. Paul was reassured by their attitude. Happy people seemed unlikely to do harm to him, the outsider.

Paul also noticed that the natives, although naked, were diligent about cleanliness. None of the tribe was ever seen with dirt or food stains on his or her body. They washed regularly and bathed in the nearby stream almost daily. Although there was no furniture other than hammocks, they squatted on their heels without any part of their body touching the ground.

During the first few weeks with the tribe, Paul attempted to shave on a regular basis. A razor was one of the items he rescued from the plane. He was clean shaven on his flight to South America, and he was comfortable in his appearance. After about six weeks, however, his razor was unusable, and he switched to shaving with a sharpened shell every other day. After a few weeks it was every third day. Shaving with a shell was not as easy as using a razor, and it hurt because the shell was not as sharp as a razor, plus he had to use water as a lubricant rather than shaving cream. (After about a year, Paul quit shaving altogether and let his beard grow thick on his neck and face.)

Paul thought back to his trek from the plane to the village. The jungle was like nothing he had seen in his life. During daytime sunlight, it was as dim as twilight. There were tall trees everywhere, with an undergrowth of shorter palms, ferns, and flowering plants. Vines as thick as hawsers ran between the trees. The graying effect of the dense forest, blocking sun and wind, accentuated the ever-present humidity. Mosquitos were plentiful. Moss covered much of the ground. Orchids were everywhere, and colorful birds perched in the trees. At night, croaking frogs sounded their call. Whistling bats swirled overhead. Paul was fascinated by the jungle. As long as he remained in the clearing around the *shabono*, he was unaware of the dangers surrounding him. He would later learn the jungle is a friend to no one.

12

Piarucu's Family (1929)

Piarucu was Paul's daily companion. Every day he would find Paul, and they would have a conversation of sorts, and then engage in some activity together. It could be hunting or fishing. Some of these activities would involve Piarucu alone and some would be in the company of a group of men.

As the months passed, they became adept at communicating with one another. While they continued to have difficulty speaking one another's language, they could communicate with hand gestures, body movements, and facial expressions. And while language differences continued to be a problem, they were slowly learning one another's favorite expressions. Paul would use the term, "*Me-a-re*" for hello or goodbye. Piarucu would say "Alrighty" or "OK" to signify agreement.

One morning Piarucu came to Paul's quarters with two children, one a girl, appearing to be about ten years old, and the other, a boy of about thirteen. Paul had seen both before, since they were among the group that followed Paul around, but he never connected them to Piarucu. As they stood in front of Paul, he instantly recognized from their faces that they were Piarucu's children. He pointed to them and then to Piarucu with a questioning look. Piarucu's proud look in response acknowledged their relationship. He was their father.

Just then Paul noticed a woman, noticeably pregnant, standing to one side. He was not introduced, but he guessed it was Piarucu's spouse.

As Paul approached the children, their faces lit up with wide-eyed smiles. Paul greeted them, "Hi Ya!" He reached out with his right hand to shake. But the children were not familiar with hand shaking, and they hesitated. Paul took the initiative and reached out and took them by the hand. As he vigorously pumped their hands, he reached out with his left hand and rubbed their heads. They all laughed. Paul said, "Y'all can call me Uncle Paul." He repeated, "Uncle Paul," and the boy responded with "Unca Pol."

From the day they met, Paul called Piarucu's son, "Junior." The boy looked a bit confused by the name, but after a few repetitions, seemed to accept it.

Uncle Paul and Junior made an unlikely pair. They were different in age, color, and language, but they seemed to enjoy each other's company. Piarucu paired them together, and planned to teach Paul and his son the skills of creating and using the tools of hunting at the same time.

Paul's name for Piarucu's daughter was "Tootsie." Whenever Paul greeted her, he would say, "Hi Ya Tootsie!" in a loud friendly voice. Sometimes, Paul would shout the greeting to her across the yard. The little girl would giggle at the greeting every time.

On most days, Piarucu met Paul and his son to discuss hunting, and he would explain the methods they would use for the hunt. Piarucu would show them the tools used in hunting, including blow pipes, bows and arrows, spears, and clubs. He was educating both Paul and the boy at the same time. Both Paul and Junior were novices when it came to hunting. Paul recognized that his skills were about equal to that of the thirteen-year-old. He accepted that realization without shame.

Yanomami mothers and baby

Piarucu explained that the first project was making a blowpipe. The three of them followed Piarucu into the jungle and searched for a suitable, long, straight tube. Piarucu demonstrated each step of the process. A ten-foot-high palm stalk, chosen for its vertical straightness, was cut for each of the two learners. The trunks, about two inches in diameter, were cut into five-foot lengths, considerably shorter than an adult's blowpipe of ten to twelve feet. Next a notch was cut into one end of the stalk, and it was separated by hand into two halves. The malleable center core was scraped out with a stone blade.

A mixture of water and sand was rubbed by hand throughout the two sides of the stalk to smooth the center track of the blowpipe. It took several hours to get the tube slick enough to ensure the arrows would not be impeded by bumps and grooves in the interior. The two halves of the trunk were then fitted back together, and the two lengths of palm were bound together with a strip of cut bark wrapped in a spiral around the tube. Finally, the tube was sealed with a coating synthesized from a rubber tree. It took most of two days to complete all the steps in the process.

The following day Piarucu showed how to select a chunk of wood suitable for use as a mouthpiece. One end was carved into a flare to fit one's mouth and the other had a small hole in which to fit over the blowpipe with glue to make it airtight. Paul carved his mouthpiece three times before it passed inspection by Piarucu. Piarucu's son took a bit longer to complete his blowpipe, but it passed muster on the first pass.

Paul was amazed that all the ingredients to make a blowpipe could be found within a quarter mile of the shabono. He asked Piarucu how he had learned to make a blowpipe. Piarucu indicated he had learned from his father. He professed not to know how long his tribe had been making blow pipes. He did indicate it had been a long time. Piarucu explained that the tribe had originally been taught the skill by the spirits of the jungle. Paul was impressed. Making a blowpipe was a clever undertaking. The tribe may have been living in the stone age, but its members certainly had extraordinary talents.

The following day, they found sticks that they cut into eight-inch arrows. At one end they inserted feathers to encourage stable flight, and, at the other, they made a sharpened a point. Finally, they coated the point with a *curare* poison obtained from a *Chondrodendron tomentosium* vine that climbs on the tallest trees.

Shooting at targets over the next few days, they were taught the two-handed grip to hold the blowpipe. Paul was impressed with the speed of the arrows. Traveling from the blowpipe to the target, the arrows were merely a blur, and could not be seen clearly.

Finally, after much practice, the two novices went out with their blowpipes to hunt birds and other small animals. Right away, Junior showed an affinity for hunting, whereas Paul was a bit clumsy in stalking his prey. He could not seem to avoid brushing aside the underbrush causing the leaves to rustle. And worse, he stepped on dried branches, which caused a *snap*! sound that alerted the game to his approach. However, after several intense days, both novices were successful in finding and killing a slow-moving armadillo.

Both Junior and Paul walked back to the *shabono* carrying their blowpipe and an armadillo. They both beamed with pride after spending a week making their weapons and perfecting their hunting skills.

As they approached the center of the courtyard, a few of the old men squatting around a fire, looked up and spotted the two. Once they saw the size of Paul's blowpipe, they pointed and laughed. Paul was embarrassed, but managed an uneasy smile as he raised the armadillo in his hand for inspection. Piarucu's wife ran to her son and hugged him, taking the armadillo to be cooked, while ignoring Paul.

Other hunting trips were scheduled to improve the pair's hunting skills. Junior killed a small deer. Paul got a large anteater. Both bagged some birds.

In the following weeks, Piarucu took Paul and Junior on similar trips to find materials to make bows and arrows, clubs, and spears. In each case, the size of the weapon was reduced to fit the size and strength of a thirteen-year-old. Piarucu also assisted both students in making a hatchet with a sharpened stone head.

All in all, the indoctrination took several months and continued to evolve as the two pupils gained experience. Both Paul and Junior were permitted to join the elders on short hunting forays called *rami*. *Rami* hunting trips are led by the elders on an almost daily basis. On these hunts, lasting a day or less, small animals are stalked and killed, and fruit is gathered.

The older tribe members' hunts were called *heniyoumou*. They lasted several days and involved hunting for bigger game. It wouldn't be until later that Paul and Junior were permitted on those hunts.

13

Back to the *Port of Brunswick* (1929)

Every day Paul thought about returning to the States and Gertrude. It was a gnawing feeling that would not go away, and grew eventually into an urgent concern. In his thoughts, Paul outlined the equipment needed for such a trip. This led him to think of the items he had abandoned in his plane.

One day, shortly after daybreak, Paul sought out the headman, Shapora, and requested help in visiting the *Port of Brunswick*. He told Shapora that the spirits from the sky had given him some gifts that he would share with the tribe if he could retrieve them from the plane. Paul got out his revolver and pointed at it, then pointed in the direction of his plane. He thought the tribe would be motivated to assist if another weapon might be available. Besides, another weapon would come in handy when he escaped into the woods.

It took about fifteen minutes of pointing and gesturing for Paul's message to get through to Shapora—or, at least he *thought* it had gotten through. The headman gestured, holding out one open hand as if to say, "Stay here."

In about fifteen minutes, three tribesmen plus Piarucu showed up and motioned for Paul to follow. Paul had a rough idea where his plane was located. At least he remembered where he had entered the settlement that first day. He remembered the long arduous hike on a broken leg to the camp. Now, it only took about a half hour.

While the others seemed to glide along, Paul half-walked and half-jogged with a slight limp to keep up. By the time they arrived at the tree that still cradled his plane, Paul was breathing heavily, while the others had continued to talk among themselves throughout the trek. When he noticed Paul bent over, his arms resting on his knees with his chest heaving, Piarucu pointed at him, and the rest had a playful laugh.

While he was bent over, Paul noticed something on the ground. It was the box used to hold the beads and trinkets. The lid of the box was open, and its contents were strewn across a swath of ground ten feet in length. Someone had dropped the box out of the plane, and the lid had been thrown open. Paul was worried he had lost the contents. Piarucu pointed up at the plane above Paul's head, saying, "*Guaharibo!*," the word for monkey. Apparently, monkeys had explored the interior of the cockpit and had been interested in the box. Now Yellow Feathers and the other men picked up the contents and excitedly held them up for the others to see. Paul was happy to hear the explanation, because his first thought was that someone had been in the cockpit and had stolen his weapons and charts, the real object of his trip to the tree.

Paul held out the box to the men, who returned the trinkets. Once he had collected them all, he took a few out and gave each of the men two items. He had plenty remaining for future goodwill gestures.

Each man accepted the trinket handed to him, but then handed Paul a gift in return. Some offered arrows, or a length of string. Others offered a feather, or other adornment. Paul realized they did not wish to accept the trinket as a gift but were willing to trade.

Looking up at the *Port of Brunswick*, Paul noticed it had sunk below the very top of the trees and was resting on a lower branch than the one that supported it in the tree when he crashed initially. It now sat below the leaves at the top of the trees. Paul decided he better test to determine if the plane would still support him when he got to it.

Piarucu took a single leap and reached the lowest branch, scampering up to the cockpit. It was a move Paul would not even attempt. He had no spring in his step, especially since his broken leg had not regained its former strength. In fact, he doubted he could have made it to the first branch—even *before* the crash injured his leg.

Now, it was Paul's turn to jump up into the tree. He stood a minute, and then motioned the other men over to the base of the tree. He grabbed one man's hands and showed him how to intertwine his fingers with both hands and rest them backside-down on his knee. Leading the group to a spot under the lowest branch, he had the man pose with his hands on a knee. Paul stepped up and tried to reach the lowest branch. But, as Paul attempted to step up, his foot slipped, and he began to fall backwards. Natives standing nearby quickly caught him before he fell.

Again, Paul studied the situation. He pulled another man over to the spot under the tree and arranged the two men with each holding his hands interlaced on his knee. Paul stepped up with his left leg and positioned his foot on their hands. This time the men held steady. He reached for the lower branch and pulled himself up. From there, he climbed up the branches of the tree as if going up a ladder. He did not dare look down, as the plane was higher than he had remembered. Finally, he arrived at the main branch holding the plane in place. He grabbed the bottom edge of the window and gently rocked the plane to test its stability. It seemed secure. Paul stepped into the doorway and with a great effort, grabbed the back of the seat, and hopped into the cockpit.

For a few seconds, he remained motionless to catch his breath and make sure the plane was not going to give way and fall out of the tree. Once his breathing had settled down, he looked around. It was just the way he had left it.

Paul grabbed the folding rifle, some ammunition, and his hand-made charts. Looking around, he also snatched his thermos bottle, took off the lid, smelled the stale coffee odor, and shoved it into a pants pocket. After a thorough cleaning, it might come in handy when he took off for home. At the last moment, he also reached out for his leather jacket that was lined with lamb's wool. It would not be needed for its warmth, but it was one of his prized possessions. Paul thought he might use it as a blanket, or as a cushion. He dropped the jacket out of the cockpit onto the ground below. He grabbed one other thing: Professor Breckenridge's nine-page letter, which was yellow with age, and the ink faded. After a quick glance at the letter, he shoved it into a back pocket.

Before leaving the cockpit, Paul noticed one of the five-gallon metal petrol cans on the right-hand seat. He checked the cap, then picked up the jerry-can and dropped it out the door to the ground. He had a plan for it and the leftover fuel inside.

Piarucu and Paul lowered themselves to the ground, Piarucu in quick hops and Paul in carefully measured smaller steps. He was careful to land only on his good leg, as he made the last jump down. As he landed, Paul lost his balance and collapsed on the ground. The men around him laughed, as Paul pulled himself up. At first, he was embarrassed, but then he also laughed along with the others. The four men divided up the stuff retrieved from the airplane and trudged back to the *shabono*.

The tumble reminded Paul that his leg had not thoroughly healed. He was beginning to think that it would be sore most of the time. Upon his return, he sought out Yanokiritana, the *shaman* for assistance, and took the pain-killing drink he was offered.

After a couple months, Paul began following Piarucu when he and other men left the camp on hunting forays. At first, he went on the shorter hunts of less than a day, called *rami*. The men always hoped to find game on *rami* ventures. Even if game was not found, the *rami* served as inspection trip to insure there were no interlopers within fifteen kilometers or so of the *shabono*. As time passed, he started going on overnight ventures, called *heniyomou*. He was accepted as a member of the hunting party, but not permitted to carry a bow or blow tube. Paul had a pistol, but he left it with his other belongings next to his hammock. By hand gestures, he was instructed where to walk, when to remain silent, and how to carry a heavy basket on his head with the hunting crew's bounty. At times, he fell behind the group, but always caught up before the hunting started. The *heniyomou* hunting trips would last an indeterminate number of days. They would not return until sufficient game was gathered.

On one occasion, he watched with interest as they stalked, killed, and dressed a tapir, a stout, short-legged, and hoofed animal with a large snout. The tapir reminded Paul of a baby elephant. He was impressed with the tribe's ability to silently maneuver through the forest at night, slowly surround the large animal as it grazed before it was aware of their presence and bring it down with the poison tipped arrows. The bows were fashioned from six-foot tree branches and strung from bark twisted into string. Each hunter carried arrows in a quiver made from a cup cut from bamboo and covered with animal skin. Once hit, the lumbering tapir showed remarkable speed in attempting to escape, but within about twenty seconds, it lay on the ground. One man was sent to dispatch the creature with a club to the head. The other men then quickly butchered the animal using knives sharpened from bamboo and placed the edible parts in baskets to be carried back.

It did not escape Paul, who was smaller in size than a tapir, that he could be dispatched similarly if he were caught trying to escape. With his bad leg he was not going to outrun anybody. And, even if he got away, he could not survive in the jungle by himself.

This was hunting like Paul had never witnessed. With a rifle, one could hit a moving target from one or two hundred feet. On the other hand, the natives using a bow and arrow had to wait until they were much closer from their prey before unleashing their arrows. First, they would surround the prey. As they slowly closed in, the prey would be unaware. Each native could lift a foot, but not take a complete step until he was sure the prey remained unaware. Finally, after queuing up on the beast, several fired their arrows in unison. The procedure was like a silent, graceful dance. Getting in place took time, but it was over in a minute once they had surrounded and sealed the tapir from escape. Paul was impressed by the skill and patience of the natives.

It was obvious that the natives were at ease in the jungle and that their skills at stalking and hunting were far advanced. The men were fast and stealthy. Paul understood he would have no chance to escape if the tribe became aware of his absconding and they wished to stop him. He could be overtaken and dispatched in short order.

On that same expedition, he watched as they impaled fish from a stream with spears. The men would perch on overlooking rocks and wait patiently to fling their spears into the stream. There was a notch cut into the palm wood point of the spear to hold the fish from wriggling off. The fish were then placed in wooden baskets for transport back to the village. The women were eager to take the fish upon their arrival. Some of the fish were cooked over a fire immediately for the next meal, and some were fileted and dried for use in coming days.

Paul thought he should do something humorous to ingratiate himself to the tribe. He planned a trick in his mind to show the men that he was amiable and not a threat to them. As they were returning to the settlement, Paul decided the time was right. They came to a small hill. On the way down, Paul acted as if he tripped and fell, tucking his shoulder and sprawling out on the way down. He was careful to protect his right leg. This was a variation on his high school days when he would fake a spill on the stairs. At first, the men rushed to help him as he remained still on the ground. Then Paul jumped up and gave a little bow, all the while laughing so everyone of would know he was kidding. As the ruse was revealed, everyone laughed.

After arriving back at the camp, Paul placed a basket on a tree stump as a target and asked for Piarucu's bow and arrow. He was going demonstrate he could use the bow. Paul was taller than any of the natives, but as he pulled the string back, his arms began to tremble. It was clear he would be unable to properly aim while his arms shook from the strain. Piarucu laughed at Paul's ineptitude followed by chuckles from the other men.

Paul learned that handling the bow as a weapon took more strength than he had available. Paul's smile was a bit shamefaced as he handed back the bow.

As he observed the natives, and their skill at hunting and fishing, Paul began to think they were not so backward after all. They had proficiency in all they did. It was obvious they worked with high functioning tools and weapons. He had a much higher opinion than the first day he saw them. He no longer thought about their lack of clothing. In the hot, humid climate of the jungle, bare skin was suitable. Paul thought about going naked himself since his clothes were showing signs of wear and tear but concluded he could never be at ease without clothes in public and dismissed the idea.

On subsequent hunting trips, the men pursued monkeys, by using poison darts propelled from long, eight-foot blow tubes. The men would gather under the trees and find cover. Then the waiting would start. Within an hour or so, a troop of monkeys rollicking in the treetops would appear. On a signal, the hunters picked out the smaller, younger ones to harvest.

The poison on the darts was made from a vine soaked in hot water with vegetable ingredients added to make it sticky. It was spread on the points of the darts and then wrapped in leaves to keep the rain from dissolving the poison. The poison, called *warali,* acted as a nerve toxin, relaxing the muscles, and causing the animal to lose its grip and fall from the trees. This toxin used for hunting small game did not kill.

Once on the ground, the monkeys are quickly dispatched with clubs, and packed in baskets. On one hunt, a coati, with a striped tail like a raccoon, and with pointed teeth and sharp claws showed up and began ripping apart one of the monkeys within seconds of it hitting the ground. The natives scurried to shoo the snarling coati away.

Once they had packed the monkeys in baskets, they began to walk back to the settlement. Paul attempted to carry a basket, but it was too heavy for him. He walked along the trail with the others carrying nothing. His experience with the bow and the basket made him realize he lacked the strength to survive on his own. To cover for his ineptitude, Paul kept up a steady commentary about the day's activities. The others listened and occasionally made comments of their own. Paul could only partially understand them just as he was not generally understood.

As they approached an open area where a large tree had rotted and collapsed, the man leading the procession stopped and by hand gesture ordered the whole party to halt. Everyone was stopped in their tracks, when off in the distance, they spotted an ocelot stalking a baboon. The baboon was on the ground gathering plants to eat and the ocelot was hiding behind a large palm leaf about ten feet away. While the baboon was larger than the ocelot, the cat had the element of surprise on its side. After silently stalking, the ocelot pounced on the back of the baboon and with its powerful jaws and sharp claws quickly killed its prey. The ocelot settled in for its meal tearing meat from the baboon's bones. As that was happening the hunters silently walked well clear of the scene to avoid attracting attention.

Over time Paul realized that the tribe was careful to take only what they needed, and nothing was wasted. All parts of the plants and animals were used and extraordinarily little was thrown out. It took skill to find game and other food and only rarely was game not found. Usually, an unsuccessful hunt would be followed by a fruitful one. There was an unending food supply year-round if it could be found.

The little community of natives shared everything. They cooked together and ate together. They made tools in groups. They hunted in groups. Bands of women cultivated and picked fruit and other food from trees and plants. The various factions functioned collaboratively. Their cooperative life reminded Paul of the Amana Colonies of Iowa that he had read about in the *Columbia Star*. There, the community shared all their farm products based on need and assumed equal labor from each family.

Occasionally there were conflicts among members of the *shabono*. For example, there were major disturbances over adultery, and minor ones over hording. Disagreeable members of the tribe would engage in chest pounding contests to resolve issues. Disputes, when they became public, were settled by the headman. But normal daily life was calm and quarrel free.

Paul wondered why the coati was deprived of its kill, while the ocelot was permitted to feast on the baboon? Why did the men not rush to save the baboon for themselves?   After all, they had protected the remains of the monkey.   Piarucu explained that the ocelot had initially hunted the baboon, so the jungle spirits supported the ocelot's right to its catch. The coati, on the other hand, was trying take advantage of the work of the hunters.   The jungle spirits favored the tracker who had stalked the prey, not the interloper. Therefore, according to the karma of the jungle, interfering with the ocelot would bring bad outcomes to the tribe. But the coati had no right to the monkey that had been stalked and shot by the natives. This was a matter of morality to the tribe. In the reasoning of the natives, the hunter was always favored over the intruder.

Paul continued to be interested and curious about the tribe's belief in spirits. He thought it odd that they had no belief in one god as he did, but instead believed in good and bad spirits.

Paul went to Shaporo with questions. Paul asked about the tribe's belief in spirits. "Where do the spirits reside? Have you ever believed in God? Instead of answering the questions directly, the chief recounted a story about some missionaries many years ago. The missionaries came to the village by boat and brought with them some natives that had been taken out of the jungle as servants.

The priests who came to their village had many new rules that they insisted be followed. The natives were told they must be immersed in the river for baptism. They must marry in a ceremony. They must wear clothes and cover up their bodies. They must attend a daily service. The men with more than one wife must give them all up except one. And they were told they must all learn a new language: Spanish.

These things were new and different and violated long-standing practices. The *shaman* told the tribe that the spirits would surely retaliate if the tribe abandoned its customs. The tribe did not perceive any reason to change, but saw plenty of reasons to continue their ancient traditions. There was widespread resistance.

The final straw occurred when the tribe's *shaman* was found dead from a blow to the back of his head. The *shaman*, who was beloved by the tribe, was last seen leaving the *shabono* with several of the native servants of the missionaries. He was found by a group of young natives out on a *rami* hunt. The missionaries denied any involvement in the death and blamed a Waika tribe that lived nearby. The leader of the tribe questioned the servants and found their story to be suspicious. It did not help the servants that the *shaman* was the father of the leader. Based on a dream, the leader concluded that the missionaries were to blame.

After a week of listening to the missionary's servants, and questioning the annoying priests, the tribe met *in toto*. The leader listed the demands of the priests as far as clothes, marriage, and praying to their god. He explained his suspicions about the murder of the *shaman*. After urging by the Leader, the tribe agreed they did not want to make changes to their way of life. The old ways passed down for generations were preferred to the new rules of the missionaries. The tribe saw no reason to wear clothes or the rest of it. In addition, they thought it too dangerous to give up their belief in spirits.

They had all witnessed the effect spirits had on their lives. They had no use for the missionaries' god. It had been taught to them throughout their life that Oman created the universe, and his power sustained it. Oman created the Yanomami to take the place of the Ahma Teri people who were evil cannibals. To the Yanomami, to forsake belief in Oman was to invite destruction.

The men of the village met with the priests and told them of their decision. The missionaries were ordered to leave. The missionaries were determined to stay. On the third day after the ultimatum was given, one of the priests turned up dead with a cracked skull. It was a similar fate as befell the *shaman*. Within hours the missionaries left. Shaporo added, "Since that time, we have no use for outsiders. But you are different, since you were sent to us by good spirits. We have always trusted in the spirits who live in the sky."

Paul continued to go with the men on their trips to hunt food. He learned how to find game and it seemed that on each hunting foray the hunters found enough food for at least a week or two. Food in the jungle was plentiful. Once game was located, the natives were excellent trackers. Whether a hunt was successful depended on the hunters' skill in stalking. The crack of a stepped-on twig would send an animal scurrying away. Or the sound of a slap aimed at a mosquito could ruin a chance at sneaking up on game. Learning how to be silent and avoiding quick movements took time.

Over the years, Paul became somewhat skilled at tracking and hunting down prey.

Paul was proud of his ability as a stalker, although he recognized his skill was deficient as compared with the natives. When Paul began to go on hunting trips, he was relegated to the rear so as not to spook the game. But now the hunters could trust him. Now he was permitted join in on the tracking and stalking of game. On the latest hunt, his party returned to the village with three tapirs, five monkeys, two deer, and a hog. This was enough to last through the following month and perhaps longer. They had only been out hunting since morning and were back at camp a day early.

Paul did not use his pistol, and he was not strong enough to use a bow, but he joined in with the other men as they surrounded the quarry just prior to bringing it down. Paul was an apt pupil. He learned the tricks involved in stalking game on a hunt.

On the way back to home, Paul carried one of the heavy baskets with pieces of the hog. He was pleased to help. He noted that his leg was no longer hurting on long walks. It was time, he thought, to escape for home. He felt confident in his ability to make it out of the jungle.

Paul had been living with the tribe now for about five years. He felt accepted by everyone and felt as if he was contributing to the wellbeing of the group. His plan of laughing and joking with the group seemed to be working. He was not being treated as an outsider, but rather as a part of the tribe.

As they walked back to the *shabono*, they happened to find the trail was flooded by recent rain showers. Paul looked down and observed his reflection. He was dazed at the sight of his countenance. What he saw was a man who had aged. The lines in his face around his eyes were pronounced. He had lost significant weight which gave him a sickly appearance. His beard was thick and long. Although he was only twenty-seven years old, the hairs in his beard were beginning to change to salt and pepper. Up until that moment, Paul imagined his appearance was the same as when he left Georgia, but what he saw was a skinny older man.

Paul stood looking at the likeness in the water. He had glanced at his reflection in the past, but this time he studied it closely. He could not believe what he was seeing. His appearance changed his thinking immediately. He had noticeably lost weight. With the new wrinkles he looked old beyond his years. He needed to get back home. He could not rely on a rescue. The need to return to Gertrude was critical. He had to leave now.

There was one factor holding him back. What if he found an impediment to finding civilization? Could he safely return to the *shabono* once he had departed? Would his leaving undo all the good will he had accrued in the last five years? Paul decided he would have to take the chance and make a break for it. He needed to get back to Gertrude. Paul came to the realization that a rescue was unlikely.

14

The Waika (1930)

Life in the jungle was relatively peaceful—or so Paul initially thought. During the afternoon one day, a male tribesman was found dead only about a hundred yards from the yard surrounding the *shabono*. The man had been stabbed in the back and was discovered only about an hour later. Next to his body was a stick jammed into the ground that had a small bone with a broken end tied to it. Paul asked Piarucu to explain. Piarucu said it appeared the victim had been urinating and not paying attention when a Waika tribesman sneaked up from behind and speared him. Piarucu explained that the Waika were dangerous and often targeted other tribes for murder without a reason. The stick with the bone attached was the calling card of the Waika warrior who had killed him. The other half of the bone would be tied around the neck of the killer as a symbol of his prowess.

Paul got the impression that it was not uncommon for an attack like this to occur. He wondered why Piarucu said it was Waika as if that were a sufficient explanation. Upon Paul's further questioning, Piarucu explained that Waika tribes in the area were vicious. He said they were always at war with other tribes. Although they might not hunt a man to attack, they *would* kill a male native if they found one alone. Stray females were taken as slaves.

Paul got the feeling surprise attacks between the Yonomamo and the Waika tribes were common. It was explained that the feud between the two tribes was many years old. While it was unclear just what the genesis of the dispute was, it had resulted in many murders over the years.

Paul thought he had been reckless in going out into the jungle solo many times since he had been living in the jungle. It never occurred to him that there were enemy tribes in the area. At some point, he decided he would be extra cautious when venturing out on his own.

Fierce looking Yanomami native

The following day, the victim's body was cremated in a large hot fire, which created a thick plume of smoke at the edge of the forest. Piarucu explained the smoke was freeing one of the deceased's souls into the sky. When the fire went out, the remaining bones were collected and crushed. A thick soup of plantain and water was boiled for hours. When it had thickened, the powdered bones were added to the soup, and relatives lined up, with each one swallowing a ladle of the soup. Observing the process, Paul thought it a very strange tradition. Piarucu told Paul that eating the bones symbolized unity between the dead person and the remaining living relatives. The relatives believed by eating the bones they would acquire the best qualities of the deceased. Paul wondered whether this practice accounted for Dr. Breckinridge claim of cannibalism by the natives.

At the end of the day, a dozen men gathered in the courtyard and began shouting. There was no apparent organization to the yelling, and the men kept it up even after darkness had set in. They were expressing outrage over the killing. Paul asked Piarucu about the incident, and he said the loud demonstrators were the *unokais*. The *unokais* were those in the tribe who had killed a Waika warrior. They were urging each other to avenge the murder of their fellow tribesman. Paul took note: the men involved acted as if they were proud to be killers. These men were highly respected in the tribe, and it seemed to Paul that their fierceness was more of a show and less than genuine. However, the following morning they left the *shabono* in search of revenge.

Three days after marching off, the band of the unokais warriors returned to the village. At the evening campfire, one of them told the story of their quest. They had traveled for more than a day to an area near a settlement of Waika. As they approached, they saw a Waika man walking toward a nearby stream to fish. As he was concentrating to find fish in the stream, the unokais crept up behind him using the noise of the stream as cover. The unokais were excellent stalkers. The fisherman heard nothing when the poison arrow burrowed into his back, puncturing his heart. He died a quick and painless death, and fell into the water. Piarucu explained that this act of revenge was the customary response to an attack by the Waika. Paul reassessed his opinion of the unokais. They were not only full of braggadocio, but they were also genuinely fierce.

To leave the message that it was revenge, the fisherman's body was dragged to the shore, and the bone retrieved from the earlier victim was left on a stick next to the victim.

On the second morning of the unokais' absence, Paul woke up to the distant growl of an approaching airplane. He sat up in his hammock. His heart began to race. He ran out to the yard and scoured the sky, then scrambled back to find his flare gun from the bag near his hammock. Hurrying to the center of the courtyard, Paul pointed the pistol skyward and pulled the trigger.

The flare lit the sky above the courtyard and the natives gawked. Within thirty seconds, the engine sound that had been so strong began to fade. In a minute, the flare went out as it hit the ground, and the roar of the engine gradually dissipated into silence.

Paul frantically searched the skies for the airplane, and began waving his arms. He circled in place while searching the sky. It took him a minute to realize the plane was gone. Paul called out to the sky in his loudest voice, "Blast! Come back!"

Paul's first thought was that the pilot must have seen the flare and had rushed off to send a rescue party to fetch him. He thought of the phrase: "All good things happen to those who wait." But then, he realized that if an airman *had* seen the flare, he would come to investigate before heading for help. Instead of coming to investigate, however, the plane had immediately flown out of sight. Upon deliberation, Paul reluctantly surmised that no search party was coming after all.

Paul fell into a dark, discouraged mood for the next few days. He realized he had been unprepared. How could he have been so careless? He vowed to have the flair ready to launch the next time a plane was in the vicinity. He could not believe he had not been able to fire his flare gun immediately upon hearing the airplane. He went back to his quarters and repositioned the flare pistol, so that it was on top of the stuff in one of the baskets.

For the first time, Paul realized it had been a mistake not to have made room for a radio in the plane. He was stuck in a village of natives with no way to get out. He had no way to communicate with any rescuers. Prior to the flight, he was convinced he would make it to Brazil. There was no doubt. He *would* make it. He persuaded himself that the hundred-pound radio would be a hindrance on takeoff. He had not envisioned any possible reason for failure. His optimism had prevented him from even thinking about the possibility of a landing in the jungle, miles from civilization. Now, he regretted his decision.

Hearing the airplane led Paul to another mistake in judgment. Since that airplane had been heard, Paul thought others would soon be in the area searching. He thought he should be patient and wait for the next airplane to find him. It was reasonable to assume another airplane would soon be overhead. This idea was a mistake, and it contributed to Paul's hesitancy to attempt an escape on his own.

He placed the basket containing the flare gun near the doorway, in a spot that was easy to reach. He did not want to be caught unprepared again.

Over the next weeks, Paul gave no thought to escaping the *shabono* on his own. He was convinced there would be other airplanes searching for him.

Unbeknownst to Paul, the airplane that had flown nearby was Jimmy Angel's. Angel was on a flight from Caracas, Venezuela, his plane loaded with mining supplies for diamond miners near Georgetown in British Guyana. He had spotted the glint of the morning sun's reflection off the *Port of Brunswick's* cockpit window from about ten miles away. Although he was in a hurry to Georgetown, he had made a bee line to the wreck. The number on the tail section was NX-773. He had seen the plane before, but there was no sign of life the first time he saw it.

Angel had lowered his altitude and circled the wreck two times but did not see any trace of Redfern, so he had resumed his trip, thinking there were no survivors. The *Port of Brunswick* was about four miles from the *shabono* where Paul lived. Angel could have seen Paul as he circled the wreckage had he looked in that direction. Unfortunately, Angel's attention was on the plane, and he did not glance toward the *shabono*. As a result, he never spotted the village *or* Paul.

Paul was vigilant during the following weeks, hoping the airplane might fly over again. But there were no more sightings. As time went by, with no plane heard from, Paul became less attentive to the possibility of another airplane.

The following week, two natives from Paul's village were reported dead from drowning. It was said that their canoe capsized in the flooded river while they were fishing. Their bodies were not found in the rushing stream. Piarucu pointed out that Paul had been with one of the men on a recent hunting trip. Paul recalled the man and was sorry that he had perished. He began to appreciate that living in the jungle was dangerous. There were several ways a person could meet his end in the jungle. It occurred to Paul that the number of men in the community was adversely affected by the various fatalities that seemed to be common. He took note of the fact that the jungle was a dangerous place.

After a few weeks, on most nights, just before dozing off, Paul would think of Gertrude and wonder how she was doing. The loneliness of not having her with him would well up in his chest. He thought about his plight, with no real prospects for getting back to her. He loved her deeply and resolved to return to civilization. He reverted to doing something he had done as a child. He said a short prayer asking for help in devising a plan to get back to her. On some nights, he asked for the courage to leave the village. As a child, Paul had prayed nightly. Now he chuckled to himself, realizing he was returning to that routine as an adult.

15

We Must Find Paul (1930)

In 1929, there was not much to discuss about Redfern's disappearance at the meetings of the Board of Trade. The Board had considered various courses of action over the previous year. But a majority had never agreed on any plan. Every suggestion was stalemated. At first the hesitation was due to not knowing where Paul was. They did not have a specific place to look in the vast jungle of several hundred square miles.

Now, in 1930, after three years, there were repeated rumors making their way to Georgia of a crippled white man living with a native tribe. The rumors were vague but persistent. Speculation was that the poor man *could* be a prisoner. However, some members pointed out there had been no actual sightings, so the chance that Paul was still alive was doubtful.

It was clear at this point that Paul's flight had been a failure. There had been numerous newspaper editorials condemning the flight. Criticism was especially sharp on the heels of the Dole Race debacle in which nine airmen and one female passenger, Mildred Doran, lost their lives attempting to find Hawaii from Oakland, California. But, over the years since, the Board had enjoyed a huge increase in the flow of goods in and out of the Port of Brunswick. The men were divided as to the cause of their prosperity. Was it due to the publicity surrounding the flight? Or was it due to the overall economy that was continuing to grow? In any event, the men in the room were in the best financial condition of their careers.

At the November 1930 meeting someone suggested forming a search party. The subject had been raised before, but never really given much consideration. It was unclear from the discussion whether the suggestion had its origin in a genuine feeling of responsibility for Paul's welfare or was the result of pressure by the public.

Paul Varner got up to speak. "I got to know Paul over the years leading up to the flight. We both were regulars at the Elks. At the time, Paul and his wife, Gertrude, were living in Savannah, just a few miles from here. I asked Paul to devise a publicity stunt that would put both the city of Brunswick and our businesses on the map nationally. Paul came up with the idea of flying to Rio, and I worked to put his flight together. We should have known that the flight was dangerous, but Paul's enthusiasm was infectious. His confidence was contagious. We went along with it. If not for the Board of Trade, there would not have been a flight. Paul may be responsible for his own fate, but we encouraged him. The Board of Trade paid for the flight to Rio de Janeiro. I don't know where Paul is, but if he is alive, he is clearly in trouble. We have the resources to launch a rescue effort, and we owe it to Paul to try to find him. I know we are in an economic depression, but we have the wherewithal to lead an expedition to South America. We *must* find Paul."

Other members pointed to the uncertain economic conditions as a reason not to do anything. After all, their income had been materially reduced by the decline in business, even though they were still in "profitable territory."

A subcommittee of three members was assigned to investigate the logistics of a search. Interestingly, Paul Varner was *not* put on the subcommittee. The subcommittee was made up of George Hunter, Dick Kauffold, and Richard Huskes. Of course, nothing was done at the end of the year due to the holidays, but in April a meeting of the group was held at noon at a secluded table near the rear of the Main Street Café on Newcastle Street.

A member of the group, George Hunter, owner of East Georgia Imports, Ltd. was one of the most successful businessmen in Brunswick. He was a cotton exporter, shipping cotton to both Europe and Asia. Immediately, he took charge of the meeting. While the other two came with no agenda in mind, Hunter had done his homework and distributed a sheet of paper headed "Finding Paul Redfern," with five questions:

1. **Where should we search?**
2. **Who should oversee a search?**
3. **What equipment will be needed?**
4. **What do we say to the public?**
5. **How much will a search cost**?

The discussion lasted about two hours, which was unusually long for a subcommittee discussion. At the conclusion, Dick Kauffold agreed to contact representatives of Stinson Aircraft and Wright Engine to discover the answers to questions one through three. Richard Huskes was assigned to contact Gertrude, since he was on good terms with her.

Shortly after the meeting, Hunter called on the editor of the *Brunswick Star*, a local newspaper, to pass on the outline of a rescue plan. Most importantly, he would let the editorial staff know that the Board had voted to fund a search. In the conversation, it was agreed that Hunter would also explore with the editor how to get the story out to all the nation's newspapers. They were hoping to get nationwide publicity favorable to the Board of Trade. Despite the failure to create a successful and spectacular flight, they were still interested in getting the City of Brunswick propitious publicity.

Shortly after meeting with the editor, a story appeared in the *Star*. That story was picked up by the Associated Press and found its way into about twenty-eight Hearst newspapers across the country, including the *New York Journal*, Hearst's flagship newspaper. The article recounted Redfern's flight and followed up with a broad outline of the Board of Trade's plan to attempt to rescue him.

A month later, Kauffold spoke to plane manufacturer Eddie Stinson. Stinson said, "I don't have a clue where the plane went down. If it were me, I would start by air at the coast and follow the route set out in Paul's charts. I saw Paul's hand-drawn chart showing his compass readings, and that would be the best place to look. I think he left a copy with Gertrude. As to how to form a search party and equip it, my only suggestion is to contact the National Geographic Society."

Both Kauffold and Morass had heard of the report of Paul's sighting from the captain of the steamship *Christian Krohg*. The captain had been confident that Redfern had made it to the coast of South America. He had had remarked, "Redfern was close enough to shore when he encountered the *Krohg* so a crash into the ocean was unlikely."

If Redfern had landed in the ocean there would be no trace anyway. There had been another reported sighting of Redfern's plane by a fisherman within ten miles of the coast of Venezuela. Most importantly, there were rumors of a white man who had come down from the sky living in the jungle. The Captain and Morass recommended looking along Redfern's planned route in the jungles of South America.

Kauffold had seen a news article about Jimmy Angel spotting the *Port of Brunswick* in the treetops in the jungle. Jimmy ran an air service out of Caracas, carrying supplies to the gold and diamond miners in the region. The article did not say whether he had kept any coordinates of the exact location.

Seeking more facts, Kauffold sent a letter to Angel:

"Dear Mr. Angel,
My name is Richard Kauffold, and I am a member of the Board of Directors of the Board of

Trade for Brunswick, Georgia. The Board of Trade sponsored Paul Redfern to an airplane flight from Georgia, USA, to Rio de Janeiro. Mr. Redfern took off on August 25, 1927, in an airplane named *Port of Brunswick,* but never showed up in Rio.

Our understanding is that you have discovered his plane in the jungles of Venezuela. We are interested in an expedition to find Mr. Redfern, and wonder if you can be specific as to where the plane is located? Would you be able to find the airplane again? Would you be willing to lead a search party to the airplane? Did you see any sign of Redfern in the vicinity? Is there any hope of finding Redfern alive?

Please answer this letter and let us know your thoughts on our quest to find Paul Redfern.

Very truly yours,

Richard Kauffold"

After a wait of about three months, Hunter received a hand-written reply:

Dear Mr. Kauffold:

I am receipt of your letter of March 23, 1930. I did indeed see the airplane, The Brunswick, in the trees here in Venezuela back in 1929. I wrote down the license number written on the tail—NX-773. I was flying to Georgetown. It seemed to be intact, but not flyable as one wing was badly damaged. Unfortunately, I did not see any sign of life. I can only assume Paul Redfern either did not survive, or had left the scene. From what I could see of the plane, it appears feasible, but not certain, that Redfern may have survived the crash.

I could probably find the location of the plane again. But the only way to do that would be by air. The jungle in that area is too dense for trekking. I could not agree to going by foot over land to get to the site. If I were to fly over the area, there is no place to put the plane down in the area.

So, you know, I have heard stories of a white man living with one of the tribes in the vicinity. These rumors may or may not be true. The Indians in that area are not friendly and could possibly have killed Redfern. However, the fact of the rumors gives hope that he may still be alive. I will ask around and write again if I hear anything. Oh, in answer to your question, I did not write down any coordinates for the plane.

Yours truly,

James Angel"

A month later, at Huskes' request, Gertrude mailed a copy of Paul's chart that she had found in his home office. It was a crude, hand-drawn map. It was not detailed, but did show the compass heading changes planned every five hundred miles. If he kept on course, he would have made landfall ten miles south of Trinidad-Tobago, after which he would then have followed the coastline toward the mouth of the Orinoco River.   From there, he planned an eight-degree right turn toward Rio as he flew over Venezuela and then British and Dutch Guiana.   The distance from the landfall to the British Guiana border was about one hundred thirty miles. The Board felt the best place to search in Venezuela was from the Atlantic shore to the border of British Guiana.

But, what the Board could not have know was that Paul had deviated from his proposed flight, circling and searching for a suitable landing spot, and had crashed into the jungle about thirty miles to the south of his proposed route. The Board of Trade had no idea of this change.

The editor of the National Geographic Society magazine responded to correspondence from George Hunter and said the Society was in favor a search. Indicating that the organization would seek funding for the expedition first, Gilbert Grosvenor said the Society was "definitely interested" in the project and asked for the Board to be patient until an estimate of the expenses could be determined. Their letter also estimated that equipping and manning the search party would probably take six months to a year.

It had already taken the Board nine months to get to that point, far longer than anyone on the subcommittee could have anticipated. But no one in Brunswick had any expertise in such a project, so they could do nothing but wait for the Society to find the funds and organize the trip to Venezuela. There was nothing left to do but wait. Besides, the offer to fund the expedition by Grosvenor was a welcome development.

In their initial letter to Grosvenor, Hunter forwarded the letter from Angel and suggested that Grosvenor contact Jimmy Angel. Now, three months into the project, Grosvenor wrote to say that Angel had been found in Caracas and verified that he knew where Redfern had gone down. He had seen the plane hanging in the treetops in Venezuela and would assist in any search. Angel reportedly said, "The plane has sunk a little since I first spotted it. But, whenever I fly over it in the morning sun, the reflection off the plane's window shines like a beacon."

Grosvenor also indicated the Society could collect $400,000 toward the $500,000 needed to fund the search, but was hoping the Board of Trade would kick in the rest. Hunter was dismayed over the $100,000 cost. But after polling the members of the Board, he was pleased to report the Board of Trade would act upon Grosvenor's request.

George Hunter sent a progress report to the Board and to Gertrude the same day. It was the best news Gertrude had heard since the day of the flight. The $100,000 price tag sent to the Board of Trade was equivalent to $1.2 million in today's dollars. It was not an amount that was easy to swallow by its millionaire members, but in the end, an amount that was within reach. Pursuant to the decision made at its meeting, the group in Brunswick sent $50,000 to Grosvenor to get things started. The remaining $50,000 was sent two months later.

Dr. Geoffrey Haskins at the Society began a European-wide hunt to recruit a search team of approximately five paid members. In England, he would also look for a few additional unpaid volunteers willing to donate six months of their time. The National Geographic organization had successfully used this tactic, using unpaid volunteers, in the past. They would hire porters once they got to Caracas. Oddly, the Board of Trade found no one in their midst who desired to join the expedition. The Board members felt neither they nor their employees could give up running their businesses for the six-month time commitment.

The society placed a request for donations in the next issue of the National Geographic Society magazine explaining the project. They included a heartfelt letter from Gertrude about her husband. In the letter, she said, "My husband, Paul Redfern, took off in 1927 from Brunswick, Georgia, for Rio de Janeiro. Since then, we have heard persistent stories of a white man living in the jungles of South America with natives. I believe that white man must be my husband. I am desperate to have an expedition go to the jungle to find him before it is too late. I pray each of the readers of the *National Geographic Magazine* will donate toward such an expedition."

In the same issue, Gilbert Grosvenor made a similar request for donations, adding some details as to the timing and other plans for the expedition. He predicted the search party could begin in 1930. Once the magazine was published, readers from all over the globe sent in donations. The magazine was popular everywhere.

In a boost to the endeavor to reach its goal, the Society was aided by a well-known aviatrix, Amelia Earhart. Her husband, George Putnam, made sure to publicize her achievements throughout her life. That meant a plethora of radio interviews. To her credit, she mentioned the National Geographic project several times, the mention of which showed up in several news articles around the country. Records were not kept as to the amount of money collected because of her mentioning the cause, but Grosvenor estimated that her encouragement brought in about one hundred thousand dollars.

Overall, the campaign was successful. Within six weeks they collected almost eighty per cent of the total budget. After ten weeks, the Society had the full five hundred thousand dollars.

Haskins' press release announcing the Society's success predicted the expedition would reach Venezuela by late August 1931, which was later than predicted, but was a more accurate estimation. August was the last month of the annual forty-day rainy season. So, the search would take place in relatively dry conditions. August 1931 also marked the fourth anniversary of Paul's flight.

* * * * *

While the National Geographic expedition was being planned in 1930, Frederick Redfern, Paul's father, received a letter from George P. Putnam. Putnam was a New York author and publicist, and most notably married to Amelia Earhart, although she had refused to change her last name after the marriage.

The one-page letter from Putnam told Frederick Redfern that Amelia was interested in Paul's flight to Rio and concerned with his disappearance. He opined that if Amelia were engaged in the search for Paul, it would generate public interest across the country. He noted: "The world watches everything Amelia does, and her involvement in a search could generate very significant donations. By her becoming the chairwoman of a rescue expedition, the public would take notice of Paul's situation and donate to the cause. Amelia would lend her name to the campaign to finance Paul's return to his homeland in return for half of any funds raised." He included a photo of Amelia taken during her ticker tape parade celebrating her 1928 flight from Newfoundland to Wales.

Frederick read the letter and was perplexed. He was aware of Amelia's already existing support for the National Geographic search. But Putnam's letter seemed to indicate he was unaware of her support. He was, however, keenly aware of the worldwide interest world in finding Paul.

It was not at all clear what role Amelia would take in the search. After reading it several times, he concluded that Putnam was suggesting she would lend her name to a fund-raising effort, but she would not be personally involved in the search. Furthermore, Putnam was requesting half of the fund for her involvement. In essence, he was asking for half the fund for the use of her name.

Frederick, a college professor, had received several letters like this one, offering to disclose Paul's whereabouts in exchange for cash. But nothing in the letters indicated any reason to believe the claims. He concluded the deal offered by Putman, like the others, was not in his interest, especially considering the efforts of the National Geographic.

He put the letter in his correspondence file and did not reply.

16

A Platonic Wife? (1930)

While the condition of his right leg was the main cause of his hesitation to leave the *shabono* in the first years of his life in the jungle, the leg, with the help of native medicine, did gradually improve. As it got better, his ambition to leave grew stronger. He spent time each day mapping out in his mind a plan to escape. However, his leg continued to be sore at the end of a hard day, so he kept postponing the actual escape.

His relationship with the natives continued to be on good terms. As time passed, the tribe generally became friendlier. He had conversations with everyone who would listen although the extent of understanding was still somewhat in doubt. Paul continued to repeat himself and use facial and hand gestures, which he felt increased the natives' understanding.

Paul was invited to join hunting parties and general tribal meetings. On occasion, he was even asked for his opinion. On one such occasion, Paul recommended two things having to do with drinking water. First, boil all drinking water. Second, only take water from upstream of the *shabono*. The headman, Shaporo, agreed to defer the issue to Yanokiritana. Paul spoke to Yanokiritana and explained the sanitary reasons behind his suggestion. Paul was surprised when the following day,

Yanokiritana made Paul's suggestions the new rules of the *shabono*.

During this time, Paul continued to wear the clothes he wore during the flight, minus his flight boots, which had fallen apart after about six months due to the constant dampness of the jungle. His shirt was torn in a few places, but it continued to be his staple with the sleeves rolled up. His pant leg, which had been ripped open was sewn up. Paul acclimated to going barefoot. After a few months, his feet were as tough as the terrain. He kept his leather flight jacket under his hammock and never wore it.

The children were fascinated by Paul's hairy arms and face. The natives had little body hair. Paul's facial and body hair were a novelty. It was not uncommon for a giggly child to run up to Paul for the sole purpose of running fingers over his arms, or to touch his clothes.

One day, Paul unwittingly made the children laugh. He unknowingly sat down on a log that happened to be infested with fire ants. As soon as they attacked, Paul jumped up and repeatedly yelled, "Whoa! Whoa! Whoa!" while slapping at his thighs and bottom. The children thought this was a wonderful act. Paul spent the next hour carefully picking ants off his body, but not before they had eaten several small holes in his pants and shirt.

Paul's relationship with the children was especially genial. He always took time to talk and play with them whenever he was out and about. The children especially liked to hear Paul sing songs. He had a deep voice and a happy presentation. After hearing him sing for several months, the children began to sing along. As time passed, more of the children sang along. *Frere Jacques* was a favorite that the children sang with a strong accent. They laughed heartily at the end of each song. Occasionally, a few adults would wander over and join in singing; they always sang off-key.

Perhaps it was because Paul liked the children that he noticed there was an inordinate number of them. Every family had several offspring, and many families had two or three mothers with one husband. It seemed that there was a high percentage of widows. Yet, more than half of the settlement were children. The mothers practiced birth control of sorts by not having an additional child until the first was weaned at about three years. Children were universally looked after and shown love by all the adults in the settlement.

At the same time, Paul also noticed there were not many older men. Men over forty were especially rare. He was intrigued at the difference in demographics between the settlement and the population he was familiar with in the States. There were more women, children, and fewer older male adults. There was definitely a shortage of adult males. Paul thought he should attempt to determine why the shortage existed.

Over the next few months, Paul paid attention to the deaths among the natives, and quickly realized it was the men who engaged in dangerous behavior daily. Men were more likely to be attacked by animals, drown in rivers, or fight battles with other tribes. Therefore, it was the men who were subject to premature death. The jungle was a treacherous place, and men spent more time in the jungle than did the children and women. Paul thought it was no wonder he had been prevented from leaving the grassy courtyard when he first arrived at the *shabono*.

Paul thought that exposure to the dangers of the jungle was one factor in the paucity of men in the tribe, but there must be other factors. He thought of the unokais urging each other to engage in life-threatening behaviors, such as attacking the Waika. And he thought of the widespread use of coca leaves. The use of coca gave men a false sense of power and strength, thus promoting dangerous

Yanomami native (note sticks protruding from face)

behavior. The endorsement of fierceness in the tribe was a contributing factor to the high death rate among men.

Paul continued to be sociable with the members of the tribe, talking and asking questions. He smiled most of the time. One day at dusk, he was escorted to the largest campfire in the courtyard and given a seat on a log. Most of the men of the settlement joined, squatting and sitting on logs around the fire. Paul started to wonder if he was about to be "the meal of the day." His fears subsided when he noted no malice in their facial expressions. The men talked to each other and, on occasion, gestured toward him indicating he was the subject of the conversation. He saw several men make the familiar hand gesture demonstrating his airplane falling from the sky. From then on, the discussion group met each evening and included Paul. He began to feel less anxious and more at home with the tribe.

Once Paul began walking without crutches, he was invited to go on hunting trips with the natives. At first, the hunting excursions were day trips, but later he was included on overnight excursions. The hunts began on well-worn trails until game was discovered. Then, the group would leave the trails and bushwhack through the jungle. Paul quickly learned which of the plants they encountered had "prickers," or saw-like edges. On his first few hunts he returned to the village with bloody hands and arms. However, the natives seemed to glide through the forest without injury.

Paul was not a fast walker, and often was behind the others as they skipped along on the outside edge of their feet. He was soon out of breath, and had to drop behind. However, the natives would occasionally stop and wait for him to catch up. Even after regrouping, though, it didn't take long for him to be left lagging behind again. But the hunters were patient with Paul's slow pace and did not seem to mind.

On one occasion, the men decided to play a joke on Paul. They let him fall behind and then, instead of waiting on the trail, blended into the jungle on both sides of the trail, and waited. As Paul approached, they were all hidden, and when he came around a bend and looked, no one was in sight. He started to panic, because he did not want to be alone in the jungle. He glanced in all directions. At that moment, the natives jumped out and yelled at him. All of them were laughing. Paul laughed too, except for him it was a sign of relief. He was delighted to be a part of the joke, but did not want to be left alone in the jungle again.

Of all the attempts at communicating, Paul and Piarucu seemed to make the most progress. Piarucu took his time in conversation and would repeat words so Paul could discern their meaning. In response, Paul spoke slowly back to Piarucu. Facial expressions, repetition, and gestures also were employed to give meaning to the words.

One day, Piarucu mentioned that the tribe did not like white men.

"White men are bad. They do not respect Yanomami."

"Why do you say that?" Paul asked.

"White men came to us long ago searching for gold and brought sickness. We did not want the sickness. Their digging for gold polluted the rivers with poison. Other whites wanted us to put on clothes. We do not need clothes. That is a white man's idea."

"I see. So, what about me? I am a white man . . ."

"You are different. You came out of the sky. You were sent by the good spirits of the sky."

This observation was not entirely new to Paul. He had realized his crash from the sky had a special significance to the natives. To them, his showing up in a treetop was a sign that the sky spirits had sent him to them.

Paul wondered whether the tribe had frequent or even rare meetings with other white people. In all the time Paul had been living with the natives, he never heard rumors about white people being in the vicinity. Could he expect someone to come looking for him? Or, if not specifically to find him, could someone stumble into the s*habono* by chance? He thought the best way to escape his predicament was for someone to find him and take him home.

Paul brought up the question of contact of white people with the tribe in several conversations. Some denied knowing of any encounters. Most were too vague to be of any help. Some mentioned the events relating to missionaries, events of no consequences to the present day.

Paul spoke to some of the elder members of the tribe. Several tribesmen had mentioned there had been encounters with white men in the past. Paul thought the older men of the tribe might remember something important. He asked about their encounters with white people. Some refused to talk. Others spoke guardedly and did not disclose much information. But one old man was forthcoming. He told of the missionaries who had visited many years ago. He said they arrived by boat and stayed almost a year before they were forced to leave after a vote of the tribe.

One day he noticed a man squatting in the courtyard. He had white hair and skin that sagged. He was looking off into the distance. Paul interrupted his reverie with a smile and a hearty, "Hi Guy!" Looking up, the man said, "Me a re." The only people in the world available to ask were the ones living in his *shabono*.

The old man told Paul there had been several visits by white men over the years, but nothing lately. When they were discovered in the area, the tribe would give one or two days to vacate. If they dallied, they were killed. Paul was stunned at the off-hand way this gentle-looking man spoke of death

Paul decided to turn to Piarucu for answers, since he could count on him to be truthful

Over the next few weeks, Piarucu told of old contacts with other white men such as missionaries, explorers, and gold diggers. As Piarucu told it, some of these encounters had been disastrous for the natives, because the whites had brought deadly diseases. In addition, some of the white people attempted to force the tribe to adopt the white man's religion, including giving up their belief in spirits and becoming immersed in the river. The missionaries insisted the natives wear clothing, which the natives thought was unnecessary.

The white men who had visited the tribe ordered them around as if they were children. They insisted that the natives wear clothes, something they had never done. They wanted the natives to give up their belief in spirits and adopt the white man's religion.

Praying to the white man's god seemed to be without effect. The tribe finally concluded it had no use for the white man's religion. The tribe's reticence to change angered the white men, who then changed their approach from making suggestions to issuing haranguing demands. The tribe soon resented this and ordered the white men to leave.

Ever since those encounters, the tribe had nothing to do with white men, nor did they encourage visits by whites. They made it clear they did not desire any interaction. Whenever they came in contact with the white men, the men displayed their weapons and motioned for the whites to leave. The natives thought nothing of killing anyone whom they perceived as a threat. After several disastrous encounters, the tribe had concluded death was the most efficient way to keep white men away. Piarucu explained that Paul was an exception because he was jolly and came from the sky where the good spirits lived. Paul listened intently. He interpreted the conversation as a warning: Don't try to change the tribe's way of doing things.

The normal daily routine was that Piarucu would see that Paul had food each day. But then there was a change. A woman began to bring him food regularly rather than Piarucu. No one explained the change. Paul did not know what to think of this development, but he accepted it. The woman's most distinctive features were the maroon circles that covered her body. Paul began to refer to her as "Circles."   He learned that the various sized circles had been painted on her by her mother when she was young and were now permanent.   Paul did not initially spend a lot of time talking with her.   He did make a prayerful, palms-together gesture to her whenever she brought food to show he was grateful.   He was careful not to make any gestures that could be misinterpreted, and he tried not to stare at her body which like all the natives was uncovered.

After a week, Shaporo, the headman, sought out Paul.   They went to the courtyard fire and while Paul sat on a log, Shaporo crouched next to him.   Shaporo told Paul that the tribe wanted to demonstrate that he was a welcome guest.   Paul answered with a thank you.   The headman went on to explain that as a guest the village was obligated to treat Paul hospitably.   Shaporo added that Circles was a widow and was available to be Paul's wife.   Circles' husband had been killed the prior year by an attack of piranha after his canoe capsized.

Shaporo explained it was tradition that if the tribe had a male visitor, he would be welcomed by the tribe and that included the gift of a wife from among the available females. Shaporo told Paul that Circles was available to be his wife.

Shaporo said, "This woman will move in with you. I have told her she must obey you. She will make you happy."

Circles was a pleasant woman, and had been bringing him food for the last few days.   She was talkative and happy, laughing at the drop of a hat. Paul enjoyed the short conversations they would have whenever she approached him. However, he had no thoughts of taking her for a wife.

Paul wondered if Circles had any say in the matter. He answered that he already had a wife who was waiting for him at his home far away and he was hoping to get back to her. Shaporo commented that there was no reason Paul could not have more than one wife and that he should forget about leaving the compound. Shaporo turned his back and abruptly walked away. Apparently, Shaporo was giving Paul an order to accept Circles as a wife and no longer wanted to discuss it.

Within a week or so of Paul's conversation with the headman about his new wife, Circles moved into the area of Paul's hammock. She strung up another hammock next to his. There was no marriage ceremony. Merely placing her hammock next to his signified marriage.

Most marriages were prearranged. Many times, a man would plan the marriage with his future wife's family while the woman was still a juvenile. Upon her first menstrual period she would move into the man's quarters. In those circumstances, the man would donate property to his wife's family as a gesture of respect. Since Circles had already been previously married, Paul was not required to make a marriage gift.

It was customary for married couples to make love in the forest away from the lodge. So, placing her hammock next to his was not necessarily an invitation for sex. He did not make any advances, but the two did converse regularly, although in a hesitant fashion. Over time, they became friends.   She became his second friend; Piarucu being the first.

After Circles settled into Paul's quarters, she took the role of his wife in all the household duties. She did the cooking and cleaning. She also had her own garden, and brought fruit to Paul regularly. She did not show any resentment that Paul was not interested in her physically. He remained faithful to Gertrude.

Paul attempted to explain to Circles that he had left a wife who was waiting for his return. While he thought it was clear to her that he could not marry her, she did not move out from his section of the hut. Piarucu spoke to Paul and explained, "In this tribe, it is not forbidden to have more than one wife." Based on Piarcucu's explanation, Paul did not insist that Circles move her hammock.

17

The Black Devil (1932)

One day, as they returned to the settlement, Paul sensed a great dejection and consternation among the members of the tribe who had remained in the village. He learned that a twelve-year-old girl had gone about a quarter mile to the river for water. When she did not return, a search party went looking for her. They found her lying on the riverbank, bleeding profusely, with one arm and a leg torn open.

Paul rushed to the girl's location. She was in bad shape. Her mother and siblings were crying out to the spirits for assistance. Shaporo was attempting to sew up the wounds with a thick string made of twisted vines and a needle fashioned out of a fish bone. Her wounds were no longer bleeding, but she had lost a good deal of blood before she was found. Paul thought the wounds looked fatal. The *shaman*, Yanokiritana, was in a trance induced by *yopo*, a hallucinogenic snuff made from the ground seeds of the Anadenanthera peregrina tree. He was reciting a chant to the spirits.

Paul asked what had happened? He was told it was the "Black Devil"—a Black Panther. A jaguar, sometimes referred to as a panther, had attacked the girl. After attacking her, the panther had departed, leaving her with serious wounds. It had not killed her for food. She was still alive, but barely. This was the first that Paul had heard of a Black Panther. It was explained to him that the black cats were bloodthirsty and sometimes would attack purely for sport. While such attacks were rare, they did occur from time to time. Because of its trait of attacking for no reason, it was called the "Black Devil."

Black panthers are not a separate species. Their parents usually have orange fur with black dots. Most litters have two or three kittens, with an all-black kitten being an anomaly. The fact that black cats are rare also promotes the belief that they are especially malevolent. The natives all believed that the Black Devil was more vicious than its normal siblings.

A black panther uses its dark coat to its advantage, especially in the shadowy atmosphere of the jungle, where its dark color makes it almost invisible. Moving silently through the foliage, it always has the upper hand when on the attack. Piarucu explained that black panthers have been known to stalk men for days, waiting for a chance to surprise its prey. He told of an incident where Piarucu himself was the intended victim. "It followed me for three days and then disappeared. It gave up because it could tell I was ready to fend off any attack."

Despite the entreaties by Yanokiritana and the songs and chants by the village, lasting the whole day, the unfortunate girl died. The entire village, including Paul, was saddened by the girl's death. Paul had noticed that the village was especially fond of its children, the outpouring of grief for the girl reinforcing that belief.

Paul thought about the danger posed by the panther. It was just another way one could die unexpectedly in the dark jungle, besides assassination by another tribe, drowning, or being attacked by piranha. Paul added attack-by-black-panther to the list.

Yanomami native fishing with bow and arrow

Paul was delighted when Piarucu asked him to join the hunting party to find and kill the brutal panther. Piarucu explained that while it was common for a *shaman* to take a normal spotted panther as his "mirror soul," and add spots to his body, none picked the Black Devil. Yellow spotted panthers with black dots were more plentiful. The scarce black panther was considered the personification of evil. The panther attacked the girl and left her bleeding but did not bother to use her as food. Therefore, to the tribe, it had evil intent. It had to be killed.

The eight hunters assigned to find the black panther started at the water's edge and found a few faint tracks. It was impossible to tell the direction taken by the panther, because its footprints were pointing in random directions. Piarucu studied their surroundings for a few minutes. He then proclaimed, "We go this way!" pointing downstream. They quietly followed the stream for several hours without spotting any additional tracks.

Piarucu ordered everyone to set up camp early, right at dusk. The men had a quick meal and lounged around a large campfire. Several of them sharpened their arrowheads and checked their bow strings. At midnight, they broke camp and split into two factions. Paul, Piarucu, and two others continued downstream, parallel to the river. The other four temporarily stayed behind. After about a half hour, Piarucu sensed the panther was in the vicinity, even though he had not actually seen it. He whispered to the others, "We are close. We will stay at the water's edge."

They turned left toward the river, when suddenly, there were flashes of black in the underbrush as the panther began prowling just wide of the trail to their right. The beast was unafraid of allowing the natives to intermittently spot him. Piarucu cautioned the men to keep going. Without giving any sign of having seen the cat, the group trudged on.

As the group reached the large rocks at the river's edge, it appeared they were trapped. The water could be infested with piranha, making it impassable, while large rocks blocked their way to the right. The panther was behind them, but unseen.

Appearances can be deceiving, however. The other four men had secreted themselves in the undergrowth on the other side of the river. They were hidden from view about thirty yards away, about the maximum for a kill shot with a bow. As the panther jumped into the open on a nearby rock perch above the hunters, ready to tear into the men at the shore, two of the marksmen from the second group rose and fired their arrows. One of the arrows struck the side of a hind leg and fell harmlessly to the ground. The second arrow, however, struck the beast in the chest just aft of its neck, and penetrated deeply. A high-pitched scream resounded from the injured panther. Within seconds, the panther collapsed like a sack of potatoes on the rocks. The poison-tipped arrow had punctured its heart.

Piarucu stripped off the black shiny hide of the panther back to camp to be used as a blanket for their leader, Shaporo. Upon close inspection, Paul noticed the faint outline of normal spots in the black pelt. To emphasize their disdain, the remains of the panther were dumped into the river.

With the hunting party back at the camp, the whole group of men, women, and children sang and danced for hours to celebrate their return. The celebration was to thank the spirits for the kill. The natives were enthusiastic in their merriment. All the men in the hunting party were congratulated. Paul was happy to be among the heroes. Shaporo proudly wrapped the panther hide around his shoulders, even though it had not yet dried.

On other occasions, if a hunting trip were unsuccessful, the chanting and dancing would be to scare away the evil spirits that had kept the game hidden out of sight. This time, however, the singing was to celebrate the success of the hunt.

Every ceremony included songs and chants to the good or the cruel spirits. The people believed strongly in spirits that could cause good or bad things to happen. For example, if a hunting trip were successful, the village would praise the good spirits. If someone became ill, the *shaman*, Yanokiritana, would lead a series of songs imploring the bad spirits to withdraw from the victim's body.

Paul was impressed by the optimistic belief of the natives that spirits existed. The villagers trusted that singing and dancing would regulate the spirits' effect on the native tribe. They believed Yanokiritana could control the spirits. Yanokirtana had spent years as an apprentice before becoming *shaman*. The belief in spirits had been passed down through generations. When Paul asked Shaporo how long the belief in spirits existed, the response was always the same: "Forever."

18

Attacked (1933)

As time passed, Paul's days began to follow a pattern. He no longer needed his crutches. He would relax around the compound for a few days and venture out on a hunting trip the following day. Most hunting trips were one-day affairs called *rami*, while others took up to two nights or more. The longer hunts were called *heniyomou*. Paul could tell that the group regularly traveled to well-known hunting areas as they almost always followed established trails through the thick undergrowth of the forest. Paul attempted to determine the direction of the trails, but there were too many bends and intersections for him to get his bearings. He noticed that after only a few steps most of the trails bent to the left or the right. Since the sun was hidden by tree limbs most of the time, Paul could not count on it for a navigation tool. He imagined his escape from the *shabono* and the fact that he would be lost almost immediately.

Paul also went with the men on fishing-gathering trips. Normally, they used a spear or bow and arrow to harvest fish. However, in a small stream about five miles from the settlement, they had placed fish traps. The oval traps made from large bamboo culms were placed deep in the river and would fall to the bottom when the fish pulled on the minnows used as bait.

These traps were emptied two or three days a week and always seemed to have a fish in them.

While watching the men fishing, Paul realized that the streams all had to run somewhere. If he could get on a stream eventually, he hoped it would wind up at a civilized city. It was a fleeting thought and he soon forgot about it. He was correct, however, in thinking that a stream could take him to civilization. However, the distance to cities was quite a bit longer than he envisioned.

As the men were picking up their stuff at the end of the fish harvest, Piarucu spoke to Paul. "This stream turns red under a full moon. It is magic." Paul looked at the creek and observed the crystal-clear water. He could count the rocks four feet down at the bottom of the stream.

Paul questioned Piarucu, "Why does it turn red? Why during a full moon?" Piarucu did not reply directly, but only repeated, "It's magic." Paul shrugged and felt there was a language problem. *The creek turns red during a full moon. Unlikely.*

In the twilight of the next full moon, Piarucu found Paul, and, in the dimming sky, took him four miles back to the creek where they had been fishing. The water in the five-foot wide creek was still clear. Paul pointed and said, "It's not red." Piarucu urged him to wait, and they sat down on the creek bank. They sat and talked for almost two hours as the sky blackened. Piarucu pointed out the ribbon of pink that appeared running down the middle of the stream. Paul was intrigued. As the two men continued to watch, the pink strip widened and finally all the water from one side to the other was a deep red. Paul was dumbfounded.

Looking in the direction of upstream, Paul said, "I am going to go look. I want to know why the water has turned red." Piarucu said, "No, you cannot go. The spirits there are evil. It is great danger."

Paul said, "I understand. But I am not afraid. You stay here. I'll go by myself."

Paul began trudging upstream into the thick jungle while Piarucu remained seated on the bank. He jumped the creek several times to ensure good footing, and continued following the contours of the land upriver. At one spot, he was forced to climb to the top of the riverbank to avoid some rapids. Finally, he came to a place where the creek zig-zagged around several large boulders. The boulders stood above Paul's head. It was a full moon but still dark due to the denseness of the jungle.

As he came to the last boulder, Paul heard a soft moaning sound. In front of him was an opening in the trees and he saw a bright spot on the water. He heard splashing. Paul stepped around the boulder. He saw the head of a tapir above the water line. It was the tapir that was whimpering. As he got closer Paul heard another sound. It was a clack, clack, clack noise coming from the water. Paul realized in an instant it was piranha. Paul grabbed a tree branch lying nearby and attempted for several minutes to pry the tapir from his predicament. But no amount of pushing or shoving with the tree branch could free it. He threw the branch down. Paul could see underwater that the some of the white bones of the tapir were visible. The fish were stripping the tapir bare. He would soon be eaten alive. Paul thought for a moment, then picked up the thick tree branch and swung as hard as possible hitting the tapir in the back of the head. As the tapir sank into the creek, the water swirled as the piranha tore into the remains. Paul had freed the tapir from the suffering of being eaten alive.

As Paul held the branch he had used as a tool, he noticed black sticky stuff on it. He plunged it back into the water and felt it sink in the mire. He lifted it out. It was black tar. Paul thought perhaps it was a sign of oil seeping up through the ground. The tapir had ventured into the water and had gotten stuck. He was easy prey to the hundreds of vicious fish.

Paul then noticed a ray of moonlight streaming down on the pond. The luminous spotlight lit the middle of the pond where the tapir had stood. It was this glow in the dark that made the pond attractive to animals. Large creatures venturing out into the middle of the creek became stuck. It was the combination of animals becoming mired in the black tar and being eaten by the piranha that resulted in the crimson coloration of the river. Paul had solved the mystery.

As he began the trek back, Paul noticed a glint of light at the bottom of the pink watered creek. Curious, he carefully reached into the water and pulled out a small rock. Examination showed it to be a hard clear crystal stone. Then he noticed another shiny stone and collected it as well. This one was larger, about two inches wide. He had no use for either, but thought he would collect them as a memento of his time in the jungle. *These will make a good souvenir for Gertrude. Maybe they will turn out to be diamonds*, he thought. He chuckled to himself at the thought, since he was confident they could not be valuable. He dropped the two stones into his pants pocket and continued his hike back to Piarucu.

About halfway back to where he had left Piarucu, Paul was surprised to see Piarucu trotting toward him. Piarucu had worried about his friend Paul. He imagined that Paul had met a terrible fate. That concern had overcome his fear of the bad spirits. Paul explained how the moonlight of a full moon attracted animals into the water, the tar pinned them to the bottom, and the piranha did the rest. Piarucu was happy to see Paul, but despite Paul's explanation, he was not convinced. He still believed the tapir was the victim of evil perpetrated by bad spirits.

Paul was impressed that his friend Piarucu had come to his rescue. His overcoming his fear of evil spirits showed great determination. Paul said, "Not everything in the jungle is the work of the spirits." Piarucu looked back at Paul but did not respond.

As they hiked back to the *shabono*, Piarucu told Paul that the name of his tribe was "People of the Color of Blood." It seems that an earlier *shabono* close to this creek was named based on the periodic change in color of the water. After they moved to a different location, they used the old name even though the creek was no longer nearby. Paul laughed. His wife, Gertrude, belonged to a club back home called the Tuesday Club. The women had changed their meeting day to Thursday, but kept the original Tuesday Club name. The Tuesday Club met on Thursdays.

Over time, Paul and Piarucu had several conversations in which Paul attempted to enlighten Piarucu about his world in the States. He attempted to explain how his world worked. Paul talked of airplanes, automobiles, radios, and electricity. It was not clear how much Piarucu understood, but he always appeared interested in listening to Paul. When Paul talked of Gertrude, Piarucu seemed to appreciate Paul's desire to see her again. Paul was comfortable talking about Gertrude with Piarucu.

One day, on the second dawn of a hunting expedition, Paul noticed a different attitude among the hunters. Instead of their normal, quick-paced walk along the trail, the men were unusually quiet, and reduced their speed. They made frequent stops to look ahead and listen intently. On earlier trips, the hunters would reduce their forward progress only when stalking prey, but on this day, they seemed to be overly cautious. Paul sensed a look of apprehension in their eyes. He was about to ask someone what was going on.

Paul was walking along side Piarucu and suddenly they heard a thud. They both flinched. An arrow had landed about five feet in front of them. Paul saw another arrow flying at them and quickly side-stepped. Angry shouts filled the air. They were being attacked. Paul's pulse was racing. From the front, left and right, arrows were falling from the sky. Two of the hunters at the front were hit. Both went down. There was shouting by both sides. Some of the hunters began unleashing arrows back at the attackers. It was clear that the attackers outnumbered the hunters. The battle had erupted suddenly from nowhere. Paul immediately ran to the rear. He was trying to avoid being hit by one of the poisoned arrows raining down. Paul realized almost immediately that with his white skin and clothes, he stood out from the rest and was an obvious target.

Shaporo shouted instructions. "It's Waika. Take cover!" He roughly pushed Paul down to the ground. Everyone immediately threw down their baskets of game and began back-tracking along the trail at a swift pace. Paul dropped the basket he had been carrying and crawled awkwardly on his hands and feet away from the confrontation. After about fifty yards, he caught up to the group that had formed a defensive line behind a thick grove of bamboo trees and waited. Paul and the others were now hidden from view by the thick stand of trees. Paul was instructed to sit behind a large-leafed palm to the rear of the hunting party. Things had happened too fast for Paul to analyze them. Now, as he waited, he realized he was facing death.

Paul's experience as a pilot helped him through this occurrence. He had learned to push fear out of his mind and concentrate on what needed to be done to save himself. He recognized he was in danger, and he was unsure what to do about it. He wished he had brought his revolver. He sat motionless and involuntarily took several deep breaths. He realized he was in the hands of the fellow natives. They were the ones that were armed.

The members of the hunting party remained out of sight while they stood behind the impenetrable stalks of the bamboo. The attackers were unaware of the hiding place as they advanced. They thought the natives had fled the scene entirely. When the attackers were about ten yards away, on the Headman's orders, the hunters stepped out and inundated the attackers with arrows and darts. Paul's comrades gave a huge shout. Several of the attackers fell to the ground after being struck with arrows. Paul turned and looked just in time to see the attackers running away. Their appearance was like that of the men he was with: they too were short and naked, and had thick black hair. The tide of the battle had turned, and the attackers quickly retreated out of sight.

Paul sat on the grass and took a deep breath.

The hunting party quickly re-grouped, picked up some of the game they had left on the ground, and hurriedly made their way back toward the compound. Several of their baskets were abandoned where they had been dropped. Four men were sent to pick up the hunters who had gone down. One of the two men who had been struck by arrows was dead. The other was alive, but unable to walk on his own, as the muscle relaxant from the arrow's tip left no feeling in one of his legs.

Two makeshift man-carriers were constructed out of two thick branches tied together with smaller cross branches and covered by an assortment of palm leaves. The two casualties were lashed to them. Two men were assigned to each contraption, and the men were dragged back to the settlement. As the others tramped through the jungle, the main group stuck together, but two of the men, armed with bows and arrows, fell behind to guard against anyone sneaking up from the rear.

To Paul, the attack had occurred completely unexpectedly, without any reason. His group was hunting in its normal territory. Paul asked and was told that the animus between the two tribes resulted from some ancient murders. The murders had occurred so long ago that none of the living tribesmen had witnessed them. The enmity between the tribes was passed down entirely from earlier generations and lived on today. The Waiki were known as particularly war-like and were quite dangerous. The Waiki were the attackers.

It was not immediately clear which tribe had suffered the most casualties. The aggressors had the element of surprise, but their attack was brief. The counterattack from behind the bamboo had been more sustained. Paul was happy that almost everyone in the hunting party had escaped the attack alive. He was especially pleased that he had survived unscathed.

Around midnight, they arrived back at their *shabono*. Paul was exhausted. There would be no sleep, however, as the night was spent organizing a defense to any continuation of hostilities. Logs were arranged at one end of the structure, so the women and children had a walled-in refuge. Arrows and other projectiles were carved and dipped in poison three times rather than the customary one time. Some men began carrying clubs made from thick root material. Paul agonized over what might happen next. Would he die in a fight in which he had no stake? He sat down on his hammock to ponder his predicament.

As he sat on his hammock, worrying, Paul came up with a plan. He quickly gathered the required items and checked them over. Everything appeared to be in working order.

It was still dark, just before dawn, when the quiet jungle erupted in shouting. Paul slipped out of his hammock to see what was happening. About forty men came running out of the jungle into the courtyard. Roughly thirty men from the village poured into the grassy courtyard to defend the settlement. The two tribes began to battle. Men were shooting arrows and darts, and, in some cases, swinging clubs at one another. The dogs of the *shabono* ran toward the attackers barking and adding to the chaos. A few of the combatants fell to the ground. Paul looked out from his hut and could not tell at a distance which tribe was which. In some cases, he recognized his fellow tribesmen, but not in every case. He decided he must act quickly.

Out of nowhere, a bright red light filled the sky above. The fighting stopped and there was silence as the natives on both sides stood gawking at the floating flair drifting down from the dark skies above. The frightened invaders retreated to the edge of the forest, and Paul's tribesmen hosts gathered close to the flickering bonfire in the center of the courtyard silently staring. Paul had retrieved his flare gun from his leather jacket and fired it straight up. No one seemed to notice him standing in the opening. And, apparently, no one had seen him fire the flare gun. Now all attention was on the bright object floating down above them.

As the flare continued its glide to the ground, it dimmed and then faded to nothing. At that moment, one of the attackers, armed with a club held over his head, let out a loud yell, "E-e-e-y-y-y!" and bounded quickly across the lawn toward the log barrier protecting the women and children. He was hoping the lull in the fighting would result in a slow response. He was intent on getting to the women and children. They were unarmed and easy targets.

The marauder quickly ran past several surprised men in the yard. Paul moved on instinct. He ran toward the attacker. He was less than graceful and looked as if he could fall over at any moment. It was the first time he had attempted any movement faster than a walk with his broken leg. Despite the pain, Paul strained to get to the assailant. Luckily, he had a short distance to travel. As their paths were about five feet from intersecting, Paul raised the revolver from his side and fired, hitting the man in the chest. The native went down, hitting the ground with a thud, bouncing once and then tumbling over twice—and then he was motionless.

The boom of the pistol brought everyone to attention. Both sides watched as the attacker went down in a heap. After a second, the attackers all ran to the edge of the forest and disappeared. They wanted nothing to do with Paul and his lethal weapon. The villagers ran to Paul shouting encouraging messages. They jumped and shouted as they congratulated him as a *unokais,* a man fierce enough to have killed an enemy. Paul found himself surrounded by about fifty happy men.

A few men followed the marauders into the forest but reported back that they were in full retreat and no longer in the area. Yanokirtana started a chant that was joined by most of the tribe. The chant praised the spirits for the victory. Everyone pushing toward Paul held out his hand to touch him on the shoulder, back, or head.

Paul was conflicted. He had never been involved in aggressive bloodshed in his life. Piarucu explained that the Waika were angry with everybody. Most nearby tribes lived peacefully with the Yanomami. There was active trading and an occasional cross marriage. But the Waika were perpetually at war. None of the nearby tribes had contact with the Waika, other than to defend against occasional attacks.

Now, on the spur of the moment, Paul had killed another human. But no sooner had the weight of his actions occurred to him, than the whole tribe gathered around him and began singing and dancing. Piarucu explained that the man Paul had killed was the leader of the Waika tribe. That meant any counterattack would be delayed until a new leader was chosen, probably in several months. Paul was a hero. His last thought on the matter was that his violence had been necessary to save the lives of defenseless women and children. Then a second thought: he may have saved his own life as well. If the Waika had overtaken the village, everyone would have been killed.

After the battle, there were a dozen of the natives lying dead on the lawn. Some were enemies and some were from the home tribe. Their dead colleagues were brought to the main campfire for cremation. They gathered up the enemy bodies and took them several hundred feet into the jungle so they could be retrieved by the Waika. Piarucu told Paul that it was a show of respect to take the bodies of the fallen enemy to a place where they could be recovered. He said, "The Waika do not show the same respect."

The tribe prepared a huge meal that morning. It was a victory celebration. Afterward, the group continued chanting and dancing around a huge bonfire for about four hours. When they were done, after a chant by Yanokiritana, they lit the fires around the dead bodies of the colleagues who had been killed the day before. As was their custom, no one mentioned the name of the deceased tribesmen once they were cremated.

Paul's leg was throbbing. It had been years since he had sprinted on his broken leg. He was not in shape to be running and now he felt it. Despite the pain, he was satisfied that he had done a good deed for his new family of friends.

Starting that day, the men and women of the colony greeted him with smiles and laughter every day. They doted on him, bringing him extra helpings of food and water. This gesture made life more pleasant. Paul realized the tribe now held him in high esteem. He had gone from being a curious stranger to a commanding and extraordinary friend of the settlement. His quick action to prevent the slaughter of the women and children had been observed by all. Now he was admired for his bravery.

In mid-afternoon, Paul gathered the children together. He was in a good mood after the Waika encounter. He thought it was a good time for some lighthearted fun. After leading the singing of *Ain't She Sweet* a few times, Paul unveiled a new song he had been working on with the group: *Frere Jacques*. Paul's voice boomed out loudly, although the children were still confused by the words until they reached the last words, *"Ding Ding Dong, Ding Ding Dong,"* which they shouted out with joy. The mothers in the village liked this song and smiled and laughed with the little choir as they sang. The fathers remained stoic, but secretly smiled.

That evening, Circles approached Paul. She smiled and reached out and touched his shoulder. Paul thought she was attempting to prompt some intimacy. He pretended not to observe the sign and pulled away. He was determined to remain true to Gertrude.

Paul noticed that Circles stared at him whenever they were in the vicinity of one another. "Why are you looking at me?" he asked. Circles said, "It is your eyes. They are so different." Paul's eye color was quite a bit lighter than any other she had seen before and that fascinated her.

That was the first conversation of a personal nature that had taken place between the two of them. Paul realized that while he was fascinated by the customs and appearance of tribal members, the same must be true of the tribe. They in turn found his appearance and actions to be curious.

The natives continued to consider Paul's activities to be the work of the spirits who had sent him from the heavens as a protector. He was considered a proxy for the good spirits. Paul realized the natives were sure he was a force for good and would not want him to leave. But neither would they harm him.

A victory celebration continued with chanting and dancing. Yanokiritana led the chanting in his high-pitched voice, with the tribe answering in a sing song manner.

Some of the men walked to the center of the courtyard near the campfire and ceremoniously took out some coca leaves and limes from a pouch. They stuffed the leaves into their mouths and then squeezed the limes so that juice dripped over the leaves. Then they began to dance to the beat of drums.

The cadence was slow at the beginning, but picked up as the evening progressed. The men whirled in circles and jumped off the ground. Over the course of the next few hours, the drumbeat increased, and the dancing became more frantic. The men moved in faster circles and leaped higher and higher. They took longer steps. Their knees acted like powerful springs. They began to leapfrog over one another. All their body motions were fast. None of them stopped to rest, and this continued for the four hours the drums kept beating. Paul thought the dancing men must be related to the whirling dervishes from Turkey he had seen in the newsreels.

Paul was surprised that once the drums subsided the men did not fall to the ground with exhaustion.

Instead, they stood in the courtyard and engaged in normal conversations.

Paul asked Piarucu about it and was told the coca leaves provided energy and endurance. In addition, the coca erased any feelings of hunger. Men going into battle used coca for added strength.

Later near the end of the celebration, the men sat down and complained of their leg muscles cramping.

In the succeeding months, Paul assessed his ability to leave the jungle and head for home. He was unsure of the difficulty he might encounter. Under normal circumstances his leg did not hurt. Although he was now firmly thought of as a friend, he was also an asset to the tribe's ability to survive, and the natives might not want to give up that benefit easily. At the time of these thoughts, he had no ability to leave even if he desired. The limp that had started to fade in recent days returned, along with an aching and stiffness when he awoke each morning. It would be a while before he could once again begin a long trek back to home.

During the next few days, Paul worked on learning more words so he could communicate better with the openly friendly tribesmen. He paid attention to the words being used by his rescuers and attempted to ascribe a meaning to as many as possible. He added words to his note pad, each one spelled phonetically.

Within a short period, he had learned several new words. Once learned, Paul would use the words in conversations. The dugout boats were called "kanawa." The peach palm was named "rasha." Paul said to the next ten people he happened upon, "I will take a *kanawa* and find some *rasha*." He listened carefully to the reply, hoping to hear something that confirmed the message had gotten through. He dutifully wrote down each new word on his note pad.

The process of learning new words fed on itself. The more he learned, the more he sought to learn new words.

It was about this time that Paul recognized something about the culture of the natives. Paul was writing down the words phonetically as he heard them. He realized the natives had no paper, pencils, or even pictures. He laughed as he thought about the several years that had passed, and he was only now comprehending this fact. The natives had no written language.

Within a day or two Paul discovered another deficiency in communication with the natives. He asked a man how many mangoes he had in his basket and the man answered in his language, "more than two." Paul asked, "How many?" And the man replied, "many."

For the next few days Paul asked several people questions designed to uncover their word for a number. He asked questions such as, "how many children do you have? How many days in a year? He never got a specific answer. He soon realized there were no words for numbers other than one and two.

Paul thought these shortcomings in the education of the tribe as odd, but he did not derogate their intellect. He looked past the deficiencies and concentrated on their achievements. He had seen the bridges that they had built that were strong enough to stand up to the yearly floods in the rainy season. He was impressed by their love of their children. He marveled at their hunting, fishing, and agriculture techniques. Paul wondered what the case would be if during his childhood he had never been exposed to paper and pencil.

The fact that they had no written language did not mean the tribe had no history. As a proxy for written materials, they had oral stories that were passed down over generations. At regular intervals, Shapora or Yanokiritana would repeat allegorical tales that told the history of the tribe. The stories were repeated often. Shapora especially loved to tell them.

Paul noticed that the natives always cooked their meal "well done" and never rare. He asked Piarucu about it and Piarucu told him the story of why food is always cooked thoroughly.

It was the story of the history of fire. Piarucu said, the original owner of fire was Iwa. Iwa thought only of himself and controlled the tribe's use of fire. To retain his power, Iwa kept all fire secreted in his throat. Therefore, while Iwa and his family always thoroughly cooked their meat before eating it, the rest of the tribe without fire was forced to eat it raw. When the tribe attempted to get Iwa to share, he guarded the fire and kept it concealed in his throat. The families without fire suffered greatly because they had to beg Iwa to build both cooking and heating fires, which he refused to do.

In addition, many families had no fire to protect against wild animals. This situation existed for a many seasons.

The tribe's storyteller thought about fire and Iwa's miserly attitude. He vowed to take fire away from Iwa. One day, during the recitation of one of his anecdotes, the storyteller told a funny joke. Iwa could not help himself and laughed. The fire tumbled out of Iwa's mouth and scattered across the ground. The storyteller was prepared. Before Iwa could retrieve the fire, the storyteller gathered up all the embers. As Iwa watched, the storyteller distributed the fire to all the male members of the tribe.

From that day forward, to celebrate having fire, the natives always cooked their meals thoroughly. Some would say extra thoroughly. Since then, by tradition, the *shaman* of the tribe always started any new fires using a flint stick.

Iwa no longer had any fire. Since that time, he had had to eat raw meat. As a result, Iwa became exceedingly angry and changed himself into an alligator, while the storyteller turned into a red-beaked songbird.

Paul thought about the story. It had several lessons: The ability to make fire is an important skill; it is better to share fire than to hoard; and those who share are happy, while hoarders are reviled. Paul surmised that the tribe, through that simple story, had summarized some important moral principles. His admiration for the natives was boosted once again.

19

The Tall One (1933)

Paul decided he needed to learn additional skills to survive in the jungle living on his own. He would be alone in the jungle once he escaped. He would have to learn to hunt and feed himself, spend his nights in the wild, and hike during the day.

Every week, he followed along whenever a hunting party left camp. He was interested in both the techniques for hunting as well as learning the trails around the camp. He watched as the men built a fire, so he could do so on his own. He was surprised that after about five repetitions, he successfully started a fire using a stick and a board. He held one stick between his two hands and twirled it back and forth on the small board until a spark was generated. Once he had a spark, he fed it with dry moss, blowing on it until he had a flame. Over the following weeks, Paul built fires every day. He wanted to be prepared when it was time to head for home.

Using his notepad, Paul engaged in conversations with the natives. He would start in English and sprinkle the conversation with a native word or two from his notepad. Sometimes he would get a reply and sometimes not. But as time went by, the natives' responses were better understood by Paul. He was slowly learning their language.

Paul found that Piarucu especially was willing to converse in broken English. He and Paul had spent time together every day and it was slowly rubbing off. Paul, in turn, attempted to use the native words he had learned whenever possible.

While flying, Paul always navigated using dead reckoning. He would follow the roads, rivers, or railroad tracks along his route. He never bothered to navigate using a sextant and he was not adept at finding key constellations used by sailors to navigate by the stars. His flights at night over unfamiliar territory were few and far between. When he did venture into the darkness, there were always well-known landmarks within range.

He found himself wondering how to find directions in the southern hemisphere. He had a rudimentary knowledge of the stars, especially Polaris, but that star was not visible in South America.

In any event, Paul had only limited views of the sun and stars due to the thick vegetation everywhere. He had studied maps of his route to Rio over the course of several weeks of preparation, so he reasoned that he needed to go North and East to the coast to find civilization. He was not aware of towns to the South other than Rio de Janeiro. Rio, according to his calculations, was still almost one thousand miles away. He would like to get his hands on his charts to verify his conclusions, but finding his plane in the trees on his own was impossible. He would have to find someone to take him back to the tree that held his plane.

Paul was sorry he had left the detailed maps of the area between the coast and Rio at home. He had been confident he would make it to Rio, and therefore, in his mind, the area between Brunswick and Rio was unimportant. It would be helpful to know where the trails and rivers were and, more importantly, in which direction they ran. If he were sure, he could follow a river with confidence as to where it would lead. Without the maps he could not be confident where the rivers led. Paul concluded it had been a costly mistake to leave the maps on the desk at home. It wasn't the first time since his crash landing that he had questioned the wisdom of his long flight.

He thought of Gertrude, his father and mother, and his many friends back in the States. He was relatively comfortable in the primitive settlement, but he missed his life back home. Paul made a list in his head of the equipment he would need to get home. He needed his chart, his weapons, the beads and trinkets for trading, and one of his compasses.

Paul approached Piarucu, asking, "Can you tell me where white men live?"

Piarucu said, "If you keep the sun on your back and walk far enough you will find white men. We are taught, be aware of the jungle opposite the sun. The white men who came to our *shabono* all came toward the sun."

"You mean in the North?"

"I do not understand North."

Paul thought he understood Piarucu's explanation, but was not sure. He did understand keeping the sun on his back as he searched for civilization.

Since Paul had some extra fuel, he had another idea. He asked Piarucu to place fifteen logs of various sizes in the courtyard as if he were going to start a fire. Paul poured some petrol on the pile and then called out to the natives mingling in the yard to come watch. Once the natives gathered around, Paul threw a stick that he had pulled out of another fire into the pile of logs. Immediately, in a whoosh, flames erupted. The flames shot up about ten feet and then settled down to about three feet. The crowd gasped in amazement. Most of the children and some of the adults ran away. The sudden explosion of fire was a mystical sight. Paul's reputation as a messenger of the spirits was confirmed once again. He enjoyed putting on the show. He laughed as the tribe stood transfixed by the flames. Yanokiritana who, as *shaman*, oversaw starting fires for the tribe, was intrigued by the explosion of flames.

The following morning, he asked Paul to show him how to use the petrol to create a fire explosion. Paul was happy to oblige and, from then on, Yanokiritana used the petrol whenever he started a new fire. The huge, abrupt flames resulting from the petrol were spectacular to the tribe. Paul noticed that Yanokiritana's standing increased with his ability to control the petrol-fueled flames.

The men in the settlement were interested in Redfern's rifle, so he demonstrated and taught several of them how to shoot. It crossed his mind that the weapon could be turned against him if he gave it to them. However, Paul felt that if he left Piarucu with the weapon for hunting, he would be less inclined to chase him when he made his getaway. Piarucu would understand that Paul was not leaving to invite other white men to the *shabono*. He was leaving to go live with his white wife who lived a great distance away.

Paul explained to the natives about the ammunition. "The rifle only works with bullets. No bullets, no shoot. Bullets should be used sparingly."

Paul brought three boxes of shells, each containing one hundred shells. There was enough ammunition to teach, so long as everyone was frugal with their shooting. However, the next time they went hunting everyone took a turn shooting at tree branches. At the rate they shot, the bullets would not last long. Paul took the rifle back and decided to concentrate on teaching Piarucu to shoot, in order to save ammunition. He taught Piarucu how to clean the rifle after every shooting session, cleaning the barrel with a stick and a wad of leaves.

Paul told Piarucu, "A clean barrel is necessary to maintain an accurate aim."

Over the next few days, Paul spent time teaching Piarucu how to shoot. He placed an old clay pot at the base of a hill and had Piarucu aim at it. The first shot was wild, and the rifle nearly jumped out of his hands. Paul laughed and helped Piarucu with his technique.

"Hold the weapon firmly, line the target up with both the sight and rear v-shaped sight, and slowly pull the trigger." After the third day, Piarucu could not miss, and several clay pots met their end. He was a natural with the rifle. Paul thought again about whether he could turn the rifle on him should he leave for home.

Other hunters were given some instruction, but Paul spent the most time with Piarucu. Once a few men had been taught, they took turns hunting game. Some were better shots than others. After about three months, there was no more instruction and Piarucu was named the designated marksman, the one to carry the rifle on a hunt. No doubt his personalized instruction was the reason.

When Paul re-read Professor Breckenridge's letter, he noticed a passage that gave him hope. The letter said, "In South America, ninety per cent of the population lives within ten miles of the coast. Almost all of the white people populating the continent can be found within that ten mile strip." So, he needed to get to within ten miles of the ocean if he was going to find any white folks. Thinking back on his crash landing, Paul remembered it had not been very long between the time he crossed the beach at Capuano and when he ended up in a tree. Getting back to the coastline would be his goal.

He decided to ask others in his village about the trip. So, he began to question tribal members as he encountered them. It was still difficult to communicate, but it was easier than it had been. He first spoke to Piarucu, since conversations with him were common. Haltingly, Paul pointed to the trailhead and asked where the path went. Piarucu responded that it led to hunting areas. Paul then said that he was interested in where the trail led *after* the hunting grounds. Either Piarucu did not know, or he was not going to tell what he did know. He said, "Bad spirits live on the other side of the hunting grounds."

Piarucu was adamant that to follow the trail would lead to doom because of the bad spirits in the area. Paul was not entirely convinced about the existence of spirits. On the one hand he tended to believe the tribe when they said something. They did not normally attempt to obfuscate. But, on the other, they sometimes exaggerated their beliefs, especially when it came to spirits. In the end, to Paul, the belief in spirits was childish and his need to get home far outweighed any fear of evil spirits.

Next, he asked Shapora, the Headman, and got a similar answer. Shapora said that the trail was not passable because of the presence of the Waika that had attacked the hunting party. When Paul asked for more details, Shapora said that the Waika lived near the footpath, and they were very war-like. He said any person who entered their territory would face a certain attack by the tribe and that the spirits in that area were in league with the hostile tribe. It would be exceedingly difficult to avoid them, even if one wanted to find a way around.

Asked if there were any trails that completely missed the area occupied by the Waika, Paul was told that yes, there was one. Anyone wanting to avoid the Waika would have to take a trail that went off to the right before reaching the war-like natives' territory.

So, now Paul knew approximately where to look for the side trail; it was off to the right. However, he had never seen this trail, and finding it could be problematic. It sounded as if missing the trail would be an easy proposition. There were no signs or blazes.

Paul asked several other men about the trails and his plan to avoid contact with the hostile tribe. None of them offered an opinion as to his chances. He concluded that no one wanted to help him to escape.

Finally, desperate, he asked "Circles." She was more talkative than most of the women, which meant she was exceedingly so. She had always been friendly and had cooked him food on a regular basis. He had named her "Circles" based on the way her mother had decorated her body with circles of ink in different sizes. Paul had been circumspect with Circles, but she always acted as a helper, unlike other women who kept their distance.

One day he asked if she had ever seen any cities with white people. She looked back at Paul with a blank expression on her face. Paul took it to mean she had not. *Well that just about does it,* he thought. *I'm stuck here without any way of getting out.*

The following week, Circles brought another woman to see Paul. Circles told him that she did not know anything about the location of white people, but that the woman with her might know something. Paul had seen the woman before, but had never spoken with her. He noticed immediately that she was taller than anyone else in camp of either sex. In every way, her appearance was the same as the other women of the tribe other than her height. Paul decided her name would be "Tall One."

Paul began a conversation by asking about her background. In the ensuing conversation, he learned through a combination of pointing and a few words that she had been captured by natives when she was a small child. She held her hand just above her knee to demonstrate her height at the time of her capture. She had been playing near her hut in the vicinity of a village called Tucupita, when a tribe from the forest had scooped her up and taken her back to their encampment quite a distance away. There, she was treated as a slave. She had no friends and, unlike other young children, was forced to work.

When she reached puberty, she escaped that tribe, and began to search for her mother. She wandered in the jungle for several weeks and almost died of hunger. A group of Yanomami hunters found her and brought her to their village. Since then, she has been treated as a member of the tribe. She was raised by several women and not treated as a slave. By the time she reached adulthood, she was the tallest person living with the Yanomami, but it made no difference. She was about the same height as Paul.

Paul asked, "When you lived near Tucupita were there any whites living there?

The Tall One replied," "Yes, I remember seeing whites at the trading post."

"Do you think you could find Tucupita?"

"I think so. It is several days from here, but when I get close, I think I can find it."

Finally, Paul asked if she had a husband. The Tall One looked suspiciously at Paul and did not answer immediately. She thought Paul was asking her to be his wife. She was married to an older man, who took her as his younger third bride. The reason for the question was to ascertain how much trouble it would cause for her to leave. Based on her husband's age and the fact he had two other wives, Paul thought it would not be a serious issue. He guessed she was close to twenty years old. He posed a final question, "Would you like to go home?" She responded immediately, "Yes."

Paul allowed himself to think again of Gertrude as well as his parents. He was more resolute than ever in his decision to get back to them. Having the Tall One to help guide him was a bonus. She once lived in the vicinity of a town with white people. Even though she had been young when she was captured and taken, it was a possibility that she could find Tucupita and the white people living there.

Some in the village noticed Paul spending time with the Tall One over the next few weeks, but did not become suspicious. It was a male-female relationship, and that could mean only one thing in the eyes of the villagers. They assumed it was a sexual encounter, although there actually was none of that. Paul was making plans to leave the village and not return. That took a lot of talking and planning.

Paul was anxious to leave, and asked the Tall One several questions, among them: How many days to her mother's house? When would be a good time to go? The Tall One had an answer for each questions: "It's at least three days to my mother's" and "The next full moon would be a good time to go." She explained that it had been a long time since she was kidnapped and so she was not entirely positive of the way. But, she said, "I can find my mother. I remember the hut we lived in."

A few days later, there was alarming news. A young man was reported missing. All the members of the group were alarmed. The boy, about sixteen, had gone out by himself to gather vegetables. This meant he would not be far away from the center of the camp. But, by nightfall, he had not returned, and it was too dark in the jungle for them to search for him. So, the following morning, a group of the men went out looking for him.

Since Paul was planning his escape, he joined the search party. He was anxious to learn about the surrounding jungle and, by tagging along, he got an opportunity to do just that. The posse soon found the boy's tracks and began following the signs. Eventually, they found his body hidden under some low hanging branches. There were pink blots on his back that were clear evidence he had been poisoned with several darts from blow guns.

For the next two days, the tribe mourned the loss of the young man, before they cremated him in a tree just outside the camp. There was singing, dancing, and crying, and his family, especially, was visibly upset by the loss. It was unclear whether he was killed by someone within the tribe or by a native from another tribe. However, once he had been cremated, no one in the village would ever mention the boy's name again.

Paul and the Tall One continued to make their plans. Paul had her make a basket with a large strap so he could carry the stuff he would need on the journey. In it he placed a pistol, ammunition, a knife, his jacket, and some of the glass trinkets for trading. He also added some dried meat and plantains, as well as *cassava* bread. Although Paul thought that the Tall One was willing to go, he did not know for sure. When he told the her they would leave an hour before sunup the next morning, she just stared at Paul without any expression on her face. Paul repeated, "One hour before sunup." He hoped her prior commitment would hold up. He needed someone who had been in the area before. But now he was not sure whether she would follow through. He decided that even if she did not show up, he was ready to go alone regardless.

That evening Paul had dinner with Piarucu. Paul sat on a log by a fire, while Piarucu squatted beside him. They talked about their experiences together. Paul recounted his first day when he landed in the tree. He mentioned how Piarucu had jumped up to his plane with his blow gun. He did not mention it was his last night in the *shabono*, but he was thinking about it to himself. They chatted well into the evening and finally each retired to his respective hammock. Paul thought the person he would miss the most when he was gone was Piarucu.

Paul was still experiencing some pain in his broken leg. The discomfort would be slight in the morning, however, by bedtime, there would be quite a bit of pain. He worried about how the leg would hold up on a long, multi-day hike to civilization. He worried, too, that he could end up miles from his settlement but still miles from civilization and not able to go any further. But he always concluded that it was worth the risk to get home to Gertrude. *No one is coming to rescue me*, he thought, and attempting to escape was the only way he would ever get home.

Paul awoke the following day when it was still dark, except for the light provided by a full moon. He went to find the Tall One, but could not find her. Since she was nowhere to be found, Paul decided she was not coming. Everyone in the village was still asleep.

Paul ducked into the forest and circled around the outside of the courtyard behind the thick underbrush of the jungle. He made it to the trail on the other side of the opening and looked back one last time at the hut. It was still dark, and no one was stirring. As he turned to start down the path, he jumped at the sight of another person in the shadows. It was the Tall One. She had beaten him to the start of their escape. Paul's attitude brightened. He had decided she was not coming, but now he had a companion. They exchanged *me a re's* and were off.

For almost two days, Paul and Tall One talked constantly on the trail; it was easy to follow and the two of them could walk side by side most of the time. Paul still did not know the language. He made comments from time to time about where they were going, but he had no idea if the Tall One understood. Any comments from the Tall One were likewise only partially understood by Paul. When they approached intersections, usually the Tall One pointed and they followed the trail they were on disregarding any cross trails. It had rained the first day, but they made good time. The second day was sunny. Paul judged they had gone about twenty miles when they stopped for a brief time to eat. His leg was throbbing, but there was no thought of returning to the settlement. He was about to escape the jungle for home, and he was determined to not turn back.

The trail was vaguely familiar. In fact, it was on this trail where Paul and the other hunters had been attacked and followed back to the village by a rival tribe. It made Paul wary of being discovered by any members of that tribe. He kept his attention focused in front of him in order to spot any members of that tribe before they could see him. He had not noticed a trail to the right as he expected.

As they got up from lunch on the third day to continue the journey, Paul heard rustling from the brush off to his left. He stopped and motioned The Tall One, who was about fifty yards behind him, to stop. Then the noise stopped. Paul stood motionless for a moment longer, but then, thinking the noise was made by an animal, he resumed the hike. He was not finished with his first step when nine men, all with bows and arrows, silently stepped out of the forest from all directions and surrounded them. Paul knew instantly they were not from his village. He thought they were probably from the Waika tribe that had attacked him and the others a few weeks ago—and, he guessed, probably friends of the Headman who Paul had killed in front of everyone.

Paul froze in his footsteps, his eyes wide. His pulse was racing. All the natives were pointing their weapons at him. He calculated that even if he reached down and pulled the revolver out of the basket, he could only kill one or two before he would be struck by a poison arrow. Escape was out of the question. Instead of taking out his gun, he pulled out the box of trinkets and threw it on the ground at his feet. Beads and trinkets scattered across the ground. The men quickly ran forward and picked up the stuff. As they did, the Tall One, who had stepped behind a bush, broke free and ran into the woods behind her. One man took a step to follow her, but then, thinking better of a pursuit, stopped, and continued picking up the trinkets. Paul assumed the Tall One would continue the journey to her mother's home without him. He was frozen with dread and unable to move.

Once the natives were through gathering the bounty, they motioned for him to walk forward. Paul decided his best chance was to cooperate. Stirring up trouble would bring certain disaster. He walked down the path, followed by the men, and, after walking for an hour, they arrived at an opening in the jungle.

It was roughly equivalent in size to the village he had left three days prior. There was a hut in the form of a semi-circle, facing a courtyard of more than an acre of grass. It was noticeably larger than the one at Paul's *shabono*. He was walked to the center fire by several men, who motioned for him to sit on the grass. He obeyed. One of the men took a homemade rope, tied it to Paul's ankle and then to a nearby log. Paul took note that he could untie the rope whenever he desired, but also knew he would not last long before he was hit with a poison arrow shot by one of the men standing nearby. Paul sat down and decided to wait to see what would happen next. He noticed the bag with his weapon was on the ground about twenty feet away. Since he had killed this tribe's chief during the attack a month ago, he figured he was about to meet a similar fate. He would die soon. The only way to save himself was with that revolver.

As he sat, Paul thought about Gertrude and how she must be longing for him to return. His attempt to join her had been a failure. He had barely hiked three days before he was caught. Now it appeared he would be killed.

Just then, a group of men appeared. Each carried a weapon, and they did not look happy. Paul thought, *This is the end. I'm a dead pigeon.* One of the men reached down and untied the rope from around the log and tugged on the rope indicating Paul should follow. Paul got up and followed the man to another fire. As he walked by, he looked down at his basket. Only his leather jacket was in sight. The pistol and flare gun were tucked underneath it. He still was in no position to make a move for the gun, being surrounded as he was by a group of about six men.

They walked to the edge of the wilderness where he was urged to sit on the ground. He sat and watched as one of the men started a small fire. Then, the other men left and returned with more wood for the fire, which was soon burning brightly. It grew larger than any fire he had seen at his own village. As the flames blossomed, all the village came out to the fire and began chanting and dancing. Paul realized he was witnessing some sort of ceremony. *It's probably a run-up to my death*, he imagined, *but if I can reach the pistol, I'll have a chance to survive.* He glanced back to where he had been sitting on the log and noticed his basket was still lying on the ground in the middle of the opening.

After about an hour, the villagers started retiring to their quarters for the night. Paul was left with two men, who were squatting about twenty feet away, talking to one another. He concluded that the ceremony was over, and inferred they were going to take care of him the following day. The fire was beginning to fade, and Paul's mind was racing. He knew he had to take a chance, but first he had to act passive and bide his time. He pretended to be sleeping.

After about an hour, Paul sneaked a look at the two men, one of whom looked asleep. The other was leaving in the search for more firewood. They had not retied the rope; it was loose. Paul decided it was time to act. He stood and scrambled toward the basket, which was about thirty yards away. He would have to hurry. As soon as he began running, he heard a commotion behind him, as one of the men shouted out. Paul got about halfway to the basket, when he felt the prick of a dart on his back. He was surprised to hear more men than the two that were chasing him.

At first, as he ran, Paul did not feel the effects of the poison. He dove for the basket and reached for the revolver. Sprawled out on the ground, he felt inside the basket, but then things started to get blurry. He looked up toward the men who were running after him and realized he could not see them very well. He was getting dizzy. He felt himself losing consciousness and, within seconds, he had blacked out. Just before passing out, he tucked the pistol back inside the basket and under his jacket.

20

The Haskins Expedition (1933-1934)

The search party sponsored by the Brunswick Trade Association and the National Geographic Society was taking shape. Sufficient money had been raised by the Society and the Board of Trade. In addition, readers of the Society's magazine had responded to a solicitation in that publication. School children had contributed with pennies, adults with dollars. And Paul's father, had sent in a sizeable four-figure check.

Dr. Geoffrey Haskins, of Oxford University, was chosen as the leader of the expedition. He arrived in Caracas on August 18, 1933. He recruited three white men who were familiar with the jungle. One member was Jose Mendoza, a reporter from the *Caracas Dario*, and he, as a local, was chosen to shop for supplies. Only one of the unpaid volunteers was from the States. Six Indian guides were recruited by Haskins to carry supplies and operate the three river boats waiting in Tucupita.

Mendoza took daily notes and outlined an article to be submitted to his editor upon completion of the expedition. He would soon be famous, regardless of whether they rescued Redfern or not. His story of the search for Paul Redfern would spark great attention. Everyone throughout the world, it seemed, was interested in Redfern's fate.

Each of the matching three boats was twenty-two feet long and powered by an Evinrude outboard motor. The two natives manning each vessel would stay in the rear. Gear was to be secured at the bow covered by a waterproof canvas. A cotton rain shell fit over the middle section. Haskins and the other white searchers stayed under the tarp.

On July 28th the U.S. volunteer boarded a ship leaving from St. Augustine, Florida. After five days, he disembarked at Caracas. He and the men from Europe checked into the Santa Maria Hotel and, together with Haskins, took a week to plan their next steps. They spent time studying the maps of the rivers that they would take. In consultation with their native escorts, they learned as much as possible about the native tribes in the area. They also looked over the letter from Jimmy Angel describing the area in which he had seen the airplane, *Port of Brunswick*, sitting on top of the trees. In addition, they spent a fair amount of time eating and playing poker.

Tucupita is a village on the Cano Manamo River, a tributary of the larger Orinoco River. It was inhabited by natives who decided to give up their tribal life. Most of them worked for the whites in town, in stores and trading posts. Surrounding the town on three sides was a swamp dotted with hundreds of Mangrove trees. The Santa Maria Hotel was almost full due to an oil exploration company that had come to town a few months earlier from England. At the spot where the Cano Manamo meets the Orinoco, the water goes from fresh to brine, as the Orinoco dumps into the Atlantic Ocean only a few miles downstream, forming a huge delta.

Geoffrey was a natural leader. He had taught anthropology at Oxford for more than twenty years and acquired an authoritative manner. Haskins had led several of the Society sponsored trips to Africa, although none were for the purpose of locating lost explorers. His experience in Africa gave him experience living in the wild and dealing with a crew made up of natives.

After five days of getting acquainted and studying maps, the men loaded up their trucks and started down a dirt road to the South. The road was passable, but rain had made some of the way muddy and slippery. On three occasions they had to push the trucks out of bogs that had formed in the road. After a two-day journey, they came to the Cano Manamo River and followed it for another twenty miles to Tucupita.

Tucupita was a primitive town, and it was obvious that zoning had not yet been introduced. The buildings were a hodge-podge of styles and colors. At the center of town was a combination trading post and general store owned by Andy Patel, originally from India. There were members of about five Indian families who worked in the store. The structure itself was made up of several distinctive additions, each with its own style. The newest addition was a large building, filled with wooden shipping boxes, with a tarp for a roof .

Across the street were a hotel and a tavern/restaurant with a German owner by the name of

Detlef Lind. There was a combination hardware/barber shop next to the hotel, also managed by Lind. One of the hardware store clerks was also the part-time hair cutter. The tavern was always busy after 5:00 p.m., when the oil workers got off work. The hotel rooms were perpetually murky and damp. As a result, the men were anxious to spend time in the tavern.

Finally, there was a large storage warehouse, filled with oil exploration gear owned by Standard Oil, located at the river's edge. Periodically, goods were shuffled in or out of the cavernous stockroom in boats manned by local Standard Oil employees.

The other buildings in town were mostly a variety of shacks, constructed with paper, wood scraps, and thatched branches, used as housing by the local natives. Each ramshackle hovel looked like it would collapse if rain hit it.

While in the trading post, Haskins spoke to Patel and asked him if he had any idea where Paul Redfern was.

"I have heard rumors of a crippled white man living with the natives," replied Patel. Haskins was intrigued by this and asked where that might be.

"Supposedly, he flew into the jungle and never came out," said Patel. "I would guess it was to the east of here, but I can't tell you much more."

Haskins pulled out his map and pointed to the area where Jimmy Angel had indicated the plane might be found. "Do you think this would be a good area to search?"

Patel responded, "Yes, but that area is impassable, and the natives are not the least bit friendly. If you go there, be careful."

Lind was even more emphatic. In a heavy German accent he said, "The natives will have nothing to do with you. White men are *feinds* . . . er . . . I mean enemies. Whites are unwanted. The natives may make *krieg* . . . er . . . war." Haskins listened and took note. But the expedition was already equipped and ready, and he was going to forge ahead.

The group settled in at the hotel and began to map out their plans. They would launch their boats in the river and head upstream to the South. According to Jimmy Angel, the airplane was about three miles east of the Capo Manamo River about eighty to a hundred miles away. They would float the river until they got close and then take one of the many tributaries to the East. After that, plans were uncertain. Luckily, it was past the rainy season and the river was unhurried. They would look for the plane and hopefully run into some natives who could guide them. Depending on the conditions, they would leave their boats to conduct the search. But, based on the reports by Patel and Lind, they would remain cautious.

Haskins spoke to his native helpers, and soon learned that they had been city dwellers in Caracas too long to be of much help. None of them had ever been in this locale before. As it turned out, none of the hires had knowledge of native dialects in the area. Each could speak some English and Dutch, but it was unclear how they would interpret the native tongues found in this area.   Haskins realized he had made a mistake by recruiting in Caracas, but decided not to admit his error to the others. The workers, even if not good interpreters, would be useful doing the heavy work on the trip.

Finally on their way, the group settled into a routine. Up at dawn, breakfast of coffee and toast, and off they went. They would have lunch on the go, and dinner in camp an hour before sundown. The river was smooth with no rapids to navigate. Occasionally, they noticed an alligator or snake swimming in the river, but no wildlife on shore. The jungle was thick with brush and had a foreboding appearance.

Once they beached the boats for the night, the natives pitched the tents and cooked dinner over campfires.

After a day and a half, they left the Capo Manamo River and headed East on a stream that looked promising. It was larger than most of the other streams they saw and as far as they could tell it headed in the right direction. There was no sign of civilization. There were no huts or roads.   Haskins was impressed by the denseness of the jungle. For mile after mile there was nothing but a green curtain at the river's edge.

On the fourth day, they spotted several natives in an opening in the jungle barely visible through the thick underbrush. They pulled to shore and waited. Within a few minutes a group of men came to them. They were all naked and each one sported a bowl-cut hair style.

Haskins had been advised to expect the natives to be without clothes.

Haskins spotted a man in the group with feathers adorning his head, arms, and ankles, unlike the others who had far fewer adornments. He shouted to him, "Hello" and then, "Greetings." To Haskins' surprise the man answered, "*Hola.*" They quickly learned that the man was the chief and he spoke a little Spanish. Haskins offered the man some colorful trinkets as a token of friendship. The man searched his bag made from the skin of an ocelot and handed Haskins a dozen plantains. He was willing to trade, but would not take a gift. In the ensuing conversation, they learned that the tribe Haskins had stumbled onto was aware of a white man living with another tribe.

The chief explained that his tribe, the Guarocoaueteri (pronounced Garo koe tarry) and the Yanomami tribe that lived about a day's travel upstream periodically traded tools and weapons in the jungle halfway between their two camps. The Yanomami bragged about holding a white man who fell from the sky. He was a prized possession and supposedly communicated with the spirits. The white man was considered an oracle who had saved them from attack by the Waika using magic. In addition, he was an advisor to their *shaman*. He was described as a happy wise man.

The chief admitted he had not been to the Yanomami's *shabono* and had not laid eyes on the white man. But he said based on the detailed description of his heroic skills by the Yanomami, he did not doubt his existence. Based on all the information about the white man, the chief was sure the Guarocoaueteri man was truthful. He explained that the Yanomami lived about a day's travel upstream and their *shabono* was about a mile from the river.

Haskins broke off his conversation with the chief and ordered his men to launch the boats. They now knew they were on the right track. The paddling that afternoon was a bit more enthusiastic than earlier in the day.

As the sun began to set on the fifth day, they set up camp on a grassy spot along the stream. Based on the chief's directions, they thought they must be close to the Yanomamis' settlement. After unpacking, they started a fire and pitched their tents. As the evening started to cover them in darkness, they put dinner on the fire. It was baked beans and sausage that evening. As the men gathered around the fire, a faint sound was heard coming from the jungle surrounding them. Haskins thought it must be a large animal and ordered his men to be alert.

Then, out of the woods came a dozen or so natives. All were armed and this sent a few of the men into their tents for firearms. The natives, naked except for body paint, stood in a half-circle and stared at the search party. Once his men had armed themselves, Haskins got up and slowly stood to face the natives. He asked the porters to bring the beads secured in a box. He opened the leather case, reached in, and pulled out a handful of colorful beads that he distributed to each of the natives. As had happened with the other tribe, the natives reached into their packs and handed the searchers items found there, such as arrow heads, leather pouches, and feathers. After the exchange, the natives began to talk excitedly to one another. Haskins acted unafraid and asked one of his native porters to translate. In the background, Mendoza filmed the conversation with a small motion picture camera. Of course, no one would see the pictures until they were developed after the expedition. There was no sound recording of the conversation.

Haskins asked the leader if he and his men would join them for dinner. The offer was declined. He then spoke to them all, "Hello. We are here to find a lost comrade. He was in an airplane that fell from the sky. Have you seen him?" As he spoke, Haskins used several different hand gestures. After the translation, which was questionable, one of the natives spoke in his native tongue. The interpreter translated his words as "We know of such a man who fell from the sky."

The interpreter was able to pass on the information that the tribe knew of a man who fell from the sky or that they had heard of such a man. The information was not clear. Haskins asked if the natives could bring the man to the camp. The answer to the question was also vague. Haskins thought the leader agreed. Mendoza agreed. However, the interpreter felt differently. "No," he said. "He did not agree to bring him here."

Communication was difficult because of the language difference. Statements were made on both sides, but no one was clear on what was said. It was all vague. After a long back and forth with no definitive answer about bringing the white man to them, Haskins ended the conversation by saying to the natives, "We will see you in the morning."

It was getting late, and the expedition party retired to their tents for the night. The porters were assigned night watchmen duties, with two at a time on guard. Haskins had noticed the fact that the natives all kept their weapons in hand during the whole encounter. He worried it was a sign of hostility. The natives moved to a spot one hundred yards away and built a fire. Haskins assumed they also were bedding down for the evening. In any event, Haskins had ordered the natives to bring Redfern to the camp, and Haskins was accustomed to having his orders obeyed.

The next day, upon awakening, Haskins was shocked to see that the natives were gone, and their fire had been extinguished. The porters who had stood guard reported that they had heard nothing and were just as surprised as Haskins that the natives had left. Haskins suspected the guards had fallen asleep.

Unfortunately, the natives had disappeared before Haskins could inquire any more about Redfern's whereabouts. However, the encounter with the natives gave the rescue operation fresh hope. The fact that the natives had heard of a white man falling from the sky meant they were in the right area and, if he was alive, Redfern was probably nearby. They waited all day, but heard nothing.

The following morning, they dallied, hoping the natives would either bring Redfern, or return for more beads and more questions. Some men passed time by leisurely fishing in the stream. But the natives did not return. At about noon, Haskins launched the boats and began moving further upstream. Mendoza began pecking at his typewriter.

The sun was hot as they paddled upstream; the porters had their shirts off and the sun reflected off their wet skin. The stream was relatively flat, but the current was persistent. On their right was a cliff about fifty feet high. There was nothing to see above, as the cliff rose directly from the edge of the water. To their left, the riverbank was level, with jungle foliage reaching to within twenty feet of the edge of the river. To the right was a sandy strand.

Haskins thought the right bank looked like a comfortable place to settle for the night. They pointed the boats toward the shore. They were about seventy-five yards from their landing spot, when a fusillade of arrows rained down on the water in front of them. Surprised at first, the natives at the controls hesitated. There was yelling by several men at once. Then Haskins shouted out an order that stood out from the other noise. "Stop! Head back! Get out of here." At that command, the men at the controls quickly maneuvered the boats downstream and retreated from the area.

It was unclear whether the attack had come from the tribe they had spoken to the night before, or from someone new. In any event, it was evident that the expedition was unwelcome. Haskins was not sure whether the arrows missed intentionally, to serve as a warning, or whether they missed their intended target as a result of poor marksmanship. It didn't matter, he thought. If they had gotten closer to shore they would have been attacked. Of that he was certain. Either way, they could not take a chance.

That night they stayed in their boats and kept drifting downstream all the way back to the Capo Manamo River.

In the morning, the explorers held a meeting. They argued again about whether the natives said they would bring Redfern. *What to do next?* thought Haskins. They discussed the situation and concluded that it was too dangerous to go over land to search for the crash site. There were no roads and the trails were unmarked. They decided to go back to Tucupita to see if anyone there had a suggestion. After packing the boats, they continued the trip back, until they reached Tucupita, where the expedition checked into the Santa Maria Hotel once again.

The following day, Haskins met with Patel and Lind. They were unanimous in their advice: "Don't go back. It's too dangerous." Haskins concurred and had already decided not to press on with the search. Patel and Lind were just preaching to the converted.

The following day, they packed their trucks for the return to Caracas. From there, they would head for home. The whole crew was disappointed it had not found Paul.

Once settled at home, Mendoza wrote a four-part piece for the *Dario,* and six months after returning, his longer commentary about the expedition appeared in the *National Geographic Magazine.* There were color photos of the expedition leaders and several photos of natives showing their lack of clothes as well as their weapons.

Someone gave a copy to Gertrude, who read the article multiple times. Each time she read it, there were tears in her eyes. She was beginning to realize that she might never see Paul again. She remembered his statement that he would eventually walk out, but now it had been six years. Her hopes were vanishing.

21

Bitter Pickles (1934)

The next thing Paul remembered was waking up in a dark room. There were three men next to him and they were all pushing at various parts of his body. He felt hands pressing on his back and stomach, and against his arms. What was happening? It took him a moment to adjust to the fact that he was alive. Then, he realized the three men were trying to force him to wake up from a hazy sleep. Paul let out a groan and slowly sat up in the hammock, placing both feet on the ground. The men surrounding him emitted agreeable sounds, and it was obvious that they were happy he had woken up. Slowly, it came to Paul that these men were from his own village. He was in his own hammock.

One of the men continued to rub Paul's shoulders, while the others stood and stared at him. Paul's head cleared. It was Shapora, the Headman, who was rubbing his shoulders, with Piarucu standing in front of him. *What are they doing here?* he thought. He started gesturing and talking. "Where am I? How did you get here?" As the words came out, Paul's head began to clear. The last thing he could remember was being shot with darts and passing out on the lawn in the enemy's *shabono*. Now he was in his own hammock.

Piarucu began to explain. Two days ago, the Tall One had run back to the village to report his capture. The tribe had known Paul was gone, but was unsure as to why he had left. From the Tall One's report, however, the reason for his absence was clear.

Shapora ordered a search party of four to go find Paul. Paul was an asset to Shapora, one that he did not want to give up. The fact that Paul had been captured by the Waika was another incentive. The tradition of the tribe was to keep visitors safe while they were in the tribe's care. Shapora wanted Paul and his transcendent powers back in the village if at all possible.

The searchers easily found tracks on the trail and followed them. The four men followed the footprints and found evidence of the confrontation between Paul and the hostile tribesmen. Next, they followed the tracks to the *shabono*.

They arrived outside the enemy village after dark, and huddled in the underbrush as they surveyed the situation. They spotted Paul by a fire, tied to a stake. He was guarded and asleep. Initially, there were villagers milling about. But, as time passed, there was less activity as the village retired for the night. By midnight, only a handful of men could be seen. The four waited almost four hours, keeping well hidden. They were still waiting when Paul leaped to his feet and sprinted toward them. Acting instinctively, the four men all jumped up and sprinted toward Paul.

The rescuers ran across the lawn. The single man chasing Paul was concentrating on catching him and did not notice the four rescuers until it was too late. He was struck by two of the four poison-tipped arrows shot at him by the rescuers.

By the time they reached Paul, he had passed out on the lawn, a result of being struck by the poison-tipped blow pipe darts fired at him. Piarucu and another man propped him up and dragged him out of the area. The other two fought off the other men of the tribe, who had staggered half-asleep from their hammocks, and were now chasing Paul. One rescuer scooped up Paul's basket as they sprinted toward the surrounding jungle.

There was a brief skirmish as they started to leave with Paul. The four men stood their ground, but sadly one of Paul's rescuers was killed. However, before most of the enemy tribe awakened, the saviors had escaped the encampment and were scurrying home. The Waika were unprepared for battle and decided not to follow the rescue party.

Piarucu told Paul that the natives were happy that he had gone to the village of the enemy to retaliate for the death of the boy attacked by the Waika. Paul was surprised at the words. *What boy?* he thought. Then, he recalled the boy who had been murdered just a few days ago. Judging from the expression on Piarucu's face, Paul could tell Piarucu knew his being captured in the enemy's *shabono* had nothing to do with the boy.

The headman reiterated that Paul's motivation for going to the enemy's camp was revenge. It did not occur to anyone other than Piarucu that Paul was attempting to escape.

One of the rescue team said in his native tongue, "We went to rescue you. You had gone to the enemy *shabono* to seek revenge for the murder of the boy. You were captured. We saw you lying on the grass. We had surprise on our side. So, we took action."

Piarucu pointed to Paul's basket, lying in the corner. They had recovered it in the grass and brought it back with them. This discovery reinforced their conclusion that revenge was Paul's motivation to leave the *shabono*. Paul correctly surmised his pistol was still in the bottom of the basket under his jacket. He didn't understand how his intentions had been so completely misinterpreted, but he decided not to correct their understanding.

A large tumbler, fabricated from a bamboo stalk and containing a warm beverage, was placed in Paul's hand. He was urged to drink. Yanokiritana, the *shaman*, said it would help to counteract the poison. The liquid tasted like bitter pickles, but Paul drank the contents of the whole cup with a tormented look on his face. He felt like going back to sleep, but the men did not let him lie back down and kept pushing and prodding him to keep him awake. Paul assumed the rough massage must be an additional remedy for the poison.

Paul whispered to Piarucu, "This drink you gave me might be worse than the poison." Piarucu smiled.

In any event, Paul's first attempt to leave had been a failure. He would have to plan another escape, but not now. While not physically constrained, he nevertheless felt like a prisoner. He could not just wait to be rescued. He could not *rely* on a rescue. He had learned a lot from his failed attempt—mainly not to get caught. He resolved to be more careful the next time.

Paul stayed awake until everyone left. About fifteen minutes after they had gone, he fell into a deep sleep and did not wake up until late the following morning. When Paul awoke, Piarucu came to him with the news. "While you were gone, some of the tribe met a group of white men and their native servants. They were looking for a white man who they said they heard was living with us."

Paul was shocked to hear this news. He ran as fast as possible to Shapora and asked about the encounter. The chief explained that an expedition of white men had been "exploring the area." Shapora told Paul they had met for a few hours, but the white men left. The headman claimed he ordered the white men to leave.

Paul asked, "Where did they go?" Shapora said he did not know. Paul suspected he was hiding something. He asked several additional questions to get a better understanding of what exactly had transpired. Shapora let it slip that the white men were interested in finding a white man who had fallen from the sky. The headman mentioned that at the time of the meeting, Paul was missing. The headman's explanation was confusing to Paul. He could not believe that the search party had left the area. If only they had waited. He was back now. He desperately wanted to meet with them.

Paul then approached Piarucu to interpret what Shapora had said. Piarucu said the headman was embarrassed. Strangers who show up at the *shabono* are routinely taken in and shown hospitality according to tribal obligations. Shapora was not sure why Paul was missing when the rescue team arrived. He understood the search party was looking for Paul. Since Paul was gone for unknown reasons when they arrived, Shapora was concerned he had not lived up to his hospitality responsibilities. To cover his embarrassment, Shaporo decided to put an end to the discussion about Paul's whereabouts. Piarucu said, "During the night, the natives left the white men on the river's edge and returned to the *shabono*." Shaporo did not want to admit that he did not know where Paul was.

The news sank in. During his attempted escape, the tribe met some white men who were looking for *him*. Now they were probably gone. But Piarucu was not sure, because the expedition was abandoned on the river's shore. Paul's pulse began to race. How could he locate the search party now?

That afternoon Piarucu took Paul on a four-hour hike to the grassy spot near the river where the tribe had met with the search party. There was no sign of them, other than some discarded camp boxes and the remnants of three campfires. Piarucu, after a study of the scene, opined that the expedition had left only a few hours earlier at about noon.

As they stood at the water's edge, tears started to flow over Paul's cheeks. It was the first time that he felt total despair. In the back of his mind, Paul thought he would someday be rescued. Now, he had missed connecting with the rescuers by less than a day. A search party had been on the spot earlier that same day where he now stood. Now they were gone. It was an emotional realization.

Piarucu saw the tears and said, "If they come back, I'll bring them to you." Paul stayed in his hammock most of the next week and hardly spoke to anyone.

When he did venture out, Paul approached the Tall One and asked her if she would want to make another attempt at escape. She asked for a day to think about it and then said, "No, I will stay here. Leaving is too dangerous." Paul did not try to dissuade her of that decision. He could see that she was too determined in her resolve to stay put. He was having doubts about attempting another escape with her anyway, and so he readily accepted her decision.

* * * * *

While Paul yearned to get back to Gertrude, the days had turned into months, and the months into years. He was hesitant to make a break for it. He was not only wary of his sore leg, he also feared the reaction from the tribe. He was not sure they would allow him to leave.

Paul continued to go with the men on their trips to hunt food. He learned how to find game, and it seemed that on each hunting foray the hunters found enough food for at least a week or two. Food in the jungle was plentiful. Once game was located, the natives were excellent trackers. Whether a hunt was successful depended on the hunters' skill in stalking. The crack of a stepped-on twig would send an animal scurrying away. Or the sound of a slap aimed at a mosquito could ruin a chance at sneaking up on game. Learning how to be silent and avoiding quick movements took time.

Over these last few years, however, Paul had become somewhat skilled at tracking and hunting down prey.

Paul saw how the other men would silently sneak up on the game. When he began to go on hunting trips, he was relegated to the rear of the hunting party, so as not to spook the game. But recently, the hunters could trust Paul. Now he was permitted join in on the tracking and stalking of game.

Today, on this hunt, his party returned to the village with three tapirs, seven small monkeys, three deer, and several large *pauji* (wild fowl). This was enough to last through the following month and perhaps longer. They had only been out hunting since morning and were already back at camp a day early.

As the men came back to the *shabono,* the conversations among them were animated. They were happy with the amount of food they were able to harvest. It was a very good hunt. The villagers at home would be grateful. Paul was especially happy, as he had joined in the hunt. He did not participate in the kill, because he was not yet strong enough to use a bow. But he did help to silently surround the quarry just prior to the kill. He was proud of the success of the hunt and the skillfulness he demonstrated.

As was the custom, the village immediately sprang into action upon their return. Fires were lit and several women left the village to gather plantains and bananas from the cultivated fields at the edge of the forest. The food would be served as soon as it was cooked, and everyone would join in the feast.

22

Gold Prospectors (1935)

The Spanish and Portuguese began colonizing Central America in the 15th and 16th centuries. Before they arrived, the Aztecs and Incas extracted gold and silver for jewelry and trinkets. The Europeans saw these items and decided to take whatever they could from the natives. Once that source of gold and silver was gone, they enslaved the natives and forced them to work the mines. For hundreds of years, gold and silver mined by slave labor, was packed up, and shipped back to Europe.

In 1595, Sir Walter Raleigh repeated a widely repeated rumor he heard of a Gold City in what is now known as Venezuela or Guiana, near the Orinoco River. The story was that the city of gold, called Manoa, was located on the banks of a lake. In the city, everything was made of gold, even the buildings. Raleigh, at the time, was in Columbia, several hundred miles from the Orinoco. The story was a hoax. No matter, the rumor was believed, and several expeditions sponsored by Spain and Portugal explored the area around the Orinoco in the next centuries.

The natives whom the explorers met played along and encouraged prospectors they encountered to believe that the City of Gold was just a bit further. "Keep going and you will find it," they told the explorers. It was their way of ridding themselves of the gold hunters and persuading them to move on. There was no lake near the Orinoco River, but the explorers continued to search. However, there were never any substantial sources of gold discovered in the area.

By the late 1920s, there were no longer any governmental sponsored expeditions to hunt for the city of Manoa. The rumor of a City of Gold was officially disbelieved. Governments no longer financed searches in the area. However, Raleigh's extravagant promise of a huge fortune still resonated with some. The fact that Raleigh's rumor mongering was old oddly lent credibility to it. As frequently happens, the lure of gold cast a wide net, encouraging overeager explorers to vainly search without success. During the Roaring Twenties, a few adventurers mounted small expeditions once again, searching for Raleigh's gold in the Orinoco-Essequibo region.

One of those expeditions was headed by John Schneider, from New York City. Schneider in his mid-twenties was a successful stockbroker who had found references to Manoa, the City of Gold, in an antique book. The lure of untold wealth pulled at him. The fact that no one had found such a city in the centuries since Raleigh's tale did not faze him. He was sure he was clever enough to find the City of Gold.

This was his first trip to the area. With him were three native porters and a fellow New Yorker, named Paul Gerard, a former classmate from Cornell University. Gerard was a senior bank manager. The two had started their journey into the wilds of Venezuela from Georgetown in August, 1936, in a large flat-bottomed barge, and had made their way up the Essequibo River. As they proceeded up the river, they searched the riverbanks for gold. They panned for the precious metal in the cascades, and dug for gold in areas that looked promising.

Their search was largely unproductive, although, after three quarters of a year, they had two bags of gold dust weighing a total of forty ounces, yet still not hardly enough. At a value of close to thirty-five dollars an ounce, it was worth approximately one thousand, four hundred dollars ($1,900 in today's dollars). However, they were searching for the *tons* of gold it took to pave the streets, and they had not gathered gold sufficient to even pay for their trip.

Their journey took them to the Caroni River. On their third day on the Caroni, they ran into a hunting party of Yanomami Indians. While the tribe was of the same family as Paul's tribe, the two groups lived independently.

They had been searching for gold for nine months and were almost ready to give up. During their time in the jungle, they had found only one small nugget about the size of a marble, even after considerable digging. They were more successful in finding gold *dust*, but the effort it took to find and collect it was excessive. Standing in a river bed, bending over for hours at a time was tedious and back-breaking.

By this time, the expedition had unsuccessfully run into several groups of natives. Schneider had no respect for the Indians and assumed, based on appearances, that he could boss them around. In his mind, the natives were stupid and should be beholden to him. He spoke to the natives in a brusque manner, and always with the expectation his commands would be obeyed. He visited the Indians' *shabono* not for hospitable reasons, but to nose around for evidence of gold. The natives, in turn, offered no assistance.

The Yanomami tribe he ran into was sociable with Paul's tribe. The two neighboring groups of natives had regularly traded goods with each other and banded together sporadically to fight off attacks by the Waika. Occasionally, men from one tribe took wives from the other. They spoke the same language. The two tribes maintained a friendly alliance.

As was their habit when meeting natives, Schneider handed out colorful beads and other cheap baubles. He was not aware this act was taken as an insult by the tribe. The natives were willing to trade for the stuff, but not willing to accept a gift from a stranger — especially a white one. One by one, they handed back the bounty. Undaunted, Schneider peppered the tribe with questions designed to learn of the existence of gold deposits.

The Yanomami tribe wanted to be rid of Schneider's expedition as soon as possible. Through observation and rumor, the natives believed that gold prospectors had little respect for the land and rivers of the jungle. In their search for riches, they stripped the land of trees, leaving a muddy mess. The mine tailings of their search poisoned the rivers killing the fish and other wildlife that lived near the water.

The tribe attempted to persuade Schneider to leave as quickly as possible. After a discussion among themselves, they decided to mention Paul's existence to Schneider in the hope that would be enough to induce him to move on.

The chief told Schneider there was a white man who was living with a neighboring tribe. Schneider only became interested because the white man might be someone with whom he could converse easily in his search for gold. He hoped the white man might be willing to share information of nearby gold deposits. Schneider asked how to find the *shabono* where Paul lived. By then, Schneider was satisfied there was no gold in the hands of the group with whom he had been conversing. They sent him on his way hoping never to see him again. They did not care if Schneider found Paul or not.

Schneider set out to find Paul based on the directions given to him by the tribe. His first clue as to the intent of the natives should have been how garbled the directions were. Despite the tribes living only four miles from each other, it took Schneider five days to locate the area around Paul's *shabono*.

As Schneider's group got close to Paul's *shabono*, they were traveling upstream on a lazy waterway. But upon disembarking, Schneider found his way was blocked by a group of six hunters carrying weapons, who were determined not to let him pass. The tribe had made it a practice not to permit white people to see their *shabono*. Their stern manner made Schneider decide immediately not to attempt an end run.

Schneider asked, "We are looking for a white man. Do you know how we can find him?"

Piarucu was in the group of six and walked up to Schneider to speak. "A white man stays in our *shabono*. His name is Meh Paul. Do you wish to speak with him?" Schneider was pleased to hear Piarucu speak his heavily accented English. Schneider replied, "Yes. I do."

Piarucu answered, "Wait here. I get him."

Piarucu hurriedly skipped through the jungle to the *shabono*. He found Paul and told him there was a white man about a half hour away who wished to see him. Paul was stunned by the news. He collapsed to his knees, holding his head in his hands, and cried out, "Oh my God!" His stumbled as he attempted to get up. The thought of a white man wanting to see him momentarily took the strength from his legs.

Within an hour, Piarucu picked up Paul, and the two of them scurried down to the river to meet Schneider.

Paul spotted the two white men about twenty-five yards ahead and called out, "Boy am I glad to see you." As he trotted up to them, he added, "I've been waiting for years for you to show up. Where are you from?"

Schneider looked Redfern over and could hardly believe his eyes. Paul's hair was long, and was falling over his collar. He had a dark brown beard and moustache that covered his face. Paul was dressed in a torn, long-sleeved shirt with the cuffs rolled up. The shirt appeared as if Paul had been run over by a train in it. It was dirty, and fire ants had eaten a dozen or more holes in it. His pants were also torn in several places, with one leg carelessly sewn up to the knee.

In addition to the condition of Paul's clothes and hair, Schneider noticed Paul had a slight limp. He thought Paul looked pale and thin. His first thought was Paul looked too weak to traipse through the jungle.

Gerard spoke up, "You look like you could use a shave. I'll lend you my razor."

Schneider added, "I've got an extra shirt in my bag that I'd be happy to let you have. You'll be far more comfortable in it."

Paul thanked them for their offers. Schneider went to the barge and returned to the group, handing Paul a nicely folded shirt. Paul was genuinely grateful for the shirt and thanked Schneider profusely.

Schneider replied, "We're gold prospectors. We heard you were in the area and wanted to talk to you. Our purpose in coming to South America is to find gold."

Schneider's comment was disappointing. Paul assumed they had come to rescue *him*. After a second, he asked, "Well now that you are here, can you take me with you?"

As Paul spoke to Schneider and the others, he took note of their appearance. Schneider and Gerard were both dressed out in trim khaki shirts, Sam Brown belts, and creased pants. Each sported a safari helmet made of pith. Their spiffy appearance made them look as if they were out for a Sunday stroll.

Schneider asked, "How is it that you live here?"

Paul explained, "I was in an airplane flying from the States to Rio de Janeiro when my engine failed. I landed in a tree and was rescued by this tribe. That was eight years ago, and I've been here ever since.

Schneider asked, "Why haven't you gone home? Don't you have family in the States?"

Paul explained, "I hurt my leg crashing into a treetop and wasn't able to walk out of here at first. When I did attempt to leave, I was captured by an opposing Waika tribe. They were going to kill me when my tribe rescued me. Since then, I've been afraid that if I leave the natives I live with, they will chase after me and try to stop me. You see, I am a hero to this tribe, ever since I used my pistol and saved the tribe from an attack by the Waika."

Just then, Gerard walked back from the barge and handed Paul a pair of scissors and a razor. "Here, you can return these any time."

Paul changed the subject, asking, "What makes you think there is gold here?"

Schneider then explained, "I read an old book that quoted Sir Walter Raleigh. He said he had heard the area around here was teeming with gold. Raleigh said there was so much gold, some of the streets were actually paved with the stuff. Even if his story is only partly true, I want the gold that sparked it in the first place. We think there must be some basis to back up his tale and we are exploring this area. Have you seen any precious metals in the hands of the natives?"

Paul replied, "I've been here for eight years and have not seen one piece of gold. The natives here do not use money and, as far as I can see, there are no gold traders. It would have no value to the tribe I'm living with. No, I don't think you will find any gold around here."

Paul went on to say that there were other tribes in the area, some friendly and some not so much. He cautioned that the native tribes had no use for white people and would say anything, once they appeared, to get them to vacate the vicinity in a few days.

Paul repeated what he had heard from Piarucu. "As I understand it, they don't want to have anything to do with whites. I am a special case since I came from the sky. They believe I was sent here by the good sky spirits."

After about five minutes of conversation, Paul said, "I really want to get home. I'm ready to go with you anytime, okay?"

The request took Schneider by surprise, and he thought about the idea for a few seconds. "We still have a month to go before we end the expedition and leave the area. It would be better if you joined us on our way out of this area. Right now, we are intent on finding gold and you would just get in the way. We'll be back here in about three or four weeks, and we could take you with us then."

Paul begged them to reconsider. "You are the first white people I have seen in eight years. I really want to leave *now*. It's time for me to get out of here, *please*."

Schneider then disclosed the actual reason for their reluctance to take Paul then. "Our provisions are not sufficient to feed an extra man. If we took *you*, that would deplete our food supplies that much sooner. No, you need to wait here until we turn around and head back. Then we could take you with us."

Paul persisted. "I can hunt while you all concentrate on prospecting. I've learned a lot about stalking and hunting while I've been here. You can count on me to find food."

Gerard countered. "If the natives chase after you, they will be chasing *us*. I don't have time to take care of you and at the same time avoid a confrontation with them. Look, we'll pick you up on our way out of the jungle. It's only a month until we start back. Be here at the riverbank and you can jump on board the barge. We'll be heading straight back then. We'll be able to go full speed."

After a bit, Paul asked, "Can you show me a map of the area that shows how to get back to civilization?" (Paul had wondered for eight years how he could escape, and this was his chance.) "A map could be useful," he added.

Gerard spoke up and said, "We have a map showing the rivers and streams. If you follow the rivers, they will take you to Georgetown." Gerard stepped away and went back to the barge. He returned and handed Paul a map printed on wax paper. "Here, this is an extra. You can keep this."

The only map Paul had was his hand-drawn chart showing the way to Rio. Since he had not considered that he would ever fall short of Rio, there were no landmarks filled in for the area short of Rio. He wanted to study Schneider's map to memorize the details to his hand-drawn paper.

Paul carefully opened the paper into its full size and looked first at the streams. He was immediately surprised by the fact that none of them were anything like straight lines. Each it seemed curved left and right to one degree or another every mile or so. Some of the curves were so extreme that in some places, within a mile, the river doubled back and flowed in the opposite direction. But then he noticed Georgetown near the end of the Essequibo River. It was a welcome sight.

Paul borrowed a fountain pen from Gerard and traced a line over it, all the way to the Atlantic Ocean. He then drew the course of the stream near the *shabono*, the Capo Manamo, Essequibo, and Orinoco rivers. Also, he marked Tucupita, Georgetown, and Caracas. He was nervous about Schneider's promise to stop for him on their return and wanted insurance of his own. He was suspicious that Schneider was more concerned with finding gold than rescuing him, but he could not force himself on Schneider.

Paul finally agreed to wait, saying, "I'll be ready to join you when you come back here."

For the next few days, Paul showed Schneider around the region, but there was no gold to be found. Nevertheless, Schneider had his porters clear several areas. It disturbed Paul that Schneider's men were tearing apart the embankment around the stream. They cut down twenty trees in three days. Doing so left the area bare to the elements and turned the stream from clear to brown. Piarucu observed that the rainy season on the bare soil would wash away any tree sprouts.

Trees would not grow back in the disturbed soil for several years.

Paul remembered the stones he had recovered in the moonlight from the crimson river. He had given one of them away to Tootsie, thinking they had little value, but still had the larger one. He thought it would make a good memento for Gertrude. He found the crystal in a basket of knick knacks he had been saving at the *shabono* and brought it to Schneider and handed it to him.

"I don't know if this is a real diamond," said Paul, "but I tested it and it's pretty hard."

Schneider's eyes widened as he inspected it. He did not reply for a few minutes while he rolled it over in his hand. He probably thought, *This is a diamond. If I can't find gold, diamonds would be a nice substitute.*

Schneider asked, "Where did you find this?"

"I found it in this stream about five miles up just past the rapids. It was near a spot where tar was oozing out of the ground."

The following morning, the Schneider party left early before Paul made it to their camping spot. He was stuck, and felt abandoned. Now he had no choice but to wait for Schneider and Gerard to return.

Every day thereafter, Paul visited the riverbank daily hoping to see the two men. But they never showed.

Paul was frustrated. He had been suspicious when Schneider left suddenly. Once three weeks had stretched into five full weeks, Paul finally realized Schneider and Gerard were not coming back for him.

Paul suspected Schneider never planned to return for him and he had been deceived.

Paul confided to Piarucu that he wished he had gone with Schneider. He had missed the Haskins expedition by a few hours. Now it appeared he had failed to join Schneider's party and a chance to get back to Gertrude. At the same time, he was determined to leave one way or the other.

23

Surucu! (1936)

Paul was desperate. He had put his faith in Schneider to help him back to civilization. But Schneider never showed up. Paul was confused and frustrated. On the one hand, Schneider could have been deceitful. On the other, there could have been some confusion over the details of the pickup and Schneider unintentionally missed Paul by accident. Or Schneider may have postponed his departure.

Paul was uncertain whether or not the Yanomami tribe would permit him to leave. Furthermore, he had no plan. He did not feel like he could leave on the overland trail again, and he questioned the ability of his leg to handle the long hike. He would have to try to leave by boat.

In addition to his other concerns, Paul was worried about possible confrontations with hostile tribes in the area. If he were captured again by the Waika tribe, he expected to be killed immediately. He had heard reports of several other disputes with neighboring tribes. He was aware there were other hostile tribes in the area in addition to the Waika. Despite all that, he wanted urgently to escape, and to return to civilization and his family. The thought of a getaway was on his mind every day.

By now Paul was considered a full-fledged member of the tribe. His life was comfortable. He went on hunting forays, fished, and picked fruit for the settlement. His ability to defend the settlement with his pistol brought him admiration. On occasion, he was asked for advice by the headman or the *shaman*. And the natives enjoyed his laughter and happy demeanor. The children especially were enthralled with his antics and singing.

The folks in the settlement were treating him well in their own way. He had a roof over his head, food was assured, and, in case of an attack, the settlement would protect him. They had saved his life more than once. It was not the worst situation except for one thing: He wanted to return to the white man's world. Returning to Gertrude, as well as his life in the States, were a priority. He assumed his chances of a rescue party finding him had come and gone. He would have to take the initiative and make a run for it.

That evening, as Paul was about to fall asleep, he thought of Gertrude. But, in his mind's eye, she had no face. He was forgetting what she looked like. The following morning, he decided his fears would have to be set aside. He was going to try to make it back to Gertrude.

Paul looked at Schneider's chart of the streams of the area. The map was detailed and gave him enough information to get started. He realized the only way to civilization was downstream. That was a plus. He remembered Professor Breckinridge's statement that white people generally live within ten miles of the sea.

Paul spoke to Piarucu in confidence about leaving to go home. He thought if anyone would understand his desire to leave, Piarucu would. Piarucu agreed to keep Paul's plans secret. Paul explained that he would have attempted to leave earlier except he was concerned about the condition of his weak leg. And when he wound up captured by the Waika, it was not to seek revenge, but he was attempting to go home. Piarucu chuckled and told Paul, "I knew it, but I did not say anything."

Paul asked Piarucu to help him catch up to Schneider. His best guess was that Schneider had passed by during the night to avoid a confrontation. If he could get a canoe and catch Schneider, Paul thought Schneider would have to take him to civilization. Waiting for a rescue was no longer an option.

Piarucu asked, "If he has already gone, how can we catch him?"

Paul said, "You saw how he searched for gold here. He'll stop and cut down trees and dig along the way. There is a good chance with both you and I rowing, we can catch him. If we don't catch up, you can drop me off at the first place where we find a white settlement." Then, almost as an afterthought, Paul asked, "Do you think the tribe will allow me to leave?"

"If they think you go, they will tie you up so you stay. But if you gone, they do not send anyone after you."

Paul knew if Piarucu were to spread the news of his departure, others in the village would attempt to stop him. Having lived with the tribe for about eight years would not give him the right to leave.   He was the tribe's connection to the good spirits.   That was important to the tribe. Paul acknowledged that the tribe would likely attempt to stop him with force, even death.

If he were to try to hike out, he could run into a hostile tribe as he did the last time. Even if armed, one person could not survive an attack by several natives armed with poison arrows. The prospect of waiting for a rescue party seemed less risky. But, over a year ago, rescuers had been looking for him and he had not joined them. Paul thought the chances of another rescue party coming to find him were almost impossible.

The following day, Piarucu told Paul he would help with an escape using one of the tribe's dugout canoes called a *kanawa*. He offered that the tribe's canoes were stored by a small, but fast moving, stream about a mile away. He suggested they could "borrow" one of them, so the two of them could float downstream and eventually wind up in the white man's world. Once Paul felt he could find a white man's village, he would hike the remainder of the way, and Piarucu would bring the canoe back to the village. Piarucu said he was sad to see Paul leave but understood that he had his own world that was calling to him.

How sure am I that the river will lead to civilization? Paul wondered. He had heard the natives talk about the "River of Doubt." It was mentioned in many of the stories told by the natives. Even the *shaman* spoke of this river that had no beginning or end. In the stories, the current would periodically reverse direction.   Paul always thought the story was unlikely.   Now those stories raised doubts, especially since he was about to rely on rivers to take him home. Then, he thought about the coastal rivers near the ocean that flowed back and forth with the tide. That was the more plausible explanation to the story. He laughed when he realized how tribal stories were creeping into his thoughts.

In February 1934, Paul finally decided he would depart. All his doubts were resolved in favor of leaving. He decided that even if he were to die trying, it would be worth the effort. He could not stay in the jungle any longer.

After a series of discussions, he prearranged with Piarucu to accompany him. They met before morning light and began their short walk to the stream. Paul carried his revolver in his belt for protection. His earlier attempt at escape had been in 1930 and ended with him being taken prisoner. He hoped Piarucu would help keep him out of trouble this time. But this time, having his weapon would add protection.

Paul and Piarucu walked along the well-worn trail to the boat landing about a quarter mile from camp. They left the settlement and looped around from the back so not to be noticed. The path was narrow, and they walked single file. Neither dared to say a word until they were out of ear shot from the *shabono*. After a few minutes they left the trail and walked down a small incline to the stream. Scattered along the shore were five dugout canoes carved from tree trunks. They picked one close to the water and threw their belongings in, making sure they were quiet. Paul jumped in and made his way to the bow.   Piarucu pushed the boat into the water and jumped into the stern. They were off.

Paul and Piarucu each had a paddle, and they took turns guiding the boat downstream. Paul took one last look around as they began, then silently said farewell to the tribe he had lived with over the last so many years. While he was happy to be leaving, he felt a twinge of sadness over leaving the tribe, especially the headman, the *shaman*, and the children. He had spent longer with the Yanomami than any group other than his own family. But he had resolved to make a break for it and he was now resolved to leave.

As they began traveling that day, the stream was mostly deeper than the draft of the canoe. There were only a few rapids where they needed to get out and walk their boat. Throughout the afternoon the going was mostly smooth and steady. There was thick jungle on both sides of the steam, and no sign of any other tribes. As they sailed downstream, Paul reflected on his feelings and thought, *Every mile we float downstream is another mile closer to home.*

Piarucu did most of the paddling. His arms were stronger than Paul's and he was adept at navigating around the occasional logs or debris in their way. On two occasions, they had to portage around rapids by picking up the canoe and carrying it on their shoulders. Fortunately, on both occasions the distance they had to lug the canoe was short.

At the end of the first day, the two travelers stopped for the night. They had not seen another human along the lazy stream they had chosen. Paul was relieved not to have run into any hostile tribes. They unpacked their belongings and set up camp. Piarucu got out the manioc bread and dried meat. He gathered some plantains picked from nearby trees. Paul built a fire and boiled some water from the stream. While the bread was warming, Paul thought again about getting back home. The idea of getting back to the States permeated his mind.

As Paul unloaded the canoe, he noticed his folding camp knife in one of the baskets lying on top of his jacket. He called out to Piarucu, showed him how the blade opened, and handed it to him. The concept of sharing possessions was common among tribe members. As he gave the knife to Piarucu, he said, "Here, my friend, is something to remember me by." Piarucu looked the knife over and ran his fingers over the five-inch blade. He had never seen a metal knife before, and his facial expression was one of gratitude. He replied, "Thank you, friend."

The following morning, they arrived at a juncture with a larger stream. Piarucu, without hesitation, chose to head to the right to continue heading downstream. There were no blockages or rapids in the new stream, which was wider and deeper than the one they had exited. They still had seen no other humans, nor any other sign of civilization. The lack of an encounter did not bother Paul. He was not eager to meet another tribe like the one he had encountered on his first attempt to escape.

The next day, they came to the Cano Manamo River. They did not know its name. They chose it due to its size, which was even larger than the stream they were on. The Cano Manamo was almost one hundred feet across and deeper than the prior streams. Paul thought, *Surely this river will carry me to the coast. Civilization here I come!*

Before noon, they saw a woman dressed only in a wrap around her waist walking on the trail next to the river with a basket balanced on her head. Following behind her were two naked children about two and four years old. Piarucu seemed interested in talking to her, and they guided the canoe over to the bank nearest the woman and the two conversed for about five minutes. When the woman had finished talking, Piarucu passed on questionable assurances to Paul that they were heading in the direction of a white man's village called Tucupita. Paul was relieved, since, up until then, he had only been guessing on the course to follow.

The woman had told Piarucu that a white man's village was on this river. They began to see signs of civilization. Over the course of the day, they saw natives, all of whom were partially dressed in wraps, short pants, or pieces of cloth looped over the string around their waist. Women made no effort to cover their breasts, but wore a cloth tied around their waist that covered them from there to their knees. A few of the people they saw had push carts with wheels. Piarucu shouted out to several of the men. Some did not respond, probably due to a language difference. Two of the men, however, did answer back. Piarucu reported to Paul their assurances that they were on the right course.

According to what the men told Piarucu, they would be at the white man's village sometime after dark. It was late afternoon already, and Paul was anxious to press on. Piarucu, on the other hand, was tired and voted to stop and camp. Since Piarucu had spent the day paddling, Paul relented, and he agreed to camp for the night. Reaching the village would have to wait until tomorrow. It was late afternoon and they pulled over to a sandy beach and pulled their gear out of the boat.

Across the river, obscured by the jungle, two men watched with interest as Paul and Piarucu unloaded the canoe and built a fire. The men were careful to stay out of sight. Piarucu, wearing no clothes and Paul, in rather ragged looking garments, probably appeared to be easy targets. Paul's shirt had several large holes torn open over the years. His pant leg was clumsily repaired with green string. The two men were obviously not rich enough to have security, and based upon their appearances, probably gave the robbers the impression they were easy prey. They could swoop in and steal anything useful or valuable.

That night, around midnight, the pair crossed the river in a rowboat and made their way up the slight rise toward Paul's fire. They did not have any firearms, but they would be able to attack before Paul or Piarucu had any warning. As they got closer, they saw neither Paul nor Piarucu was awake. The leader made a bee line toward Paul. He was carrying a three-foot tree limb over his head. He held one end with both hands. On the other end of the limb was a bulge in the wood from a large knot. When he was within three steps of the sleeping man, he broke into a run and swung the club at Paul's head, as he slept on the grass. Paul did not see it coming.

But the intruder's foot slipped on the damp grass, and the club hit dirt before its intended target. The strike to Paul's head was a weak blow to the back of his skull. Since the intruder was falling to the ground, there was not much force behind the blow. Startled, Paul rose to his feet, lurching because he was groggy and having difficulty focusing. He realized that the intruder was attempting a second strike, and as he staggered to keep from falling, the man swung again. But this time the man missed completely.

Paul scampered away and grabbed his revolver from his belt. Both robbers were undeterred and followed him, expecting they could get to him and force the pistol from his grasp. After all, he had just been struck by a club. After about ten steps, the first man reached for the pistol in Paul's hand.

Piarucu, now awake, bounded up, quickly caught up to the three, and put two darts into the two robbers in quick order with his blow pipe, which was always at his side. Both robbers glanced down at the darts and immediately realized what they were. In another second, they were on the ground unable to move. Piarucu did not hesitate. He ran over to the men and with his new camp knife, knelt and stabbed them both in the chest, killing them immediately. As Paul looked on, he surmised that Piarucu was repeating something he had done before, only this time he was using the metal blade Paul had given him yesterday.

Piarucu grabbed the robbers one at a time and dragged them to the river's edge, then pushed them into the water. Within a few seconds the water around the bodies was churning with piranha feasting on the remains. Paul looked on while the two white foaming masses floated gradually out of sight with the current.

By this time, Paul was also fully awake. He was happy he did not have to use his own weapon. He had a tinge of regret that the men had been killed, but that feeling was short lived. He realized that the robbers were attempting to kill him. He would be dead had the first or second blow made rock-solid contact. After a moment's reflection, Paul was at ease with the death of the robbers.

Paul's head was throbbing as Piarucu wrapped it with a palm frond. They now knew they could not trust the local folks to be friendly. And Paul no longer felt he could sleep in the open. They could have been seen by others. They decided to find a safer place to spend the rest of the night.

Paul and Piarucu packed and got back in their boat, floating farther downstream in the darkness for more than an hour. In the moonlight, they spotted an *Araguaney* tree masked in voluminous, bright orange blossoms. They pulled the boat to shore and made camp under the tree behind a large low hanging limb filled with the flowers. The branches of the tree drooped to about three feet above the ground and hid the two of them in the darkness. Paul and Piarucu covered themselves with large leaves. It was about 3:00 a.m. when they both dozed off.

However, Paul could not sleep the night through, and he awoke about two hours later. The sun was about an hour from rising, and it was misty and dark. His mind was wandering, and the encounter with the thieves was still fresh in his mind. He got up and wandered off to relieve himself, leaving Piarucu asleep. Paul had his revolver with him.

When he returned, Piarucu had awakened, and, in the early sunlight, was packing their things in the baskets. Paul walked up to the baskets and found food and drink in one of them. He pulled the items out and began to eat some dried fish and his favorite peach palm fruit, which Piarucu called "*rasha*." The blow to Paul's head, together with a lack of sleep, had rendered him groggy. He took about a half hour to casually eat what normally would have been a fifteen-minute breakfast.

Paul turned to Piarucu and said, "I will miss you, my friend, but I am looking forward to getting back home." Piarucu smiled. "I will miss you too," he replied. Both were looking forward to arriving at the spot where they would separate.

Paul filled a basket with his belongings and carried it toward the boat, which was tied up at the river's edge about thirty steps away. As he approached the boat, Paul's gait was a bit out of kilter. His limp was noticeable, and his eyes were at half-mast.

Suddenly, Paul caught a glimpse of a blur hurtling toward him from his right. He jumped to the side. His recoil was delayed less than a second by his lethargy, but it was just enough that he failed to avoid the Bushmaster snake that sailed at him. The snake's mouth was open, and, as it landed, it sank its two fangs into the side of Paul's right calf. Paul screamed in pain, reacting quickly and pulling the snake away, before throwing it off to the side. The snake was a about ten feet long and it too was startled. It quickly slipped away, as Paul sank to the ground.

Normally, Paul would have followed behind Piarucu, because Piarucu was adept at spotting danger ahead. Several times in the past, as he and Paul traveled through the jungle, as the leader, Piarucu would stop because he sensed danger. But this morning, Paul was anxious to be on his way, and it was only a few steps from the campfire to the boat.

Most snakes sleep during the day and only strike in response to being stepped on, or otherwise being startled. The Bushmaster, however, is known for its nasty disposition, and will attack a man with no provocation. It is commonplace for a Bushmaster snake to station itself along a path used by humans, for the purpose of attack. There they lie coiled up and wait to strike. They are extremely aggressive. No matter that the human is too large to eat, the snake will strike first regardless.

The Bushmaster possesses a powerful dose of poison that it injects through its hypodermic-like, white fangs, which are always erect and able to penetrate deeply into their victim. Unlike most other poisonous snakes in the Venezuelan jungle, its venom is known to be deadly.

Paul called out to the Piarucu. Sensing Paul's distress, Piarucu rushed over and looked at the two puncture wounds in his leg. He exclaimed, "*surucucu!*" the native name for a Bushmaster. He pushed Paul to the ground. Paul's heart was racing, due mostly to the fact that the snake had startled him.

Once Paul was lying still, Piarucu ran off, only to return shortly with some plantain leaves. He sat on the ground next to Paul's body. Paul's leg ached from the poison spreading up and down his leg. Piarucu squeezed drops of sap from a handful of leaves he held over the puncture marks. Then he stroked the bite marks with the wet leaves. His concern was evidenced by the look on his face. All jungle dwellers are aware that plantain leaves can help neutralize the effects of snake venom. But Piarucu also knew that the leaves had little effect on poison that had already spread via the bloodstream. The skin around the bite marks had already turned black and the discoloration was spreading.

The surprise attack by the snake had taken only seconds. The pain in Paul's lower leg was increasing, and his calf was becoming tight due to the swelling. He vomited on the ground next to him. The venom was working its way through his body. He remembered what the natives had told him about the Bushmaster's bite: "*Surucucu* bite bad." Piarucu ran off to gather more plantain leaves. He returned to find Paul with a fever, and weaker than he'd been just five minutes earlier. He rubbed the bite again with the wadded-up leaves. There was nothing else he could think to do.

After about fifteen minutes, Piarucu got up and threw the baskets into the canoe. Then he got Paul to his feet, and held him up as he limped to the boat with one arm over Piarucu's neck. Paul got into the canoe and lay down, resting his head on one of the baskets. Piarucu pushed off from the shore, and the boat began drifting with the current.

The canoe slowly turned as it floated downstream. Piarucu picked up a paddle and began to maneuver the boat, so the bow remained pointing downstream. He scoured both banks of the river looking for someone who could help. But it was early morning, and no one appeared. He began to chant to the spirits for assistance.

Paul stared vacantly out at the jungle, and as the poison spread throughout his body, he felt his heartbeat slacken. While viewing the green jungle had a calming effect, in the back of his mind, Paul realized nothing could be done about the bite. He hoped to survive, but he was resigned to any outcome.

After a couple of hours, Paul's leg was swollen to twice its normal size, from his ankle to his knee. Piarucu paddled harder, hoping to find help. Paul was becoming bilious, and sweat was dripping off his forehead. Piarucu continued on with a long chant, an entreaty to the spirits to save Paul's life. As he did, Paul leaned over the rail and wretched into the river once again.

Paul's condition continued to worsen. In the next hour, his breathing became shallow. His words were slurred. His lips were numb. His body convulsed for five minutes. Piarucu held him down. The convulsions slowly came to an end. Then, his body was motionless. Piarucu begged the spirits to save Paul.

As he lay in the bottom of the canoe, a vision came into Paul's head. He saw Gertrude. She was at home in the kitchen, and as he approached her from behind, she turned toward him and smiled. He reached out to her, but his reach fell short, and then he lost consciousness and fell into a deep sleep. He no longer could hear Piarucu's pleading. Paul remained insentient. In another ten minutes, his heart stopped.

Piarucu realized at once that Paul was gone. He let out a loud yell. Paul had been his friend and Piarucu was devastated by his death. Tears ran down his cheeks. Even though he was familiar with death and knew of the dangers in the jungle, he could not help but react to the death of a friend he had known for the last seven years.

They were from different worlds, of course. But they had spent many days together talking and hunting. Paul had always been the talkative one and although Piarucu did not always understand precisely what Paul said, he always enjoyed his laugh and sense of humor. Now Paul was gone.

Piarucu paddled to the shore and took Paul's body out of the canoe and laid it on the sand. For the next few hours, he gathered firewood and arranged the logs so Paul's body would fit on the top of the pile. He took off Paul's clothes and placed his body on the firewood.

The following morning just before dawn, he lit the fire. Then Piarucu went through the baskets and put all of Paul's belongings next to his body. Soon the fire was red hot and Piarucu placed some of the burning logs on top of the corpse. The thick black smoke rose directly up into the early morning sky.

Piarucu started reciting a familiar mantra, repeating similar phrases over and over. "Where are you, you who used to collect the fruit from the *wapu* tree? Where are you, you who used to hunt the tapir? Where are you, you who laughed each day?"

Paul's "soul of death," one of three souls recognized by the natives, rose in the heavy smoke that emanated from the fire. It was important to Piarucu that Paul's remains be cremated so this soul would be set free and rise to the sky. He cried on and off as the fire burned for over four hours and, when it was out, Paul's corpse had disappeared.

Piarucu gathered the ashes from the extinguished pyre and put them in a container fashioned from a gourd. A few pieces of Paul's bones remained and Piarucu promptly ground them up and placed them in the gourd. After sealing the gourd with bees' wax, he took the gourd about a hundred yards into the jungle and placed it in a hole in a tree trunk, hidden from view. As was the custom in his world, Piarucu, for the remainder of his life, would never speak Paul's name again.

That afternoon, Piarucu started the return trip back to the *shabono*. It would take an extra day to make the trip, since he was heading upstream against the current. He was sad with the thought that his friend "meh Paul" had not gotten back to his family. As the afternoon passed, Piarucu feelings of condolence lessened. In the jungle, death was always close at hand.

Days later, back at the *shabono*, Piarucu told of the bushmaster attack, but did not say Paul's name. Nor did Piarucu mention Paul's attempt to escape and go home. Instead, he explained his absence as a hunting trip. Paul's death was not an unusual event. Many tribesmen died early deaths in the jungle. There was no contact with anyone outside the tribe, so no news of his death was broadcast publicly. The only person who mourned his passing was Piarucu.

For the rest of his life, Piarucu and Junior reminisced about their experiences with Paul. They laughed when they recalled his awkward hunting techniques and his inability to hit a target with his blowpipe. Tootsie could be heard singing some of Paul's favorite songs for a few months after his death. But as she matured, she forgot the songs.

Piarucu remembered Paul and wished he was still living with him and the tribe. After a while Piarucu thought of him less and less.   However, the reasons were more complicated than Paul could have guessed.

* * * * *

A week after leaving Paul in the jungle, Schneider had not found gold. He did, however, discover a dry tributary of the stream with an outcropping of raw diamonds scattered about near the spot Paul had found his diamonds. The group spent ten days gathering the stones and placing them in leather bags. Schneider calculated the diamonds were worth several thousand dollars.

On their last evening at the fruitful creek bed, Schneider and Gerard celebrated with a bottle of champagne they had hidden in the bottom of a box.

Schneider, pleased to not be returning to New York empty handed, intended to pick up Paul on their way back to civilization. They left the site and followed the river toward where they had last seen him. He had Paul to thank for the tip. However, getting to Georgetown was his priority. Cashing in was more important than finding Paul. *He's been here for several years*, thought Schneider. *He's in no danger. It's not my fault if he doesn't make it on the barge.*

Before he reached that spot, Schneider came to a place in the river with a half-mile long run of rapids. The porters had dragged the barge through these rapids on their way upstream, but now they were going downstream. They decided to stay on board and sail around the boulders in the stream, through the cascading water. As they surged in the fast water, the porters lost control. The barge turned sideways. As it flew downstream, it barely missed several rock outcroppings. Then, as they got near the end of the rapids, they hit a submerged tree and the lurching craft threw Schneider, Gutmann, and the crew into the water.

The porters in the front of the boat were closest to shore, and they all made it out of the river and onto a boulder near the bank. Schneider and Gerard who were riding in the stern, flew out over the gunwale, and were immediately trapped in an eddy, formed by the water rushing over the tree. The natural current over the tree was like a wheel with the current going in a circle. The two men were dragged under, and the current held them below the surface. Their struggle to break free was futile and neither of them survived.

The porters rescued the barge and the diamonds, and continued their journey overland through the jungle toward Georgetown. They left Schneider and Gerard still trapped underwater. Venturing into the rapids to retrieve their bodies would have been far too dangerous.

They never mentioned Schneider and Gerard, the diamonds, or their encounter with Paul to anyone. They cashed in the diamonds and left Georgetown on a ferry bound for Caracas. They had decided they could be suspected of foul play in the deaths of their employers, so silence was the best strategy.

24

The Final Chapter (1938)

Paul's death came in 1934, about seven years after his takeoff for Rio. Gertrude and the rest of his family were unaware of his demise. Due to his adventurous spirit, it was difficult for those close to him to imagine that Paul would not one day return to Georgia. They still had hope he could be found and returned to the States.

In 1937, Frederick Redfern, Paul's father, cashed in his savings and commissioned Theodore Waldeck, a New York adventurer to go to South America to locate Paul. Waldeck put together a team and launched an expedition from Georgetown, British Guyana. They made their way to Venezuela and, since it was the rainy season, hunkered down on an island called Devil's Hole in the Cuyino River, north of the Essequibo River. While waiting out the rain, one of his crew, Englishman Frederick Fox, succumbed to Jungle Fever. Waldneck may have been discouraged by the death of Fox and less diligent in his search. He reported that conditions in the jungle during the rainy season were unbearable.

When he returned to New York, Waldeck contacted Frederick Redfern and reported that he had found the wreckage of the *Port of Brunswick* and ascertained that Paul had perished in Venezuela. It is unclear whether Waldeck produced any documents or photos to back up his claims. None were ever published. Frederick was willing to accept Waldeck's report.

Shortly thereafter, in 1938, Gertrude reluctantly petitioned the court, using Waldeck's report as evidence, to have Paul declared deceased. Until then, Gertrude anticipated Paul would return to her. She could have obtained a petition to have Paul confirmed officially dead long before 1938. Gertrude must have suspected long before she filed with the court that Paul was not going to return. There had never been any confirmed sightings of him or his airplane. Paul had told her on the day

Gertrude and Paul Redfern

of the flight that if he disappeared, she should not despair, as he would walk out of the jungle "even if it takes two or three months."

Gertrude was willing to wait, even after the months turned into years and the years turned into a decade. Paul's life had been one big adventure after another. He had escaped every close call. Paul Redfern had lived a rambunctious life. Gertrude believed he could overcome any adversity and would return to her.

To Gertrude, at first, Paul's failed flight to Rio only meant she would have to wait to get him back. The reports from South America claiming a white man was living among the natives reinforced her belief in his return. But there were no credible sightings of him. Even his plane, *Port of Brunswick,* was never located even though it was supposedly seen by Jimmy Angel. Despite those facts, it was difficult to acknowledge her vigorous and skillful husband could be gone. However, Waldeck's report closed the door on ever finding him.

So, in 1938, Gertrude had to admit that Paul's great adventure — attempting to fly over fifty hours to Rio — was, indeed, "more than a man could stand."

Gertrude never remarried and moved to Detroit where she lived alone until 1981.

Sign next to a strip mall on
St. Simons Island, Georgia

Afterword

In 2012, I was invited by Ron Shelton and the late Tom Savage to attend the yearly ceremonies in Columbia, South Carolina of the Paul Reynaldo Redfern Society. By ceremonies, I mean every year on the anniversary of his flight on August 25, the group raises a glass in honor of Paul at 12:46 p.m., the time he took off.

In addition to the toast, two other events occurred that year. First, a new highway historical sign was dedicated at the curb on Millwood Avenue in front of Dreher High School, the former site of Redfern's airfield. Fortunately, the older marker it replaced was found after a no-questions-asked plea was made. So, at the same time as the new sign was placed on the street, the old sign now graces the entrance of the school.

The sign succinctly states: Paul R. Redfern at an early age showed a marked aptitude and excitement for aviation. Shortly after graduating from old Columbia High School in 1923 he built his own airplane and established the city's first commercial aviation company and flying field at this site. Later Redfern attempted a non-stop flight to Brazil. Leaving from Brunswick, Georgia, August 25, 1927. He has never been heard from again.

Second, the sons of Art Williams and Hugh King came and brought with them a silent film of the encounter with natives in Venezuela during their parents' expedition attempting to find Paul Redfern. They told the story of conversing with the natives, thinking they would bring Paul to them, and then their mysterious disappearance.

That homemade film started my thinking about what it must have been like for a bright aviator like Redfern to be existing with a naked tribe living in the stone age. After a while I started to write this account based on my imagination, but also weaving in facts known about Redfern's life. After fits and starts, hours of research, pondering, and writing, this book emerged.

Thanks to Ron and Tom. If they had not invited me to Columbia, this book would never have been written.

I also owe a debt of gratitude to my family, especially my sons Steve and Doug for their suggestions that kept the project alive.

Finally, I appreciate my many conversations with the Escarpment Press founder Joe Perrone, Jr. Each time we talked the book improved. He also is the creator of the front cover. Thank you, Joe.

The Expeditions

Below is an account of the various expeditions sent to South America to find Paul Redfern. Some of them, together with fictionalized ones, are mentioned in the book. The National Geographic search described in the book is fiction. However, I included several elements from the actual searches in the description of that expedition. While the number of searches for Redfern is often listed as thirteen, I could not find details regarding that number.

George Henry Hamilton Tate

The Museum of Natural History in New York already had a team in the area when Redfern went missing in 1927. As mentioned in the book, the museum immediately wired zoologist George Tate and ordered him to cease looking for rare mammals. Instead, he was instructed to take his group to the area around Mount Roraima in Guyana to search for Paul. Not much is known about the expedition other than they found nothing. Tate is best remembered for his book on Mouse Opossums in South America.

William LaVarre

LaVarre, a Fellow of the Royal and American Geographic Societies, and well-known explorer of Central and South America volunteered to head up a Redfern search party. LaVarre's offer was in response to the claims of a Creole Catholic missionary first publicized in 1930.

The missionary had claimed that a white man "who had come from the sky with broken legs" had been rescued by natives and was living with the natives in their village.

The white man was described as content with his life with the natives and not eager to return to society. He was also reported to be the father of several mixed-race children. In December 1932, LaVarre led a group into Dutch Guiana in search of Redfern.

LaVarre, a globe trotter and fortune hunter, originally from Virginia, had led several expeditions to Central and South America exploring for gold, diamonds, orchids, *chicle*, and rubber plants. He had already gathered a group of natives ready for the exploration. In at least one of his exploratory treks he was accompanied by his new wife, whom he referred to as "Lipstick" in his memoirs.

He loaded the boats in New Nickerie in Dutch Guiana and launched onto the Nickerie River. He described the jungle as thick as a "palisade" on both shores. He remarked that there were no animals to be seen in the thick wall of trees and was surprised there were no targets for shooting.

After about six months LaVarre abandoned the search and returned to New Nickerie. One must wonder how diligent his search was as he returned to New Nickerie with three small wooden boxes of diamonds. The money given him for the search may have been used to search for more lucrative bounty.

Some of the diamonds came from wooden boards in which the diamonds and other stones were embedded by native women for use in grating cassava roots. As LaVarre derisively wrote, "They used diamonds as potato graters."

After ending his search, LaVarre reported he found no evidence of a white man falling out of the sky into native hands. Nor did he find any proof the natives were holding a white man captive.

LaVarre returned the States to become editor of a newspaper in Greenville, South Carolina. He wrote several autobiographical books about his exploits in Central and South America.

In one of them, he wrote of encountering a white man living with natives near the border of Venezuela and Dutch Guyana. Unlike Redfern the man had not accidentally ended up in the jungle. He had voluntarily emigrated for the purpose of living a simpler life.

Art Williams and Hugh King

In 1935, Art Williams, owner of a small air service enterprise, flew over a native village during a survey of Dutch Guiana for the country's government. He watched as the natives ran for cover into the jungle. While circling the encampment he noticed a white man standing in the clearing waving frantically.

As a result, Williams, an American, teamed up with Hugh King, an employee of the Dutch Guiana government to search for the white man. They traveled by boat and after several weeks found a tribe that told of rescuing an injured white man from his plane in the trees. The story made Williams and King think they were close to finding Redfern when they turned in for the night.

In the morning they discovered the natives had gone. There was no trace of them. Their first thought was the natives had gone to bring Redfern to them. After waiting a day, the natives had not returned. They decided they could not follow the tribe through the thick jungle. After waiting a second day gave up the search and returned to Georgetown.

Alfred Harred

As reported by Harred in a Paramaribo newspaper, he and Art Williams flew to a "main tributary" of the Amazon River and then trekked across the Tumuc-Humac mountains on the border of Brazil and Suriname. After several days they came across a tribe of natives who were completely naked. There, they saw an airplane in the branches of a big tree. A few days later they met Redfern. Redfern began by speaking "halting English." Within a short time, his English became more fluid. His clothes consisted of ragged singlet and underpants. His face was worn and made him appear to be forty years old. He used crutches made from tree branches to walk. He told Harred he had broken both legs and arms in the crash but had been cured by the tribe's *shaman*. He reported that he had married a native woman and they had a son. Harred stated that when the natives suspected that he and Williams intended to take Redfern, they threatened the expedition with poison spears. Redfern suggested that to be safe, they leave without him and withdraw from the jungle and they did.

A reporter sought out Art Williams in Georgetown, British Guyana, and asked him to verify Harred's story. Williams replied, "I never saw Redfern or his plane. I do not recall meeting Harred." Apparently, Harred's story was bogus.

W.L. Farrell

A year later, an American Legion post from Panama organized a search. Its leader, W. L. Farrell, with Columbia Broadcasting correspondent James Ryan, and several other men, searched an area in Dutch Guiana (now Suriname). They financed the trip by selling five thousand "Redfern Rescue" stamp covers postmarked from Guiana. The expedition received some notoriety when Franklin Delano Roosevelt purchased two of the commemorative envelopes. They spent about three months on boats patrolling along the Essequibo River, when Farrell stumbled out of the jungle to report no sign of Redfern. Ryan, the CBS correspondent, had drowned during the search.

Theodore Waldeck

In 1937, Redfern's father, Frederick Redfern, requested that New York sportsman, novelist, and explorer, Theodore Waldeck, conduct a final rescue mission from British Guiana. Waldeck found a native who claimed to have seen Redfern crash his plane into the trees. It was the rainy season and the group got stranded on an island called Devil's Hole in the Cuyuni

River north of the Essequibo River near the border of Venezuela and British Guyana. While stuck on the island, Englishman Frederick Fox contracted jungle fever and died. Later, Waldeck reported that he found the wreckage of the *Port of Brunswick* in Venezuela and had obtained proof that Redfern had died. However, there were no photographs of the plane, nor any other proof provided.

On May 19, 1938, Waldeck telegraphed Gertrude notifying her of his conclusion that Paul was dead. Gertrude used that report in her court filing later that year requesting that Paul be declared legally deceased.

Charles F. West

In a short obituary of West, it mentions, "He is perhaps best known for his attempts to rescue Paul Redfern from the jungles of South America. On one flight he located an unfriendly Indian tribe that had water cans that appeared to be part of Redfern's equipment. He brought back pictures of the Indians and maps of the territory where he thought Redfern might have been captured."

In a cursory pursuit, I could find no other details about West or his expeditions looking for Paul Redfern.

Sources

Cisneros Collection, 1999, *Orinoco-Parima; Indian Societies in Venezuela*.

Early Birds of Aviation, Website, No. 79, 1973, *Obituary of Charles F. West*.

Foley, Bill, *The Florida Times Union*, August 23, 1998, *Port of Brunswick Remains a Mystery*.

Goetz, Inga Steinvorth, 1969, *Uri! Jami! Life and Belief of the Forest Waika in the Upper Orinoco*.

Groom, Winston, June-July 2011, *The Lost Pilot*, Garden and Gun Magazine.

Kremer, Hans, 1938, *The Paul Redfern Rescue Expedition of 1936*, Netherlands Philately, Volume 33, No. 3.

La Varre, William, 1935, *Gold, Diamonds, and Orchids*.

La Varre, William, 1940, *Southward Ho!*

Manufacturers Aircraft Association, *Aircraft Year Book 1919*. (Retrieved, 2020).

Redfern, Frederick, 1928, *Life Story of Paul Redfern, Aviator*, Rochester Alumni Review.

Savage, Thomas, and Shelton, Ron, Palmetto Sport Aviation, 1998, *A Columbia (SC) Aviator and His Stinson Detroiter Remembered*.

Savage, Thomas C., 2014, *Lost Legend-Paul Redfern and the Birth of Aviation in Columbia, SC.*, South by Southeast.

Thomasville Times-Enterprise, August 5, 1927, *Hop Off for Brunswick.*

Waters, Robert A., 2013, *Whatever Happened to Paul Redfern?*

Wheeling Register, September 5, 1927, Associated Press, *Flyer Dropped Notes to Men Aboard Steamer.*

www.ingramcontent.com/pod-product-compliance
Lightning Source LLC
Chambersburg PA
CBHW070632260626
47161CB00007B/2677